For Barbara —
Enjoy!

Billi Morrow Steelbee

Clemmie

Bili Morrow Shelburne

abbott press®
A DIVISION OF WRITER'S DIGEST

Clemmie

Abbott Press books may be ordered through booksellers or by contacting:

Abbott Press
1663 Liberty Drive
Bloomington, IN 47403
www.abbottpress.com
Phone: 1-866-697-5310

ISBN: 978-1-4582-0191-1 (sc)
ISBN: 978-1-4582-0192-8 (e)
ISBN: 978-1-4582-0193-5 (hc)

Library of Congress Control Number: 2012902064

Printed in the United States of America

Abbott Press rev. date:3/12/2012

Also by Bili Morrow Shelburne:

Blackbirds and Butterflies

For Ralph: Unforgettable

Chapter One

I felt claustrophobic every time I walked into this room—this place to ruminate while waiting for the omniscient psychiatrist who had no doubt planned my next move.

The tat-a-tat-tat of Miss Yantz's fingers laboring on her keyboard continued as she delivered a straight-lipped smile over the plastic flowers on her desk. Miss Yantz and I never spoke. She always smiled, and I tried to return the gesture with only spotty success. When Miss Yantz tiptoed to the door by the filing cabinet, that was my cue to walk into the room where Dr. Fitzpatrick would probe my mind and work his magic.

"Good afternoon, Clemmie."

"Hello."

"I must say that shade of blue becomes you."

"Thank you."

"How is your new medication working?"

"I'm tired all the time; no energy, but I don't have insomnia anymore."

The doctor nodded. What was that supposed to mean? Was he glad I didn't have insomnia? Didn't he care that I was tired?

"I'm frustrated, Dr. Fitzpatrick." I wanted to scream it at him.

"I understand. But you've been progressing since last week. You must be encouraged by that."

"I was, but I'm stuck. I can't think of anything to write in my journal."

He nodded again.

"You must keep in mind that yours is not an easy case. The medication I've prescribed may have some slightly unpleasant side effects, but it will help you reach far back into your memory."

The doctor thumbed through notes, gnawing a lower lip, one of his many habits that annoyed me.

"In our last session, you were telling me how Roy Hubbard rescued you and your mother."

"Roy was our savior. Nothing good had happened in the ten years we had lived in Chicago. Papa died when I was three, leaving Mama and me without much insurance. The weather was savage, and money was in short supply. Roy changed all that."

"So he was your financial savior."

"He was much more than that. Roy was a big, burly, ursine bundle of laughter and kindness. He brought joy into our lives."

"Did you continue to live in Chicago after Roy and your mother married?"

"Not for long. Roy was offered a position in Georgia, close to Savannah."

"No more cold winters." Dr. Fitzpatrick smiled.

"That's right. But our new home was a far cry from what we had expected."

I felt a rush. Maybe the new medicine was helping. I was remembering insignificant details of our trip south. Roy's green Pontiac was vivid in my mind. So was Mama's reluctance to take a turn behind the wheel because it had been so long since she had driven. The U-Haul trailer hitched to the back bumper was parked outside the plate glass window of a diner where we stopped for lunch. I could see it clearly.

"Clemmie?"

"Yes."

"Are you daydreaming?"

"No. I'm remembering. I think I could talk for hours."

"Ah, but that isn't what I want you to do. I want you to go to your room and write in your journal. Quick! Quick! Don't let those thoughts elude you."

The sun was trying to break through a thick cloud cover, but couldn't quite make it. I knew that feeling, and it beat me down. But as I walked down the bricked path to my dormitory, I could feel tension leaving my shoulders. I couldn't wait to get to my room and shut out the world. I would sit at my desk by the window and let the words flow the way they had when I wrote in my very first diary, the one Roy gave me for my ten-year-old secret thoughts. The first entry was vivid in my mind:

December 25, 1965

Dear Diary,

This was a very special Christmas. I'll never forget it if I live to be an old, old woman. We had a delicious turkey dinner, and Roy was a super Santa Claus. I think he must be rich. I had hoped the blue velvet box he gave Mama would have an engagement ring in it, but it didn't. It held diamond earrings, and Mama got tears in the corners of her eyes when she opened it.

I'll always keep the memory of my dear papa, but since I can't have him, I think Roy is a good substitute.

Very truly yours and AMEN,

Clementine Foster

I stared out at the manicured grounds of Still Waters, for once not obsessing about how I came to be here, but dredging up memories of times past.

Mama and Roy were in love and married before spring. I felt like a tag-along.

February 4, 1966

Dear Diary,

We're a family as of today, and I know Roy is a good catch. He's crazy about Mama, and I can tell he likes me a lot, too. I'm positive that he would never steal or commit murder, and I don't think he swears or drinks liquor. Since he has never been married, I wonder if he knows what to do on his wedding night. If he doesn't, Mama can teach him.

Yours truly,

Clementine Foster

P.S. I think he just figured it out. Good night.

Roy brought home groceries that were delicacies compared to the pots of spaghetti and beans with a hambone that Mama and I were used to stretching for several meals. Just looking at a big bowl of fresh fruit on the table or discovering a candy bar in my lunchbox was a treat, but the real bonus was getting out of Chicago. Roy's transfer came through in May, and we headed for the sunny South.

The farther south we went, the more alive with color the landscape became. I had never been anywhere in my ten years except Chicago, and the southeast looked like a fairyland to me. We came to a strip of public beach, and Roy pulled off the road. We jumped out of the car, shoes and stockings flying. I dug my toes into the sand and breathed the salty air. The ocean breeze felt like velvet on my skin.

We raced to the water and splashed our Chicago white feet in the surf.

"Oh, Roy, this is heaven," Mama said. "We're going to love living in the South. Aren't we, Clementine?"

"You bet." I giggled. "I'm going to be a beach bunny!"

I don't know what I had expected Savannah to look like. If I closed my eyes, I could imagine the scene from *Gone with the Wind* when Aunt Pittypat, furiously fanning herself, fled to escape General Sherman and his soldiers. I didn't remember seeing shiny-leaved live oaks with beards of Spanish moss clinging to their limbs. The city squares were new to me, too. All the houses looked like mansions in the movie, but I had never seen one in real life.

"Clementine," Mama said, "look at that rose garden! Isn't it the prettiest thing you've ever seen?"

"Oh, Mama, it is. It looks just like a postcard."

We didn't have any trouble finding the Mills Insurance Agency. It was on a pretty street lined with big trees. Roy would be selling insurance for the agency in hopes of becoming a manager. The house we would be living in belonged to Mills, and sales people who worked in this particular office had a choice of a company car or one year's free rent.

Our new home was a shock and a letdown. It wasn't in beautiful, sleepy Savannah, but on nearby Tybee Island. The house was the last of eight small, weather-beaten clapboard structures, all alike but painted different colors. Ours was dingy yellow.

Roy pulled up in front of the house and looked at Mama with an apologetic expression.

"I didn't know, Emily," he said, raking a hand through his hair the way he did when something didn't go according to plan. "I didn't ask for details; all I heard were the words 'free rent'."

We didn't have the ocean view I had dreamed about, but a little strip of sand that ran along the bank of Horse Pen Creek.

Mama and Roy had just lugged a bookcase inside, and I was carrying in an armload of clothes. I was halfway up the steps when something caught my eye. It was almost like a shadow. I ducked down to get a better look, but the small dark figure dashed behind a pier and disappeared.

"Hey, what are you doing under my house?" I said in a proprietary tone.

I ran up the stairs with the clothes, yelling for Roy and Mama, but by the time they got outside, there was no sign of the tiny intruder.

"Maybe you imagined you saw someone, these being new surroundings," Roy said.

"I didn't imagine anything. He was here."

People were walking across the grounds to the cafeteria. It was nearly dinner time. How long had I been sitting at my desk? I felt tired, but I must have been sleeping. I had been dreaming, hadn't I? I rubbed a hand across my cheek, and realized I had been crying, but didn't know why. Absently fingering the locket, warm against my chest, I wished for Daniel, the quick-witted, tough little black boy I had met under a house on Tybee Island.

Dr. Fitzpatrick wants me to write. How many volumes must I put on paper to get to my last four misplaced years? If I could only talk to Daniel, maybe he could help me sort things out. Or Mama Rae. She'd fuss at me for being so thin, then give me a cup of her special herb tea to sip while I told her my plight. Mama Rae would never interrupt like the doctor, and she would find a way to make me remember. Mama Rae could fix anything.

I went to the bathroom and splashed cold water on my face. The stranger in the mirror looked back at me with sad, defeated eyes. Why couldn't I get control of myself? My shrink seemed like an enemy, but I knew I needed his help.

"I resolve to whip this thing," I said aloud. Gripping the lavatory, I stared at my reflection. Somehow, I had to stop feeling paranoid; it drained me, and made my head hurt. I was not crazy, and I wasn't considered dangerous. Otherwise, I would be in a room without a mirror or a window.

If I didn't write something in my journal immediately, everything I had gained would be in the toilet.

March 14, 1978

I have searched my memory back to my father's death, and have found nothing of import. My life didn't bloom until Roy Hubbard took over as my father. I want to talk about Tybee Island at my next session. I remember details.

"Good afternoon, Clemmie." Dr. Fitzpatrick donned his most pleasant expression.

I nodded and took my seat.

"May I see your journal?"

I slid the cheap steno pad across his metal desk. It made a scratching noise like someone raking a fingernail down a chalkboard. I clenched my teeth, and felt my shoulders tighten.

The doctor read my entry, raising a bristly eyebrow.

"Why didn't you record details?"

"I wanted to see if I could retain them. If I am progressing, I want to be aware of it."

I could tell by his body language that he didn't like my answer.

I caught him up on my recollections, or dreams, or whatever they were.

"Can you continue?" he asked.

"The cottage had two bedrooms, a bath, a kitchen, and a combination living/dining room. The kitchen and bathroom floors were covered with linoleum, and the others were ugly shag that felt damp. The windows wore permanent scum, and green moss clung to the clapboards."

"You certainly are adept at recalling details today." He looked pleased, but I couldn't tell whether or not he was smiling because he fiddled with his mustache as he spoke.

"Should I go on?"

"By all means."

I tried to relax and let my mind wander back in time, hoping the doctor wouldn't interrupt my thoughts.

We had stocked the cottage and gotten rid of the U-Haul. It was Monday morning, and Roy was off to his new job. Mama and I were scrubbing the place down when we heard a light knock at the back screen door.

"How do," a pretty, slight woman said. She was smiling, and the sun illuminated her cocoa skin and pearly teeth. She wore a blue print dress and a red scarf on her head.

"Good morning," Mama said.

"I'm Delia Grover." The woman smiled. "I clean most of these cottages."

"I'm glad to meet you, Mrs. Grover. I'm Emily Hubbard. If it's cleaning work you're looking for, I'm afraid I can't help you. I do my own cleaning, as you can see."

"Call me Delia. I'm not looking for work. I just wondered if you and your little girl would care for a glass of homemade lemonade." She held up a large thermos.

"That's very neighborly of you, Delia. Come in, won't you?"

"It's nice and cool out here on the back porch by the creek," Mrs. Grover said.

I brought three glasses to the back porch and introduced myself. We sat down on the steps, and Mrs. Grover poured her lemonade without spilling a drop. It had slices of lemon floating in it, and it was delicious.

"I have a son 'bout your age," she said to me. "He's nine, but he's small for his age."

"I'm ten-and-a-half. Where's your son now?"

I would have bet anything it was her little rascal I saw under the cottage yesterday.

"Oh, he's aroun' here somewhere. I hope he's not into any mischief. He comes to work with me and plays in the sand." She took a sip of lemonade. "He prob'ly climbs trees, too."

"What's his name?"

"Daniel. He's named for his grandfather."

A strange expression took over Mrs. Grover's face. She stood up, and a hand flew to her mouth. She glanced first at Mama, then at me. The woman looked horrified!

"Oh," she said, swallowing hard.

"What is it, Delia?" Mama said. "What's the matter?"

"Please 'scuse me." Mrs. Grover jumped up and started running toward the creek, screeching like a wild woman.

"Daniel, I've tol' you and tol' you!"

It was then that we discovered what had upset our visitor. A small boy came wading from the creek, wearing nothing but his birthday suit. He was scrambling to get into his clothes before his mother reached him. He ducked behind some bushes, so the show was over for Mama and me, but we could hear Daniel's mama giving him *what for*.

"What did I tell you 'bout swimmin' down here naked as a jaybird?"

She grabbed him by the shoulders and shook him.

"You made me lose my fish," he spat. Then, he whirled and, escaping his mother's grasp, took off down the beach.

"You're gonna be losin' more than a fish when I catch you, boy! I'm gonna take the hide off your scrawny little backside."

I had to hide a grin when Mrs. Grover returned to the porch. She was panting as she climbed the steps.

"I 'pologize," she said, gulping air. "That chile gonna be the death of me."

"No apology is necessary, Delia." Mama laughed. "Children are full of surprises."

Late that afternoon I was sitting on the porch while mama cooked dinner. Mrs. Grover and her son were leaving for the day. They walked past our cottage, looking straight ahead.

"Hi, Daniel," I called.

Daniel slowed his step, and shot me a quick glance. He grinned and waved, then ran ahead of his mother and out of sight.

I was scouting around the next day when the strangest thing happened. If Daniel hadn't been wearing shorts and a tee shirt, I would have thought his mother had caught him swimming naked again. He was a blur, rounding the bend of the tree-lined beach. He looked terrified, and darted under our cottage.

I ran to the porch and squatted by the steps.

"Daniel?"

It was dark under the cottage, but I could see light all the way to the other side.

"Daniel," I called again.

"Shut up, girl!"

At that moment, three teen-aged boys came tearing around the bend. They were looking all around, and one of them pointed in my direction. I scampered up on the back porch as they trotted toward me.

"Hey, little girl."

"Hey."

I had my foot inside the screen door, and was ready to run inside.

"Have you seen a little nigger kid about this tall?" He measured to just above his waist with his hand.

I shook my head no, wondering why they were chasing Daniel.

"Are you sure?"

"I'm sure." I went inside so he couldn't ask any more questions.

As soon as the boys were out of sight, I scooted down the steps.

"Daniel, you can come out now."

I didn't see him as my eyes traveled over the little dunes. Then, without making a sound, his small body dropped from its hidey hole somewhere in the underpinnings of the cottage.

"Thanks," he said, brushing cobwebs from his hair and shirt. "That was a c-c-close c-call."

"Why were they after you?"

"They's p-prob'ly mad 'cause I untied they b-b-b-boat."

"Why did you do a thing like that?"

"How'd you l-like it if s-somebody badmouthed your m-mama; called her names?"

I don't think I had ever seen a kid look as mad and mean as Daniel.

"Well, I guess I wouldn't like it a bit."

I sat under the cottage with Daniel, trying to imagine how he felt. He told me that he and his mother lived down the road a piece. We built a sandcastle and destroyed it. Then he said he had to go.

"You know how to catch crawfish?" he asked.

"No. I've never seen one up close."

"I'll teach you tomorrow," he promised, and went to find his mother.

"I'm afraid our time is up." Dr. Fitzpatrick peered over his glasses at the wall clock.

Chapter Two

—

I was excited about my progress, and wished that I had someone I could trust to tell about it. It would feel so good to let my recollections flow like water; not worry about leaving out some bit of information Dr. Fitzpatrick might deem important. He wanted me to keep my thoughts nice and neat. Well, I didn't think in an orderly fashion, and since I had been at Still Waters, most of my thoughts seemed disjointed. Moments ago I was back in Chicago:

I was little, four or five. Mama and I were snuggled together on the sofa. We were looking at her shoebox of photographs. That was a favorite pastime on winter nights. Mama entertained me with a purpose: keeping papa alive in my memory. Each picture was a page out of his life.

I didn't remember coming to Still Waters, or how I got here, but the shoebox was in my luggage. The only time Papa entered my mind was when I took the box from my closet to pull out one of his photos.

I felt groggy. I'd fallen asleep. That was happening frequently since the doctor changed my medication. If I didn't hurry, I would miss dinner. I pulled on a pair of jeans and a sweater and headed for the cafeteria.

My eyes roamed the room as I filled my tray, and I recognized the back of Maria's head by her sleek black hair. She was seated alone. We had a nodding acquaintance, and had shared several meals.

"May I join you?" I asked.

"I'd love the company."

I unloaded my tray and sat facing her. She was one of the few people I had met who appeared somewhat normal. We made small talk while forcing down the institutional food. What else could virtual strangers do? Neither of us was going to bare her soul to the other, especially in a place like this. Maria had once made a vague reference to her past, but nothing that invited admittance into her world.

"Have you met John?" she asked.

"I don't think so."

"Here he comes now; the one in the wheelchair. John is such a sweet man. Everyone loves him."

I wanted to ask why he was here, but didn't.

"He has Down's syndrome, but that has nothing to do with his being here. I understand he suffers from depression and has some sort of fits."

The only person I had seen having a fit was the old woman called Emma. She nearly put me in a state of shock the first time I encountered her. I'd been napping. When I awoke, she was standing over me, staring.

At first, I didn't know where I was. Then I was overtaken by fear. The beginnings of a panic attack were manifesting themselves: racing heart, heavy limbs, and a feeling of helplessness. I snapped the rubber band on my wrist once. It didn't help. The woman's eyes looked wild like those of a frightened animal, and her stringy gray hair fell between my line of vision and light from the hallway as she moved closer. I made myself snap the band again, and started to feel calm radiate through me.

"Who are you?" I said, keeping my voice steady.

The woman continued to stare.

"Why are you in my room?"

"Gawd!" She dragged out the word. "That's the ugliest robe I ever saw."

"Please leave," I said.

"Ugly! Ugly! Ugly! Ugly! Ack! Ack! Ack! Bitch! Ugly bitch! Ugly robe! Ack! Ack!" Her voice kept rising.

I got up and headed for the door, ready to backhand her if I had to, when she collapsed.

The nursing staff seemed to be familiar with Emma's strange behavior. A nurse waved smelling salts under her nose and spoke baby talk to her.

"Do you know Emma?" I asked.

"Please! Deliver me from that woman. Oh, look. John's aide is bringing him our way."

"Hi, Ria!" John was waving with both hands.

"Hello, John." Maria smiled. "Won't you join us?"

The aide settled John, and Maria made introductions.

"Blessing time," John announced, holding out a hand to Maria and one to me. He squeezed his eyes closed. "Bless this food, bless these people, and bless John. Amen."

John leaned over his plate and started shoveling. He didn't come up for air until his plate was empty.

That night it struck me that John didn't seem to mind being here. He seemed happy, not depressed. And Maria generally appeared to be in a state of ennui. Everyone here had a different story, most of which I would never know. They must have come from different backgrounds, some leaving families who loved them, and some of them having nobody. A few might get to go home, but the rest would be here until they died. I wondered which would be my fate.

I turned my locket over and over between my thumb and forefinger, and went to sleep thinking about Daniel and Tybee Island.

Daniel and I became inseparable. I was so thrilled by the things he taught me that I tried to be as much of a boy as possible. Under his tutelage, I learned to bait a hook without making a face, how to catch crawfish, and the art of crabbing.

I could tell he enjoyed being in charge, and his delight in including an element of fear as part of the learning process quickly became apparent. His unorthodox swimming instruction was a prime example:

"Hold onto this rope tight," he said, "and let go when I tell you to."

He checked my grip, and gave me a hard push out over the creek. The murky water looked awfully deep from my perspective.

"Turn loose now!" he yelled.

I couldn't make myself let go of the rope. It took three attempts before I could release my lifeline to plunge into the brackish water. I could feel the slick mud on the creek floor, and knew that I was drowning.

Daniel cackled when I broke the surface, sputtering.

"See there." He laughed. "Nothin' to it."

Mama cooked breakfast each morning, but I much preferred sharing Daniel's. His mother made big fat biscuits, and Daniel stuffed their middles with gobs of butter and homemade peach preserves. He carried his breakfast in a little pail with tinfoil covering the top, and we usually ate it under the steps of our cottage.

We were munching our biscuits one morning while discussing how to spend the day. It was especially hot and humid, so we agreed it would be wise to spend most of our time in the water. We made sandwiches and packed them in Daniel's bucket.

All morning we played in the woods, climbing trees and swinging out over the creek on our rope. Both of us started to have hunger pangs at about the same time, so we headed down the beach past the cottages to a sandbar we had discovered on one of our adventures. It was the perfect place for a picnic. Daniel spotted it first and started running toward it.

I wasn't allowed to play this far from home. I could barely make out the cottages if I squinted. It would have been impossible to hear the tinkle of Mama's little bell this far down the beach, but we wouldn't be here very long. We were close to what the locals called the sound, but as far as I was concerned, it was the ocean.

The cottages at this end of the beach were much larger and a lot more expensive than ours. Wealthy families came here for summer vacations. The beach was usually crowded, but on this particular day, sun worshipers were sparse.

"Hurry up, Clemmie! We don't have all day. The tide's already on its way in."

I waded out to the sandbar where Daniel sat, dangling his feet in the water. The sun was blistering, and the shallow water was hot.

We unpacked our lunch. Daniel handed me a sandwich and started unwrapping his. Suddenly, he looked as though he were mesmerized. His little boy expression changed, and I could see fear in his eyes.

"What's the matter, Daniel?"

"Don't turn around. Just eat your sandwich." He took a bite.

I could hear splashing in the surf behind me.

"Hey, Greg, I didn't know they allowed niggers on this end of the beach," one of the big boys said.

"I don't see a nigger. Where is he?"

Daniel stopped eating. Peanut butter and jelly seeped from the corner of his mouth, and he froze. I turned to see the three bullies who had it in for him, and jumped up ready to fight for my friend.

Greg pushed me aside and grasped Daniel's neck in his big hand. He jerked him into the air.

"He's right here. Are you blind?" He laughed.

"Let him go!" I threw down my sandwich.

"What's the matter, you little piece of white trash? Are you afraid we're going to hurt your little black buddy?"

"Please." I felt tears gathering in my eyes. "He's just a little kid."

"Say pretty please with sugar on it. You lied to me the other day, you little shit."

"Let him go!" I yelled. I picked up Daniel's lunch pail and started hitting the bully with it.

"Get this pest away from me. I'm going to feed this little wiggle worm to the fish."

The next thing I knew I was on my back in the shallow water, and the bully was wading into deeper water, carrying Daniel with his limbs beating the air. He plunged Daniel's head under the water and held it, laughing back at his friends.

Daniel kicked and splashed, fighting for his life, but finally, he stopped. The big boy lifted the limp body from the water and gave it a sling, sending it out to sea, then waded back to our picnic spot.

"Let this be a lesson to you, sweet pea." He sneered at me. "Stay down at your end of the beach."

The three sauntered away at a leisurely pace while my heart raced. I didn't know whether Daniel was dead or alive, but I had to get him back to shore. I could see his yellow tee shirt riding the waves. The water was up to my neck, and I had to swim the last few yards to reach him.

"Oh, God," I prayed, "please make him be alive."

If Daniel had weighed another ounce, I don't think I could have gotten him ashore. My adrenalin was pumping as purpose replaced fear. There was no lifeguard, and the few sunbathers had left. I turned Daniel on his stomach and tried to pump the water out of his lungs the way I had seen someone do it on television. It seemed no use. I started to cry, and suddenly, Daniel vomited. I thought he would never stop coughing and puking.

"You're alive! Oh, Daniel, you're alive!"

I cleaned him up with my tee shirt and dragged him into a stand of sea oats in the shade of a *keep off* sign. He rested his head on my lap. I couldn't stand it if he died. He coughed some more, and his chest rattled when he breathed. I wanted to go and tell Mama and Mrs. Grover to find a doctor, but Daniel wouldn't let me.

"This is our s-secret," he said. "It d-didn't h-h-happen."

June 13, 1966

Dear Diary,

My best friend was almost murdered today. I, of course, was an eyewitness. I wouldn't be at all surprised if something awful happens to those mean bullies. They deserve the harshest kind of punishment.

I'm so grateful that Daniel is still alive. I can never thank you enough for saving his life. He's only nine.

Humbly yours,

Clementine Foster

P.S. It was my pleasure to help with the life saving.

Daniel didn't come with his mother for the next three days, and I was worried sick about him. The next day I made a point of being on the porch when Mrs. Grover walked past our cottage.

"Good morning, Mrs. Grover."

"Good mornin', Clementine." She smiled.

She looked happy, and that made me feel better. She wouldn't be smiling if Daniel was about to die or something.

"Where's Daniel?"

"He has a terrible cold. That child's been in bed all week."

"Tell him I miss him."

"I sure will, Clementine. Hey to your mama."

Daniel didn't show up until the following Monday, and he looked awful. He seemed tired and out of sorts, and he didn't want to do anything I suggested.

We settled on playing checkers on the back porch, and I could tell his mind wasn't on the game.

"Are you trying to let me win?" I asked, irritated. "This is no fun."

"I'm gonna get 'em, Clemmie. I swear I am."

"Daniel, don't you dare do anything crazy. They nearly drowned you. You might not be so lucky next time."

Chapter Three

"Come in, Clemmie."

Dr. Fitzpatrick didn't bother to greet me face-to-face as I walked into his dim inner sanctum, but stood at a dirty window looking out.

I laid my journal on his desk and sat down, thinking that I didn't recall ever having seen him stand before. He was a very short man.

"Squirrels are such fascinating creatures, don't you think?" he said, turning to pick up my journal.

"I had one for breakfast once." I couldn't fathom having had such a meal, but somehow I knew that I had.

The doctor looked as if he didn't think I was serious. "You must have been very hungry."

He looked over my journal entry.

"Young Daniel was fortunate to have you for a friend. Would you like to tell me more about him?"

"Yes."

"I know you're anxious to hurry through your past, but if you do it chronologically, you're likely to come across key information that will help us."

"All right."

"Let's begin."

"That window is filthy," I said.

"The window?" Dr. Fitzpatrick swiveled his chair to take a look. "Yes, it is. I'm sure the cleaning crew will get to it soon."

He turned back to face me.

"You were on Tybee Island with Daniel. Remember?"

My head started aching. I could feel pounding in my ears, and my temples felt as if they were being squeezed between two giant hands. I could see Dr. Fitzpatrick's lips move, but all I could hear was howling wind. I tried to get up, but couldn't.

The doctor came to stand before me. He lifted my chin, and his eyes bore into mine. The wind began to die down, and I felt myself start to relax.

"Are you with me, Clemmie?"

"Yes. I'm just afraid of storms."

"Were you always afraid of them?"

"I don't know."

"Is the storm nearly over?"

"I think so."

"Would you like to talk about your mother?"

"Mama was wonderful."

"Do you know where she is?"

"No."

"Do you recall the last time you saw her?"

"No, but I remember a clown's face she made with raisins on my oatmeal. She always made everything special."

"I'm sure she did."

"Roy did, too. He was a terrific father to me."

"Did your mother and Roy like Daniel? Did they think he was a suitable playmate for you?"

"They thought Daniel was a wonderful playmate. He was like a member of our family. Mama rubbed him down with suntan lotion just like she did me, and Roy took Daniel and me fishing on weekends."

"You were afraid for Daniel after that episode with the big boys, weren't you?"

"Yes, especially after Daniel told me he was determined to get even with them. I wanted to tell Mama and Roy what had happened, but I knew I couldn't say a word. Daniel would have been furious."

"So you kept his secret?"

I nodded.

Daniel had nearly returned to being the fun-loving, mischievous kid he used to be. I coaxed him back into the water, and we weren't bored anymore.

We were down at the creek pretending to be pirates, and were engaged in a vicious stick duel. I whacked Daniel's sword from his hand, and had him pinned to a tree trunk. Just as I was about to run him through, sliding my sword between his side and the crook of his arm, he pulled a fast one. He slid a hand into his pocket and brought out a knife. The sun glinted off the steel blade as Daniel jumped away from the tree, waving his weapon through the air. His eyes were menacing.

"Stop that," I choked, backing away. "That's dangerous."

"Are you scared?"

"Yes. Get that thing out of my face."

Daniel put on an evil grin and held the knife just inches from my throat. I knew he wouldn't intentionally hurt me, but if either of us made a wrong move, he might accidentally cut me. I took a step backward and tripped over a fallen tree limb.

Daniel seized the advantage. "One, two, three: I now pronouce you dead."

He clutched the knife in his fist and raised skinny arms in triumph, planting one foot on my stomach.

"Daniel the terrible wins again," he proclaimed to the creek inhabitants, and laughed like a hyena.

"Get your foot off me. I could be lying on a snake hole. And it's *pronounce*."

Daniel laughed and reached down to give me a hand up.

"Where'd you get that knife?"

"Found it. You ever see one like it?"

I took the knife from him to examine it.

"No."

"It's a Swiss Army knife. Lemme show you."

We squatted down in the sand, and Daniel proceeded to pull out the various blades and explain their functions.

"It's got this nifty red case, too," he said, as if I couldn't see that for myself.

"What do you plan to do with it except give me heart failure?"

"Clean fish, open a bottle of pop, all kinds of stuff."

"I'll bet your mother doesn't know you have it."

"I'll bet your mama don't know we smoked them cigarettes we found either." He grinned.

That evening after dinner Roy grabbed his guitar and declared it a songfest kind of night. He liked to sit on the porch and accompany the night creatures' music with the smell of pluff mud in his nostrils and a song on his lips. He and Mama both had pretty voices, and they liked to harmonize.

"Ah, Clementine, you're going to have a gorgeous voice when it develops a little more." Roy beamed at me.

"Oh, Roy, cut it out."

I enjoyed singing, but the sounds I made were reedy and timid compared to his and Mama's.

"It's a fact," Roy insisted. "You just wait a couple of years. You'll see."

We sang for a while. Then, Roy told Mama and me a silly joke. He came home with a new one every night except Wednesdays when he had meetings. We had spent many evenings like this, but there was something different about this one. I could feel tension in the air like a revelation was about to be unveiled. And a revelation it was, indeed: Mama announced that she was pregnant.

I pretended to be pleased at the prospect of having a baby in the family, but admitted to myself that I enjoyed being the only child. It was fun having Roy for a father. I had only had one parent for most of my life.

June 28, 1966

Dear Diary,

Mama's pregnant! I can't believe it. We don't need a baby; they're expensive, and I know I'll have to help take care of it. Babies cry half the night and mess their diapers. The truth is that I thought I made Mama and Roy happy. I guess I'm not enough.

Sadly,

Clementine Foster

Daniel didn't come with his mother the next day, and I was disappointed. I was upset that Mama was pregnant, and I felt guilty about my feelings. Daniel might have been able to tease me out of my selfishness if he had been there.

I piddled around the cottage most of the day, but by late afternoon I couldn't stand it anymore. Walking down the beach past the cottages, I came to the tree-lined bend where the beach was no more than a narrow strip. A sand crab ran sideways in front of me as my bare feet splashed through the water. I wondered how close it would allow me to get before dashing into a hole. It would run, then stop; run, then stop. I took a tentative step toward the crab and felt something hard under my heel. Assuming it was a shell, I squatted down to dig it out of the sand.

I rubbed off the mud and couldn't believe what I had found. It was Daniel's Swiss Army knife, or one just like it. It had some sticky looking red stuff I assumed was fish blood on it, too. I stuck it in my pocket, and started home.

I was walking around the bend at a fast clip when I saw something red in my peripheral vision. I was anxious to get home, but something told me to stop. I eased over to the edge of the trees, past the dunes where something red showed through the underbrush. Venturing a step closer, I held back a branch, and there he was: Daniel, half buried in the sand. If it hadn't been for his red shorts, I wouldn't have seen him.

He didn't move as I dug away the sand. I couldn't tell whether he was breathing or not. There was a strip of tape over his mouth. His hands were tied behind him with a piece of clothesline, and his feet were shackled and anchored to a bush with a rusty fish stringer. I yanked off the tape, then untied him and dragged him away from the brush.

"Daniel, please speak to me."

He felt lifeless, and I was so scared I didn't know what to do next. I brushed off more sand and saw his bloody chest. Somebody had carved a cross on him. I sucked in my breath and stared at it. Sand stuck to the raw flesh as the afternoon sun beat down on us.

I could feel tears in my eyes and throat, the way I felt after a long fit of crying, and wondered how I could possibly be aware of such a sensation when my best friend could be on his deathbed. Daniel's expression hadn't changed.His eyes weren't quite closed; a little bit of white showed, and his lips were barely parted.

I pressed two fingers against his neck close to his tonsil to see if I could feel his heartbeat. He was alive, and that made me less afraid. I had to get help, but I was afraid to leave Daniel alone. I knew who had done this to him as well as I knew my name, and I wondered what he had done to provoke them.

I could run home and tell Mama, or go from cottage to cottage until I found Mrs. Grover. But I didn't have much time. There had to be a faster way to get help. I told myself not to panic, to think.

There was a general store not far from where we were. Mr. Slocum who owned it was a nice man. He had given Daniel and me suckers a couple of times.

I decided on the store since I knew that Mr. Slocum had a car. Dashing into the trees, I took off in the general direction of the store. Branches slapped my face, and nettles grabbed my tee shirt and ripped at my arms and legs. I stopped to get my bearings. My surroundings looked the same in every direction, and I wasn't sure I was still headed for the road until I saw a car through the trees.

The pink stucco store was deserted when I ran through the screen door except for Mr. Slocum who was on a ladder, dusting his wares. The door banged behind me as I took in large gulps of air.

"What in the world has happened, child?" He hurried down from his ladder. "Sit down and catch your breath. I'll get you a glass of water."

"No time for water," I rasped. "Please help me. It's my friend Daniel; he's hurt."

"Where is he, child?"

"Down at the bend on the beach where all the trees are. He's barely breathing, and somebody cut his chest with a knife." I started to cry.

"Now, now, dear. Don't cry. We'll take care of your friend."

Mr. Slocum put the *CLOSED* sign on the door, and we took his car as far as we could before we had to get out and walk through the woods to get to the beach.

Daniel hadn't moved, and Mr. Slocum got down on his knees to check for a pulse. He carried Daniel to the car, and we rushed to the hospital in Savannah.

When the nurse told Mr. Slocum to bring Daniel into the examination room, I went, too. I knew I wasn't supposed to be there, but nobody told me to leave. I watched as the doctor pulled Daniel's eyelids back with his thumb to look at his eyes with a penlight. When he scraped a metal instrument down the sole of his foot, Daniel moved his leg.

A nurse cleaned Daniel's wounds. Then, the doctor examined them before dabbing nasty- looking brown liquid on them. After that came gobs of salve and rolls of gauze covering his upper body, making him look like a mummy. Daniel made small noises of protest throughout these procedures, and I took that as a good thing.

"What's your name, honey?" Dr. Holcomb asked.

"Clementine Foster."

"You're Daniel's friend, aren't you?"

"Yes."

"Call his name as if you were trying to wake him."

"Daniel," I said. "Daniel, wake up!"

Daniel's lashes fluttered, and he raised an arm to shield his eyes from the bright lights.

"Clemmie, that you?"

"Yes, it's me. How do you feel?"

"It hurts."

"What hurts?" the doctor asked.

"My chest."

I stayed with Daniel while the doctor and Mr. Slocum went to see if they could contact Mrs. Grover.

"Daniel?"

He opened his eyes.

"What happened?"

"I d-d-don't know."

"You stuttered, Daniel. You're either scared to death or lying."

He didn't defend himself.

"I found your Swiss Army knife. I have it right here in my pocket."

He squinted at me.

"It's all dirty and sticky. It's got your blood on it. I know what happened. You went after those guys. You don't trust me enough to tell me what happened, but I know who carved that cross on your chest, and I know they did it with your knife."

The doctor and Mr. Slocum came back into the room.

"Thank you for taking care of our patient," Dr. Holcomb said. "Mr. Slocum will drive you home and bring Daniel's mother back to the hospital. That's sure to make this little guy feel better."

The two men stepped out into the hall.

"I'll be right there," I said. "I just want to tell Daniel goodnight."

I leaned close and whispered into Daniel's ear. "I'm your friend, Daniel, no matter what you think."

"I know."

"I have to go now."

"Clemmie," he whispered, "hide it."

Daniel had to spend the night in the hospital. Mr. Slocum explained everything to Mama and Roy who were nearly beside themselves by the time we got home. I felt guilty about worrying them, especially Mama. Anxiety isn't good for a pregnant person.

June 29, 1966

Dear Diary,

Life is right down scary here in the South. Daniel's life was once again close to being snuffed out. I wish those awful boys would go back wherever they came from and leave him alone. He is, as you know, my favorite friend. Somehow, he seems to have a nose for trouble, and he always manages to find it. I'll keep the you know what hidden until he wants it. I wish he had never found it!

Very truly yours,

Clementine Foster

P.S. Roy wants to adopt me.

"I'm afraid our time is up," Dr. Fitzpatrick said.

Chapter Four

—

More and more I felt lonely; not just alone in the sense that I didn't know anybody, but a much deeper feeling. It was more than a lack of social intercourse and emotional emptiness. I was physically and sexually wanting. I needed to be touched, loved.

I would linger in the shower, caressing, probing, feeling my hands do their work; craving more. Closing my eyes as the water rushed over me, I would imagine the maleness I needed so vividly that I would have to stifle screams.

Sometimes I would wake in the night, feeling fulfilled, but not knowing where I was. My mind was playing tricks on me. I was in a mental institution in Louisville, Kentucky. The feeling of sexual satisfaction was very real, and I was familiar with it. I didn't know who my lover had been. Had I been imagining it?

I couldn't convince myself to write these things in my journal. They were simply too personal.

March 21, 1978

I had a setback in Dr. Fitzpatrick's office today. I don't know what happened. There seemed to have been a horrific storm in the room, and I couldn't hear anything but wind. I wonder if my new medicine is causing me to hallucinate. If it is, it will have to be changed. I'm so tired.

"Hello, Clemmie," the doctor said.

"Hello."

I handed him my journal, anticipating a lecture for the entry.

"You mustn't be upset by that episode the other day. I'm sure it's overblown in your mind. I'll remind you that it takes a while for this medicine to take effect."

"I'm having enough trouble coping without additional strange happenings. Maybe you should decrease the dosage."

I knew he wasn't going to budge.

"Let's give it a little more time. I think you'll change your mind."

"All right. A little longer."

Dr. Fitzpatrick made a quick study of his notes. His face was bright as if he were about to smile.

"So your mother was going to have a baby. That was pretty big news for a ten-year-old, but you made yourself accept it?"

"Of course, I did. It was just a shock at first."

"Everything else was the same? Roy was selling insurance; enjoying his work?"

"Yes. Everything was the same in our family, but I thought my world would fall apart because of Daniel."

"Can you tell me about it?"

———————

Mrs. Grover didn't come to work the day after Daniel came home from the hospital, but she showed up on our porch the following morning.

"Come in, Delia." Mama smiled.

"No, thank you." Mrs. Grover looked nervous.

"How is little Daniel? Did he get to come home?"

"He's home. A neighbor from down the road is lookin' after him."

"I've just made a fresh pot of coffee. Are you sure you won't come in and have a cup? Clementine and I are anxious to hear about Daniel."

"No, thank you."

Mrs. Grover looked down at the boards of the porch floor.

"Mrs. Hubbard, I don't know exactly how to say this, so I'll just say it plain and simple. I think it would be best if Daniel and Clementine didn't play together anymore."

She might as well have slapped me. I couldn't believe what she was saying.

"I don't understand," Mama said.

"I'm truly sorry, so very sorry."

"Is Daniel going to be all right?" I asked.

"Yes, but he'll always remember this accident."

It wasn't an accident. Those boys had deliberately hurt Daniel and tried to scare the bejeezus out of him. Daniel had flat out lied to his mother.

"What do you mean, Delia?" Mama asked.

"You haven't been here long. You wouldn't understand."

She picked up her bucket of cleaning supplies and turned to go.

"Goodbye," she said, and started down the beach.

I hated Daniel's mother for what she was doing. Neither Mama nor I understood her reasoning, but Mama insisted that I abide by Mrs. Grover's wishes. I missed Daniel something awful. Nothing was fun without him.

A few days passed, and I couldn't stand it any longer. I didn't care what Daniel's mother thought was best. I just had to see him.

I told Mama I was going fishing. I had my fishing pole and a can of worms I had dug up to make it look authentic, and headed for the creek. As soon as I was out of sight, I hid my fishing gear in the weeds and cut through the woods to Daniel's house. I sneaked into the back yard and crept over to his bedroom window. It was open, but I didn't hear a sound. I saw him lying on his back in bed. He wasn't snoring, but looked like he was asleep.

"Daniel?"

He shot up from his bed, looking frightened.

"Daniel, it's me, Clemmie. Are you alone?"

A quarrelsome expression spread across his face.

"Yes, I'm alone, and that's how I'm gonna stay."

"I had to tell Mama a lie to get to see you. The least you can do is let me come inside."

"Okay. Go around to the kitchen door, and I'll unlock it."

He looked like he wanted to kill something when he opened the door. I had planned to give him a little hug, but changed my mind.

"You want some juice or somethin'?" he offered.

"Sure."

I pulled out a chair, and sat down at the table while Daniel poured grape juice. We automatically clinked our jelly glasses in an unspoken toast to our friendship.

"Listen, Clemmie, we can't play together anymore."

"That's exactly what your mother said. Why can't we, Daniel? What's going on?"

"You wouldn't understand."

I was really getting tired of all the doubletalk from Daniel and his mother.

"Your mother said what happened to you was an accident, but you and I know that's not true."

"It was an a-accident."

"You're just plain lying, Daniel Grover! I know who did this to you, and I know it was no accident. In case you've forgotten, I have your bloody knife to prove it."

"What'd you do with my knife?"

"I hid it just like you told me to."

"Where?"

"I'm not telling you. I don't have to."

"Do, too. It's my knife."

"Tell me the truth, and I might tell you where it is."

Daniel started to sob, and I thought my heart would break.

"I c-can't tell you any m-more, Clemmie. And I can't p-play with you, either. You just got to trust me."

I felt so sorry for him. I knew he had some awful secret that he was afraid to tell me. I walked around the table and put my hand on his shoulder. If he hadn't been so bunged up, I would have given him a bear hug.

"Please don't cry, Daniel. I don't know why you won't tell me what's going on, but I won't ask you any more questions. I just hate being in the dark, that's all."

"I know." He started crying again.

"I'll clean up your knife and bring it the next time I come to see you."

"No. Don't clean it up. I want it just the way it is."

———

"I don't like the looks of the sky," Mama said. "I rang the bell. Didn't you hear it?"

"No. I'm sorry."

"I see the fish outsmarted you."

"Yeah, I think maybe it was too hot for them to bite."

"What does heat have to do with fish biting?"

"I don't know. It's something Daniel told me."

"I know you miss him. We don't always understand the reasons people have for the things they do. Maybe Daniel's mother will change her mind when he gets well."

"I think she's mean."

"Clementine, you know Delia isn't a mean-spirited person. I'm sure she believes she's doing the right thing."

Suddenly, lightning flashed and turned the dark sky white. Thunder cracked its warning.

"Let's get inside and latch the windows." Mama looked worried.

Strong gusts of wind swept across the water and picked up sand, slinging it through the air. A deluge of rain followed. Something was banging against the cottage.

"Get away from that window!" Mama yelled. "It's the shutter."

We were in the narrow hallway between the living room and kitchen when the power went off.

"There's nothing to be afraid of, sweetheart." Mama tried to sound calm. "Stay here while I get a flashlight."

She returned a few minutes later with a candle.

"Roy must have the flashlight in the car. This will have to do."

The storm raged, and Mama hugged me close. We had to yell to hear one another. This storm was like none I had ever seen. The wind was stronger, the rain more torrential, and the thunder and lightning were nothing less than awesome.

"I wish Roy were here," I said, unable to control my trembling and the fear in my voice.

"He'll be here any minute. Now, stop fretting."

Rain pelted the roof like snare drums, and the thunder and lightning were relentless. The wind howled, rattling the windows, and the sky was eerily bright; so bright that we didn't see the headlights.

Roy dashed inside, slamming the door, and leaned against it as if he were trying to keep out the storm. He was drenched, and his hair was pasted to his head.

"Watch the candle, Clementine," Mama said, rushing to Roy. "Get out of those clothes, honey. I'll get dry ones."

"No time for that. We have to get out of here fast. The creek's out of its banks, and parts of the main road are flooded. Some of the side roads are already washed out."

I started to cry.

Roy hugged me to him. He went down on one knee and looked into my eyes.

"Clementine, would I let anything happen to you?" He didn't wait for my answer. "Of course, I wouldn't. We just have to be smarter than the weather, that's all. Now, we're going to throw a few things into our suitcases, and get out of Dodge."

Roy carried the candle, and Mama and I followed him. He and Mama tossed clothes into two suitcases, and she packed our important papers and her shoebox of photographs.

"That's enough," Roy said. "We need to leave now."

"My diary!" I wailed.

"All right. Grab it, and come on."

Roy held the candle so I could get my diary from the nightstand. He started to the living room, but I didn't follow.

"Clementine!" Mama's voice was hoarse.

"I'm coming."

Clutching the diary, I crawled into my closet and felt around until I found the box where I had stashed Daniel's knife. I stuffed the diary into it and held it close as I ran to the living room.

The wind snuffed the candle as soon as Roy opened the door. He made it to the car with the luggage in the dark and hurried back to the house for Mama and me. It was hard to walk because of the strong wind. Roy got between us and hauled us to the car.

"I'm sorry to stop you, but our time is up," Dr. Fitzpatrick said.

Chapter Five

—

Sunshine bathed the landscape, showing off its spring colors as I left Dr. Fitzpatrick's office, and I couldn't make myself go straight to my room to write in my journal. I strolled through the grounds to a bench not far from the street, and watched traffic whiz by the tall wrought iron fence.

Nobody was holding me here against my will. I could be on the other side of that fence, but where would I go? What would I do?

Forsythia and japonica bushes were in full bloom. I was familiar with both, but it seemed a long while since I had seen either. They grew in Chicago in the late spring, I recalled. It was still sweater weather when Mama and I clipped forsythia branches to put in a tall vase to decorate our apartment. That meant we hadn't met Roy.

I couldn't imagine how the human brain worked. If I told Dr. Fitzpatrick I gauged time by spring flowers, I would never be able to leave this place.

March 23, 1978

It's beautiful outside today. I would have stayed to enjoy the spring air longer, but I felt so lonely.

I learned why I am afraid of storms during today's session. I suppose I should be relieved at the discovery, but what does it prove?

My heart goes out to the other patients here, but I confess that I find myself the most pitiful of all. Here I am, sheltered from the outside world, living one day at a time, and having little hope of getting better.

I realized I was nibbling the eraser of my pencil. That wasn't a habit of mine. I laid down the pencil, and opened my locket to look at Daniel's sweet face, remembering our ironclad childhood bond that long-ago summer.

It was strange the way Daniel and I had melded. Back in Chicago my friends had all been girls. At school girls and boys went their separate ways, except in the classroom. But Daniel and I seemed to think alike and enjoy the same things. Although he was younger, he was usually the one to make outrageous or naughty suggestions, but I always went along with them.

"You like to cuss?" he asked one morning. We were under the steps of the cottage, and I was afraid Mama would hear us. "What a question!" I said, feigning righteous indignation, but thinking it would be great fun. Daniel shrugged, dismissing the idea.

"What do you consider cussing?" I asked him.

"Just about anything you'd be scared to say in church."

"Okay, let's try it."

Daniel cocked his head to one side, tilted his chin, and rolled his eyes heavenward as though deep in thought.

"Damn!" he said enthusiastically. "Your turn."

"Hell," I whispered.

"You gotta say it like you mean it. It's not any good unless you do it right. Listen to this: sheeeit," he said, stretching the word to the limit. "See what I mean?"

I was getting into the game. "Assy," I said, trying to make it sound as dirty as I could.

"That's not a word. It's got to be a real word."

"Assy is too a word. For example: that was an assy thing to say."

"Okay, this is the last one. Motherfucker!" He whispered it, but made it sound mean, nasty, and very adult-like.

"That really sounded bad. I've never heard anyone say that."

"'Course not; it's a black cussword. White people don't say it."

I wondered where Daniel had heard that word. His mother would have skinned him alive if she heard him utter such filth.

As naughty as Daniel could be, I didn't know anyone who could be more angelic. He and his mother went to church every Sunday, and Daniel loved singing hymns. He and I had a funeral for a dead bird we found in the woods one day. Daniel preached, extolling the virtues of God's creatures, especially birds since they could fly and had pretty voices. We dug a hole, and buried the deceased, wrapped in aluminum foil from our lunch, and sang *His Eye is on the Sparrow* at the gravesite.

I closed my locket, wondering if I would ever see Daniel again.

———

I didn't intend to sit in this depressing reception area much longer. I had been waiting for twenty minutes, trying to keep focused so I could pick up where I had left off. It was all I could do to make myself stay. I wanted to run out of the building and back to my room.

I was about to tell the receptionist I couldn't wait any longer when she told me the doctor was ready to see me.

"I'm sorry to have kept you waiting, Clemmie," Dr. Fitzpatrick said.

I glared at him.

"Are you depressed?"

"No more than usual."

"You must remember it's very important for you to keep a positive attitude."

I wanted to cry. He was treating me like a child.

"I'll work on it."

"At our last session you were telling me about your family leaving Tybee Island in a storm."

"That's right."

We had a terrible time getting off the island. The storm became more ferocious by the minute. The Pontiac crawled through the muddy, swirling water. It was impossible to see the shoulder because water completely covered the road. We couldn't tell that Roy had driven off the road until after the fact, but he managed to manhandle the car back onto what was left of the gravel. There were places where the road was completely washed out, and we were afraid we might have to abandon the car and wade to safety, but Roy maneuvered us through the sludge at a steady pace.

It took forever to get to the bridge and the Savannah city limits. We were relieved, but exhausted when we checked into a motel. Dinner wasn't mentioned even though we hadn't eaten. Feeling safe and dry was a luxury.

Roy turned on the local news, and we learned that Tybee Island was under mandatory evacuation. I wondered where Daniel and his mother were. I prayed for their safety, then cried myself to sleep.

Roy called his office the next morning. His boss was aware of the evacuation, and offered Roy a few days' leave.

The island was shut down, and nobody was allowed to return for the next two days. We saw the havoc wreaked by the monster storm on the news.

"There's no point in going back," Roy said.

"Oh, Roy, we have to go see if there's anything worth salvaging," Mama said.

We returned to find the entire row of cottages devastated. Shutters were completely ripped off, or left hanging by a rusty hinge. Windows were blown out of their frames, or broken, leaving jagged shards of glass. Mud coated everything the storm had left behind. Our front door gaped open, and we could measure how high the water had risen by the muddy line on the sofa. The shag carpet was matted with sludge, and part of the roof was missing. Roy was right. There was no reason to have come back.

"We have to go to Daniel's house to make sure he and his mother are all right," I said.

"Honey, they won't be there," Mama reasoned. "The entire island was evacuated."

"Please," I begged.

"It's only a little bit out of our way," Roy said. "We'll go check it out."

The Grover house was barely standing; it listed to one side. The doors were wide open, and the windows were gone. Mrs. Grover's bucket of cleaning supplies sat in the middle of the living room floor. There was no sign of life.

"There's nobody here, sweetheart," Roy said. "Daniel and his mom are probably in a shelter or with relatives."

"So, young Daniel has disappeared," Dr. Fitzpatrick said.

"Why do you do that?" I felt like screaming when he interrupted me. He kept telling me that he wanted my thoughts to flow; that I shouldn't have to reach for what happened next.

"Forgive me, my dear. I was simply caught up in your story."

"It's not a story, doctor. It's what really happened."

"Of course. Please continue."

He had made me lose my train of thought. I couldn't recall what I had been telling him. A tall, brassy-looking woman was all I could see. She had flaming red hair, pinned up on her head, and large hoop earrings.

"Clemmie, what is it?"

"A whore, in short shorts and a halter top. She has on high heels. I don't like her, and she knows it."

"You haven't mentioned this woman before. Was she someone you knew on Tybee Island?"

"No."

"Was she a friend of your mother's?"

"No. Mama didn't know her."

"Did Roy know her?"

"Of course, Roy knew her. Daniel knew her, too. So did Mama Rae."

"I think we should probably stop for the day. It seems we have a gap that needs your attention. You have inadvertently skipped ahead. Go and rest for a while, and try to remember when you left the island."

Chapter Six

I placed a cold washcloth on my forehead and lay on the bed, willing my head to stop throbbing and the tension to leave my body. If I could make my mind go blank, maybe I could go to sleep and the pain would be gone.

Everything was red: a colander filled with berries in a kitchen sink, the amazon's fiery hair, and blood on a wall. Red was everywhere. . .

I was drained when I awoke. I hated my naked eyes. They were large and not a bad shade of blue, but there was something stark about them. I could usually remedy the problem with just a dot of eyeliner in the outer corners, but my hand was shaky, so I gave it up.

My journal beckoned from the desk. I opened it and forced myself to read the last few entries. As I read the revelation about my fear of storms, something clicked. I remembered the fury of the storm and how it ravaged the small island. I was back on track.

March 28, 1978

I recall that Tybee Island was destroyed. The storm had chased its inhabitants hither and yon. I remember fearing that I had lost Daniel forever.

Mills Insurance Agency rented a furnished apartment for us close to Roy's office. It was one of an eight-unit complex. The two-story building was dirty brown stucco with four apartments on each side of a breezeway, containing a bank of mailboxes and a bulletin board.

The couch in the living room doubled as my bed, and the unit wasn't air conditioned. It was stifling during the day, so Mama and I spent a lot of time in a little park down the street. We slept with all the windows open in the evenings and hoped for a breeze. Each night my thoughts turned to Daniel, and I hoped that by some miracle, I would see him again.

We had been in the apartment less than two weeks when Roy came home behaving very strangely. I heard him whistling as he came up the walk, and his grin lit up the earth-colored walls the minute he walked through the door.

"You look like the cat that swallowed the canary," Mama said, wiping perspiration from her forehead. She was making tuna sandwiches because it was too hot to cook.

"Girls, our troubles are over," Roy said, sweeping Mama into an elaborate embrace and kissing her soundly.

"What in the world?" Mama laughed.

"Put that stuff away. I'll tell you all about it when we're sitting in Jay's Seafood Shack with the air conditioner going full blast."

Mama donned the indulgent smile she saved just for Roy, and took off her apron.

We placed our orders in the dark coolness of the restaurant, and Mama and I trained our eyes on Roy's excited face.

"Ladies," he said, "we're off to the Garden of Eden."

"And just where might that be?" Mama raised an eyebrow.

"Hilton Head Island, South Carolina. I went there today with the boss. It's undoubtedly the most beautiful place I've ever laid eyes upon."

"What were you doing there?" I asked.

"Renting office space. I told you the company was expanding. Well, this island is booming. A gent by the name of Charles Fraser developed Sea Pines Plantation, a ritzy resort on the south end of the island. Fred Hack is developing Port Royal Plantation on the north end. The golf courses are gorgeous. And wait until you see the beachfront lots. They're spectacular, and they're selling like hotcakes."

"Does that mean that Mills is moving its Savannah office there?" Mama asked.

"No. They'll have a branch office there. They want to get in on the ground floor of a venture that's going to make us all rich. Small businesses are springing up all over the place. Don't you see, Emily? All those folks need insurance, all kinds of insurance. And I'm just the guy to sell it to them."

"Where will we live?" Mama looked worried. "We certainly can't afford to live in a resort area."

"I hope you two haven't made any plans for the weekend, because I have. Tomorrow we go to Hilton Head to see what's available."

Mama was sometimes leery of Roy's spur-of-the-moment decisions, but I treasured his sense of adventure. I could hardly wait until morning.

The drive to the paradise where we would go in search of our new home should have taken less than an hour, but it seemed more like three. Mama was sick from the time we got into the car until we got there. She made it across the bridge, but Roy had to pull off the road twice before we reached the city limits.

The island was exactly as Roy had described it. Leaves of live oaks glittered in the morning sun, and the landscape was alive with crepe myrtles and oleanders showing off their brilliant colors.

"What did I tell you?" Roy said as Mama and I oohed and aahed at the beautiful surroundings.

I had expected to see new buildings and lots of construction, but the main drag didn't appear to be exactly booming. We drove to the small building Roy had leased for his new office. It stood alone, surrounded by trees, and hardly put a dent in the landscape.

Roy showed us some of the island before stopping for lunch at a place called Katie McElven's Roadside Restaurant. The food was wonderful, and I fell in love with the sweet tea.

Aside from Sea Pines and Port Royal Plantations, the most populated area was Forest Beach. We ran across a very interesting building there. It housed a bowling alley, a Post Office, a gift shop, and a little outdoor lunch counter. I thought the wooded lots at Forest Beach were wonderful. It would be like living in the woods, but Roy axed that dream real fast. He said we couldn't afford it, at least not right away.

The place we finally decided upon was Folly Field. It was a far cry from the plantations, and even Forest Beach, but it was heaven compared to the cramped apartment in Savannah. The houses at Folly Field were small and inexpensive cracker boxes that sat on tiny lots. They were built on stilts, and the space beneath them was framed with latticework. I was reminded of Tybee Island because these houses sat in a neat row reminiscent of the rental cottages before the storm. This area had just been developed, so the homes were at least new.

Roy struck a deal with a man who had bought one of the houses for an investment. The gentleman wanted to rent it out for a year. Then he and his family planned to move into it. We would have to buy furniture, but that was something we planned to do regardless.

We arrived on the island ahead of our new furniture. The Sea Crest, a ten-unit motel, was our home for the next three days. During our stay there Mama and I learned as much about the island as we could while Roy was at work.

There were only two churches: St. Luke's Catholic and a Presbyterian Church. Being a Methodist, Mama wasn't wild about either, but opted for the latter. There was an elementary school that I would be attending shortly. The following year I would be bused to Bluffton.

Roy didn't go to his office the day our furniture arrived. He took Mama and me with him to the house, and we decided where we wanted each piece placed. Roy helped the delivery men with the uncrating while Mama told them how to arrange each room.

I tried to feel excited about the move because Roy and Mama were so happy. Getting out of that fleabag apartment was great, and Hilton Head was beautiful, but I missed Daniel so much I could hardly stand it. I would have felt a lot better if I had been able to tell him goodbye.

It was our first night in the new house. I turned on my bedside lamp and opened my diary.

July 13, 1966

Dear Diary,

Fate has plopped me down here on Hilton Head Island. I know I should be looking forward to all of the exciting adventures that await me, but I'm not. If only Daniel were here, everything would be different. I feel like I'm missing an arm.

Sincerely yours,

Clementine Foster

P.S. Maybe you could find it in your heart to give me a sign of some kind that Daniel is all right. Think about it.

Dr. Fitzpatrick was amazed that I could recall such intricate details when I shared my recollections with him.

"It appears that your new medication has fully kicked in, Clemmie. Do you have more energy?"

"Maybe. Dr. Fitzpatrick, may I ask you a question?"

"Of course."

"Can you please explain how my childhood recollections can get to the root of my memory lapse?"

"Certainly. By revisiting your past I'm confident that you'll stumble upon the problem that caused the lapse. I know you're impatient, but you'll get there."

"How can you say that? I haven't the vaguest notion how I got here. I don't know a living soul in the State of Kentucky. I . . ."

"I understand your frustration, but you must try to be patient."

"I don't want to be patient! You haven't learned a thing from what I've told you. I've looked through the Louisville phone directory, and I don't recognize any names or addresses. I've called every Hubbard listed, and they've never heard of me. How am I supposed to feel?"

"You're doing very well with your recollections. It won't be long now. I'm afraid our time is up."

The floodgates opened as soon as I reached my room. I sobbed until there was nothing left. I went to the bathroom and looked in the mirror, trying to get in touch with myself. It was a strange feeling. I looked like Mama's photos when she was young: honey-blond hair, cornflower blue eyes, dark lashes, and white teeth. People told me I was pretty.

I was meeting Maria for dinner, and arrived a few minutes early. Many of the patients weren't capable of going through the cafeteria line and had to be fed by attendants. As I watched such a scene I realized how fortunate I was.

Maria and I studied the chalkboard listing the dinner choices.

"I know what I'm having," she said.

"You sound excited."

"I am. Look! We can get Hot Browns."

"I've never heard of a Hot Brown."

"It's strictly a Kentucky dish, and one of my favorites."

"What's in it?"

"Turkey breast and crisp bacon in a tangy cheese sauce, served on points of toast, and there's a slice. . ."

"Of broiled tomato on top," I finished, realizing that I was, indeed, familiar with the dish.

I was onto something, but didn't know what. If a Hot Brown was only served in Kentucky, then I must have lived here.

Chapter Seven

Despite my growing dislike for sharing my life with Dr. Fitzpatrick, during my next session I found myself eager to paint him a perfect portrait of the paradise of my youth. I described the beauty of the salt marshes and how they flooded twice each day as if by magic. And I went into intricate detail depicting the tiny, greedy sandpipers foraging at the water's edge on their spindly matchstick legs, spotty grayish-brown feathers bathed in morning sun. My description of how the seagulls screamed, and how the slightest breeze ruffled their downy feathers most assuredly would have taken him to the South Carolina beach if he only closed his eyes.

The island was inhabited by so many delightful creatures that I didn't know where to start, so I just began ticking them off as quickly as they came to mind: the pelican, the delicate egret, the opossum, and the alligator.

I was elaborating on the art of extracting a sand dollar from the shallow waters of the ocean's silted floor, using my toes as tweezers when Dr. Fitzpatrick began squirming in his chair. It was apparent that he was only interested in my relationships with human beings, so I made myself focus on the people we met at Folly Field.

The day after we moved into the new house, Mama and I decided to introduce ourselves to some of our neighbors. We weren't having much luck; nobody seemed to be at home.

"Maybe everyone works," I said.

"I suppose it's possible," Mama said, as we climbed the steps to the next house.

Mama knocked on the door, and we heard heavy footsteps. The door opened, and there stood an overweight blond woman, wearing a two-piece swimsuit. Her face was beet-red.

"Well, hello." She smiled.

"Good morning." Mama returned the smile. "I'm Emily Hubbard, and this is my daughter, Clementine. We're your new neighbors. We just moved in a few houses from here." She gestured in the direction of our house.

"Well, come in. I'm Alice Renaker. Don't look at me, though. Ain't I a sight?"

"You look cool and comfortable," Mama lied.

Mrs. Renaker led us into the living room, and invited us to sit down.

"Have you lived here long?" Mama asked.

"Oh, about six months. Husband's work, you know. What brings you folks here?"

"My husband works for an insurance company," Mama said. "They just opened a branch office here."

Mrs. Renaker heaved a little sigh. "Well, I can't tell you how glad I am to meet such pleasant neighbors. It can git right down lonesome sometimes. All the men around here work, and most of the women do, too. I ain't met the people next door; can't never find 'em home. There's a nice young fella lives down close to you, though; a bachelor. I think he's a writer or somethin'."

"He sounds interesting," Mama said.

"I have to tell you there's some you don't want to know. My baby's not but 'leven, and she sure don't need to be havin' any truck with the likes of them."

She looked at me.

"How old are you, Clementine, was it?"

"Yes ma'am. My name's Clementine, and I'm ten-and-a-half."

"Well, now, ain't that somethin'?" Mrs. Renaker smiled. "My Gloria Jean'll be real glad to meet you. The only playmate she's got is a little girl down there a ways, but her mama and daddy both work. She's not here through the week. I guess they take her to a baby sitter. She ain't but four years old."

"Where is your daughter now?" I asked.

Mrs. Renaker put a hand to her mouth and made a strange sound, smothering a snicker. "I'm ashamed to tell you the little sleepy head's still sacked out. I'll go roust her out right now."

"Don't wake her on our account," Mama said. "We have to be going. We're still unpacking."

"I sure am gonna wake her up. Why she'd have a regular fit if I let Clementine get away without them gettin' to meet each other. I'll be right back."

Mama and I pried ourselves loose from the plastic sofa cover as soon as she left the room.

A few minutes later Mrs. Renaker returned, half dragging her daughter. Gloria Jean was the spitting image of her mother, and looked like she would probably outgrow her in the next few years. She yawned and stretched by way of a greeting.

"Precious," the mother said, "I want you to meet our new neighbors. This here's Mrs. Hibbard and her daughter, Clementine."

"Hubbard," Mama corrected. "We're happy to meet you, Gloria Jean."

"Hi," I said.

"Hey," Gloria Jean drawled. "Mama, I'm starved."

Mrs. Renaker gave her daughter a playful swat and smiled at Mama.

"Ain't that just like a youngun'? Where's your manners, precious?"

"We really do need to be going," Mama said, starting to the door. "It was very nice meeting you both."

"Don't be strangers, now." Mrs. Renaker grinned. "Me and Gloria Jean will see you real soon."

She was true to her word and dropped in for visits quite often with Gloria Jean in tow. The way she catered to her spoiled daughter made me sick. The kid was eleven years old, and she ran to her mother every time she had to blow her nose.

I tried to like Gloria Jean, but I couldn't do it. She would whine to me about being fat, then sit down and eat a half-gallon of ice cream. The two of us had nothing in common. I liked the outdoors, and she was a couch potato in front of a television set with a plate of cookies.

I lucked out when school started because I attended school on the island, and Gloria Jean rode a bus to Bluffton. By the time she got home I was either doing my homework, or I had escaped to the woods close to our house.

I couldn't imagine Gloria Jean in the woods. She was the kind who would cry over a mosquito bite, and I just knew she wouldn't be the least bit interested in climbing trees or exploring among the forest critters.

It wasn't only that I liked the sights and sounds of the woods; they reminded me of Daniel and all of our adventures. I thought of him every time I ventured into the earthy, cool darkness.

The wild ferns, Spanish moss, and prickly yucca plants were all so beautiful. Squirrels and warblers filled the trees, and butterflies flitted here and there, stopping often to gather nectar. I thought the cotton rats were outrageously brave, dashing across my path and scurrying to safety just before my footfall.

One afternoon I was looking at a cluster of berries hanging from a branch beside the path when a gravelly voice startled me.

"Go on; pick 'em. Eat one; see you likes it."

An old black woman wearing an amused expression watched me intently. She wore a long-sleeved shirt and a skirt that came down to her feet. A slouch hat shaded her eyes, and she carried a basket of things she must have picked in the woods.

"What if it's poisonous?"

"Ain't."

"How do you know?"

"I know dees woods. Dis here a puckerbush. De berries are good for what ails you."

I picked one and popped it into my mouth. It didn't taste particularly good, and smelled like bay rum.

"I'm Clementine Foster," I said, "soon to be Clementine Hubbard because my stepfather is going to adopt me."

"You call me Mama Rae." She seemed disinterested in my adoption.

The old woman hadn't said much, and the little she had said sounded pretty gruff, but I knew I was going to like her.

"I live over that way," I told her, pointing.

"Uh huh."

"What do you have in your basket, Mama Rae?"

"Herbs." She picked a handful of the berries, then stooped down to pluck something that looked like a weed.

She was definitely a woman of few words. I watched as she picked some more. The way she was haphazardly tossing them into the basket made me wonder how she would ever be able to separate them when she got home. I was about to mention my concern when she turned abruptly and started down the path.

"Are you leaving?" I called after her.

Silence was my answer.

I didn't mention my strange new acquaintance to Mama and Roy. Maybe it was because she seemed so mysterious. I did, however, devote an entire page of my diary to her.

August 22, 1966

Dear Diary,

I met a new friend today, and I have a feeling in my bones that she is going to be very special. Her name is Mama Rae, and she's probably about a hundred years old. Her face is beautifully wrinkled; it's the kind of face I had to study in art class at school back in Chicago. You may not know it, but those wrinkles are awfully hard to draw. Mama Rae dresses funny, and she wears a man's hat. I wonder if she has a husband. I'd bet against it.

Yours truly,

Clementine Foster

"Well, Clemmie, this seems to be a good stopping point," the doctor said.

He walked around his desk and sat on the edge of it facing me. He had started making friendly gestures lately, and I thought someone must have suggested that he show a little more warmth toward his patients.

It was difficult to look at him when he was so close. His Coke-bottle-thick glasses looked like a bug's eyes, and light from the window illuminated his bald pate. It was almost comical.

"I'll see you soon," he said.

That night I had a mysterious dream. People, events and places were jumbled together, and none of it made sense. Daniel was in my class at school on Hilton Head Island. The Caucasian children were taunting him, calling him *nigger* and saying horribly mean things to him. My class was more than half black, so I couldn't understand why they had singled out Daniel. The teacher and some of the other students were watching the spectacle while he stood beside his desk stoically taking the abuse.

I was crying for help, and suddenly Mama Rae appeared. She held a live chicken, its wings fluttering furiously. In a flash, she twisted the fowl's head from its body, and blood sprayed all over the room. When at last the bird was still, Mama Rae held it over her head and allowed its blood to trickle into her gaping mouth. Then, she began mumbling something indistinguishable. The sight horrified me.

Suddenly, the storm struck; the same storm that had devastated Tybee Island. The classroom was spotlight bright. The first crack of thunder signaled the tempest. Then ferocious wind lashed at anything that wasn't nailed down, sending books and papers flying, smashing children into their desks and pinning them against walls. Windowpanes blew out, and shards of glass sailed through the turbulent air, splintering upon impact with whatever was in their path. Torrential rain slammed through the windows. It was muddy, like the swirling floodwaters that washed out the side roads.

Everything was quiet then. Daniel and I were the only ones left in the room. I could hear Roy strumming his old guitar and crying.

I awoke with a start. My cotton nightgown stuck to my sweaty body, and I was paralyzed with fright.

I got out of bed and grabbed my journal. This strange, disjointed dream had to mean something, but I wasn't capable of putting it into words. I would have to sort out the components of the dream before I shared it with Dr. Fitzpatrick.

The next session with my psychiatrist was simply a continuation of the last. I didn't mention the dream.

When I came home from school the next afternoon, Mrs. Renaker was sitting at our kitchen table with Mama. They were drinking iced tea.

"Hello, Mrs. Renaker," I said.

"Hi there, sugar. My Gloria Jean sure does miss you now that school's started."

"We haven't seen much of one another lately. I guess we've both been pretty busy with homework."

I poured a glass of milk, and took an oatmeal cookie out of the jar on the counter.

"Well," Mrs. Renaker said, resuming her story that my arrival had interrupted, "what do you think they did with the poor thing's body?"

Mama looked at her questioningly.

"Put her in the meat locker right here on the island. Can you imagine that? A meat locker! Right in the same freezer with the sides of beef, hangin' on a hook with the rest of the dead meat for all I know."

"That's terrible," Mama said.

"Terrible or not, it's God's truth, sure as I'm sittin' here. They kept her there until the hearse come from Savannah. Didn't have nothin' else to do with her, the way I heard it."

My milk and cookie suddenly didn't look very appealing.

"Did someone die?" I had to ask.

"I'm 'fraid so, honey," Mrs. Renaker said. "Sweetie, could I have one of them delicious lookin' cookies?"

I carried the cookie jar to the table.

"Now, don't you go gettin' yourself all upset." She patted my hand. "None of us knew the poor soul."

I excused myself and went to change into my play clothes. Then, I took off for the woods, hoping to find Mama Rae on one of her herb gathering excursions. I went straight to the puckerbush where I had found her the previous day.

"Mama Rae?"

There was no answer.

Chapter Eight

———

Roy left work early. He and Mama picked me up after school, and we drove to Savannah to see the lawyer Roy had hired to handle my adoption. All of the legal documents had been drawn up, and as soon as Mama and Roy signed them, we walked out of the office with the same last name.

"Now you're really my daughter," Roy said, hugging me. He and Mama looked so happy, and I had to admit it made me feel good.

Roy was in one of his magnanimous moods. He took us shopping and spent way too much. Mama needed maternity clothes. The few things she had salvaged from Tybee Island were too tight, so she chose several outfits and a swimsuit. I tried on two dresses, several pairs of shorts and tee shirts, and Roy insisted that I take them all. He bought himself a new suit and an ugly pair of swimming trunks. Then he took his new family to a swanky restaurant for dinner.

The following day was a Saturday, and although Roy worked lots of weekends, he decided to take the day off to spend it with Mama and me. We packed a picnic lunch and rented a sailboat for the day. The water was calm, and we had a great time. We anchored for a while to play in the water. I practiced my diving, and Roy splashed Mama, who only wanted to sunbathe, with his belly flops. He and I had a fantastic water fight, then we let the sun and wind dry us while we ate lunch.

We were tired and grubby when we returned the boat. Roy drove to the pier behind Hudson's Restaurant where the shrimp boats brought in their daily hauls, and bought a bucket of fresh shrimp for a dollar. Mama was exhausted, so Roy cooked our dinner in a big boiling pot, and we peeled and ate shrimp until we couldn't eat any more.

"I take it this was a happy time in your childhood," Dr. Fitzpatrick said.

"Yes, it was. Roy's adopting me made me feel truly loved. I felt safe and happy, but I was still lonely for Daniel."

"Did Mama Rae become your friend?"

"Yes. Since I no longer had Daniel, she became my closest friend. I saw her as often as I could."

"Tell me more about Mama Rae."

I ran into Mama Rae in some unlikely places when I was least expecting her. There was a mom-and-pop general store with gasoline pumps out front on the main drag. It wasn't far from our house. I often went there to buy a Coke or ice cream on a stick, and Mama Rae would be there passing the time of day with the owner and guzzling a grape soft drink. She spent some of her time at the little roadside stand where we bought seafood and Vidalia onions. And more often than not she sat on the side of the main road in her folding chair with *Bait for Sale* painted on a piece of cardboard.

One day after school I was fooling around in the woods. Venturing deeper into the jungle-like darkness than I had ever gone before, I realized that I had nearly reached the far side of the woods. Patches of blue sky shone through the trees. I kept walking until I came to a clearing where I saw the strangest sight: several ordinary-looking chickens were roaming around, scratching up bugs and worms as if they owned the place.

I thought I saw the corner of a building through the leaves. The chickens seemed harmless, so I made a path right through the middle of them to get a better look. They didn't like that one bit, and began squawking and fluttering all over the place. The one making the most noise was perched on a nest right there in the woods.

"Stop scarin' my settin' hen!"

The old woman was sitting on the front porch of a tiny weatherboard house, hulling peas. She didn't seem surprised to see me. Her slouch hat was pulled down over her eyes, and the skirt she wore hit her about eight or ten inches below the knee. Her skinny legs were covered with thick, brown cotton stockings, and her large feet sported a pair of bright purple sandals.

"Mama Rae, am I glad to see you!"

"Why's dat?"

"I think I might be lost."

Mama Rae laughed. Her voice was deep, but her laugh was high-pitched and sounded like it belonged to someone else. I realized this was the first time I had heard her laugh.

There was only one chair on the porch, so I sat down on the steps. Mama Rae made me do all the talking while she finished her work. I had grown quite comfortable with her despite the fact that she had little to say, and when she did, she sounded awfully gruff. We had spent quite a bit of time together in the woods, and she had taught me a lot about plant and animal life. She always seemed to enjoy my company, but she had never mentioned where she lived. It occurred to me that if I hadn't stumbled upon her house by accident, I might never have known where it was.

Mama Rae took the peas inside, and I waited on the steps. She wasn't a person to be taken for granted, and I didn't know whether she would come back, or if this was her way of dismissing me.

A few minutes passed. Then she appeared at the screen door and invited me inside. It was dark in the house, and something about it seemed eerie. I stood in the cluttered living room looking at the hodgepodge that surrounded me. There was an old wooden rocking chair. Mama Rae told me to sit in it. She seated herself in an overstuffed chair that was nearly covered with hand-crocheted antimacassars that were yellowed with age.

She saw me admiring a row of dolls displayed on the mantle.

"Look all you want, but don't touch."

The doll collection was something to behold: The first was a large wooden doll, dressed in what appeared to be genuine baby clothes. I could see that it was anchored to the wall with a thin wire encircling it just below the arms. Its face and arms had tiny hairline cracks, and I supposed it was an antique. To its left was a beautiful china doll. Somehow, Mama Rae didn't seem the kind of individual who could have purchased such a treasure. Next was a rubber doll; it was a black baby wearing nothing but a diaper fastened with large safety pins with yellow duck's heads on them.

"I didn't know you collected dolls," I said.

Mama Rae just nodded.

The last three dolls were more in line with my idea of Mama Rae's taste: there was a rag doll, a cornhusk doll, and I wasn't certain about the one on the end. It seemed to be made of all sorts of odds and ends.

"That one's unusual." I pointed to the last one. "Where did you get it?'

"Made it." She sounded indignant.

I thought it was the ugliest thing I had ever seen, but I would never have said anything to offend Mama Rae.

After my initial visit to her house, I felt free to go there often. Instead of having an after school snack at home, I would go straight to Mama Rae's. She brewed her special herb tea and baked the most delectable tarts, oozing with sweet wild berries she had picked. I noticed that she seemed keenly interested when I talked about my family and the insignificant happenings of my school day.

Mama Rae was a virtual fount of wisdom when it came to solving problems. I knew I could confide in her, so I unburdened myself to her when things went wrong at school or at home. I even confessed that I made tracks for the woods every day after school to avoid Gloria Jean.

"Be kind to everybody," she admonished. "You won't be sorry."

I became so enthralled with my new friend that my longing for Daniel wasn't so painful. Mama Rae was a mysterious person, and she knew just about everything there was to know. She was a doctor of sorts. One day I told her that Mama was feeling tired all the time. The next afternoon just as I came home from school, she was waiting for me. She carried a small teapot. I was excited to see her because she had never come to our house.

"Mama Rae!"

She smiled.

I took her inside and introduced her to Mama. They hit it off right away. I couldn't help noticing that Mama Rae was much more talkative when she conversed with Mama and other adults than when the two of us were alone. That bothered me. After all, she was my friend. I was the one who spent time with her. Maybe she had two personalities: one for the woods, and one for the rest of the world.

Before she left, Mama Rae told Mama to drink the tea, and assured her that she would feel better. Mama downed two cups, declaring it the best tea she had ever tasted.

"Now, sleep a while," Mama Rae told her.

Mama curled up on the couch and went to sleep. I heard Gloria Jean stomping up the front steps and shushed her before she had a chance to make more noise. Joining her on the porch, I told her that Mama wasn't feeling well and that she was sleeping, so we would have to be quiet.

Taking Mama Rae's advice, I tried to feign interest, and even expressed sympathy as Gloria Jean told me about her horrible day at school. Somebody had branded her with a new *fat* nickname, and she had once again been humiliated. I reminded her of the old adage *sticks and stones*, and that seemed to appease her. Then I told her a white lie: that I had to make dinner because Mama didn't feel up to it.

Mama was filled with energy when she awoke. She was in a fantastic mood. After we ate and washed the dishes, she suggested we go for a walk. That was when I decided Mama Rae knew just about everything.

"Is this a good place to stop, Clemmie? I'm afraid our time is up."

It was warm for April, and my bedroom window was open. The curtains ballooned with the breeze. I had finished my evening ablutions and went to the desk to write in my journal. The painful truth had come to me while I was in the shower, and I dreaded giving it credence by putting it on paper. If I could force myself to pen just a hint of what I knew to be true, it would be easier to voice it to my doctor.

April 11, 1978

I don't know how I could have buried the horrible truth, but it doesn't matter now. It's as vivid as it was the day it happened. I want to write the words; I do. I know I must relive it. I have to for self-preservation, but I can't.

If I dreamed that night, I was unaware of it, but I was wrung out the next morning. I was a zombie the entire day. My thoughts were jumbled, and I couldn't focus on anything. I don't recall anything I did; I can't even remember having meals.

April 12, 1978

I can't.

"Come in, Clemmie."

I had hoped that today of all days Dr. Fitzpatrick would exhibit at least a modicum of warmth. He took the journal from my hand and nodded for me to sit. His forehead wrinkled into its familiar furrow as he looked at the entries. A scowl took over his pale face as he looked up at me, beady eyes penetrating, and causing me to look away.

"What's so horrible that you can't seem to write about it?"

Was his voice nasty, or was I imagining it? Was he being flip concerning my fears? It didn't make any difference. I would have to tell him.

"You know you must tell me everything," he reminded in a softer tone. "This could be the beginning of a breakthrough. You realize that, don't you?"

I swallowed.

"Clemmie, I want you to take a deep breath and begin. Remember, whatever you're about to relate has already happened. We're dealing with history."

—–·—–

It was Saturday, and Roy had taken the day off. Mama seemed to have gotten over her tired spell, thanks to Mama Rae. She was so happy that she seemed to glow. Her complexion was radiant, and her eyes sparkled. The baby had grown to the point that she waddled.

We had gone for a drive and were on our way home. Roy could bring out the silly side of the most staid human alive. He and Mama had been doing their rendition of Abbott and Costello's *Who's on First* routine, and I had laughed so hard my sides ached.

"Oh, Roy, pull over at that roadside stand," Mama said. "I've been dying for a tomato."

Roy eased the Pontiac onto the shoulder, took out his wallet, and handed her a five dollar bill.

"Come on, Clementine." Mama grinned. "Let's see how much we can buy with five bucks."

We walked across the blacktop to the whitewashed stand. The produce looked mouthwatering. We bought peaches, corn-on-the-cob, and ripe, red tomatoes.

I picked up the sack, and Mama grabbed a tomato as we waited for a car to pass. She rubbed it on the side of her tummy.

"When I was a little girl, I used to pick tomatoes from my grandpa's garden and eat them right there on the spot," she said.

We started across the road.

"Did you eat them dirt and all?" I looked back over my shoulder at Mama.

"You bet I did." She smiled and sank her teeth into the juicy goodness of the fruit.

Then, everything went so fast I didn't have time to scream. A bright red dervish tore over the blacktop, heading straight for Mama. The sound of squealing tires and the stench of burned rubber filled the air. Roy was startled awake from his catnap just as I dropped the sack of produce. The sports car hit Mama full force, and I watched my mother being hurled over the top like a rag doll to the other side of the road where she lay motionless in a shallow ditch.

"Emily!" Roy's hoarse cry echoed in my ears.

I couldn't move. I knew I should be doing something. This couldn't be real. Roy ran to Mama, but I stood looking down at the tomatoes on the blacktop, yellow seeds seeping through their torn flesh. I began putting them back in the grocery sack; it seemed wrong to leave them lying in the road.

A young blond woman ran toward us.

"I didn't see her!" she cried. "The trees, the curve; I just didn't see her." Tears streaked her face, and she wrung her hands as if she were trying to convince us how sorry she was.

Mama and the baby were both dead on arrival at the hospital. It seemed surreal. Roy kept saying Mama's name over and over as if he were trying to memorize the sound of it. My eyes were dry while I watched him cry for his love and the child he would never know.

The next several days are muddled. I know there was a closed casket service at the mortuary. Roy and I were the only ones in attendance except the Renakers and Roy's co-workers. Roy was an orphan, so he didn't have any relatives to call. Aunt Bess, Mama's sister, was the only relative I remembered. When Roy called Aunt Bess, he asked her to notify anyone she thought might want to know.

My aunt came to the memorial service at the church and left immediately afterward. I wouldn't have recognized her if I had met her on the street.

"Let's stop now," Dr. Fitzpatrick suggested. "I realize how painful this must have been for you."

My face was sticky with tears.

The doctor came from behind his desk and patted me on the shoulder.

"You did just fine, Clemmie. It should be smoother sailing for you now."

I lay awake that evening, thinking about Mama. I had completely shut her death out of my memory. How could I miss her so much at this moment? I went to the closet and got the shoebox of photos. Thumbing through them, I found one of Mama holding me when I was a baby. Her smile was beautiful.

April 13, 1978

I related it all just the way I remembered it. Dr. Fitzpatrick was right. I realize now that I needed to relive what happened. It reinforced the fact that my mother is gone. Even if I were fortunate enough to locate Roy, I still couldn't talk to Mama. I don't know how to reach Aunt Bess. She remarried and moved, and I don't know her last name. I suppose that means I don't have any blood relatives who know I exist.

Chapter Nine

—

Roy changed overnight. The funny guy with a ready joke had disappeared. He brooded constantly and clung to me as though I were his lifeblood. I was never out of his sight except during the school day. He drove me to school each morning, and picked me up when the bell rang at 3:15 P.M. Then, we went to his office where he worked some more and I did my homework.

We either went out for dinner, or made sandwiches at home. Roy had lost his proclivity for interesting table conversation, simply asking how my day had gone without listening to my reply.

I missed my mother dreadfully, and I ached to hear her voice and wonderful laugh. Daily I would find myself needing to seek her advice, and I would often start to call for her, then remember she wasn't there to answer. As grief stricken as I was, I wanted to be strong for Roy. His eyes were red-rimmed, and his expression was always sad.

Roy's weekly evening meeting in Savannah turned into two, then three nights each week. He was afraid to leave me alone, terrified that something might happen to me. He couldn't bear the thought of losing me, too. So when he attended meetings, he paid Mrs. Renaker to let me stay with her family and watch television or hang out with Gloria Jean. Each time, I hoped she would turn him down so I could stay at home alone and cry.

I hadn't seen Mama Rae since before the accident, and I wondered if she knew my mother was dead. Hilton Head was a small island. Surely, someone had told her. For the first time, I wondered if she was truly my friend. I shouldn't judge her; she might have come by the house in the afternoon and found nobody at home.

I had finished my homework and was sitting in a swivel chair in Roy's office waiting for him to wind up his paperwork. There was nothing to do, and I was bored. I whirled myself round and round until I felt dizzy.

"Stop that, sweetheart. You'll make yourself sick."

I dragged my feet on the floor to stop the chair from spinning.

"Roy, could we go home early today?" I asked.

"Sure. I'm almost finished."

When we got home, Roy sat at the kitchen table going through the mail. I couldn't look at him without wanting to cry.

"Roy?"

"What is it, honey?"

"Could I please go see Mama Rae for a little while?"

Roy's expression was transformed from one of sadness to panic.

"Isn't that the old woman who lives in the woods?" He swallowed hard.

I just knew he wasn't going to let me go.

"Yes, but her house isn't far from here."

Roy pulled me onto his lap and hugged me close, the way only a father can hug his little girl, for what seemed a long time.

"You're my daughter, Clementine. You can't imagine how much you mean to me. You're so much like your mama. I can't describe the happiness you and she have given me. Our marriage lasted less than a year, but I thank God every day for the time we had together."

I hugged him tight, and my tears started to leak onto his shirt.

"I've lost your sweet mama," he said, his voice cracking. "I couldn't stand losing you, too."

"I love you, Roy. You're a great father. I miss Mama so much sometimes that I want to die, too. But I'm not dead, and I'm not a baby. You can't be with me every minute of the day. I feel like a prisoner."

Roy relaxed his hug and held me away to look at my face. He ran a hand through his hair, and gave me a weak smile.

"I never thought of it that way." He swiped a shirtsleeve across his eyes.

"We're going to be okay, Roy. We're a family."

"You run on and visit your friend," he said. "When you get back, we'll go get a bucket of shrimp and I'll cook."

I kissed him on the cheek and promised to be back in an hour.

The forest was cool and redolent with pine. It felt good to be alone, hearing nothing more than the buzz of insects and the rustling sounds of small animals heading for their sundry hiding places at the intrusion of a human.

I couldn't wait to see Mama Rae. Taking the route I had memorized, I ticked off my landmarks as I passed each one until I reached the clearing close to her house. The chickens were grubbing around in the dirt. There were two setting hens, and I tiptoed past their nests, careful not to disturb them.

"Mama Rae, it's me, Clementine," I called from the front porch.

She didn't answer, and my heart sank. I needed her in the worst way. There had been nobody to talk to about Mama except Roy. I wanted to vent, and I needed advice on how to help Roy.

I was turning to leave when I heard her footsteps.

"I been 'spectin' you."

I stared at her through the screen. She had on the strangest getup. I had never seen her without the old slouch hat. A bright green turban was tied around her head and knotted at the back. She wore a long, flowing silky dress with big, exotic colorful birds on it, and she was barefoot.

She held the door open for me, and I went to sit in the rocking chair where I always sat. It would have been comforting to embrace Mama Rae and tell her how awful I had been feeling. It would have felt good to cry and get rid of some of my grief with someone who cared about me, but somehow I didn't think she would appreciate that sort of behavior.

Mama Rae sat in her big chair and looked at me. I knew she was waiting for me to say something, but I didn't know where to begin. There was so much I wanted to tell her.

"What's that odor?" I asked, wrinkling my nose.

Mama Rae's house usually smelled of wonderful berry tarts or a delicious stew. She always had something good simmering in a pot or baking in the oven. Today a stench filled the house.

"Dat not a very polite question."

"I'm sorry. I didn't mean to offend you."

I could tell she wasn't going to let me in on what was in the stinking boiling pot on the stove, so I plunged in headfirst, unburdening myself.

"My mama was killed." I could feel tears begin to sting my eyes.

"I heard."

"It was an accident."

Mama Rae nodded and felt her earlobes to make sure the broom straws were in place in her pierced ears.

"I miss Mama something awful, but Roy's so upset that I can't talk to him about it. He's the only family I have left."

Suddenly, I felt very selfish. If Mama Rae had any family, she had never mentioned it.

"He treats you good, no?"

"Yes. He's a terrific father; just a little overly protective."

"Uh huh."

"Today is the first time he has let me out of his sight since Mama died," I confided.

"I missed all your questions." Mama Rae smiled for the first time.

The conversation became easier after that, and soon it was time for me to go. As I was leaving, I noticed a saucer sitting on the table by the front door. It contained a lock of blond hair.

"Whose hair is that?" I asked.

Mama Rae shook her head and laughed. "Chile, you jes' full of questions."

I knew it wouldn't do any good to ask again.

Roy seemed to be in better spirits when I came home. I couldn't tell if it was an act or not. We went to the pier and bought shrimp. Then Roy cooked, and I made a salad. He had bought a fresh loaf of sourdough bread. It smelled wonderful, warming in the oven. Neither of us had had an appetite since Mama died, but tonight we were ravenous. We had a mountain of shrimp peels and tails when we were finished.

September 27, 1966

Dear Diary,

Roy let me visit Mama Rae today. I was awfully glad to see her. She didn't look much like herself though, all dressed up in that fancy ball gown, or whatever it was. I didn't think she appeared very sympathetic toward me, either. I'm not sure what I expected. After all, she is a truly strange person. But I like her just the same, and I have already forgiven her. Please do whatever you can to help Roy keep his chin up. I don't think he's a very strong person even if he is a man. He could use a lot of help.

Thank you so much,

Clementine Foster-Hubbard

P.S. One of Mama Rae's dolls is missing: the ugly one.

That day was a turning point of sorts. Roy relaxed his rules and didn't seem so worried about my safety. He tried to appear cheerful, but the sadness never left his eyes, and he looked tired all the time. He still attended meetings in Savannah at least two nights each week.

I dreaded spending my evenings with the Renakers, but somehow it wasn't as bad now. Mrs. Renaker still treated me like a baby, and her husband never did anything but sit in his recliner and watch television. Gloria Jean was the one who had changed. She hardly ever whined anymore, and she was dropping a few pounds. Instead of ordering her mother around, she miraculously started waiting on herself, and me, occasionally.

"So things were steadily improving," Dr. Fitzpatrick said.

"Yes, that's how it seemed."

"You're getting there, my dear. I'll see you on Thursday."

Chapter Ten

I awoke drenched, even my hair. All medicine has side effects, and I just knew that the night sweats, headaches, and nonsensical dreams sprang from the drugs I was taking. My memory did seem to be returning in clear chunks, but these horrible dreams were nothing more than scraps from my past that I couldn't quilt together in a pattern that made sense.

I went to the bathroom and took off my wet nightgown. When I pulled down my panties, I saw blood on them. Then it was gone. I sat on the commode, staring at the wall, seeing colored spots dart here and there. Then I saw heavy rain spattering on what looked like black patent leather discs, and running off in little rivers.

It was times like this I entertained the notion that I really could be mentally ill. I felt helpless. Surely, Dr. Fitzpatrick knew what he was doing, and he was going to make me better.

"Good afternoon, Clemmie," he said. "My, you look fetching in blue."

"Thank you." I wanted to scream. I couldn't stand it if he paid me that compliment one more time.

"Let's see." He looked over his notes. "Things were looking up, I believe."

"Yes."

I can't remember anything of consequence that happened over the next couple of months. Roy and I learned how to cook and do our laundry. Little by little, we managed to take control of the household.

I went to the woods to visit Mama Rae often. Sometimes she came to our neighborhood to sell eggs or her homemade pastries. I think everyone on the island knew her.

Special occasions stand out in my mind. Roy and I worked doubly hard to make things festive. At Thanksgiving we went to Savannah for dinner and a movie. We both pretended to have a marvelous time.

For my eleventh birthday Roy took me shopping for new clothes. Then we came home, and he grilled steaks on the hibachi. He had made me a chocolate birthday cake from scratch, ignorant of the fact that I didn't like cake.

Christmas was the hardest. We chose a tree together, and bought lots of decorations. The tree looked beautiful, but somehow lonely. And naturally we went shopping. I bought Roy two shirts, some handkerchiefs, and a neat pair of sunglasses. He went overboard on my gifts, but the one I liked best was another diary similar to the one I had nearly filled.

We pored over cookbooks, studying recipes, and made our first holiday dinner. We were doing fine until it was time to say grace. Roy's attempt was sincere, and I thought it was beautiful, but he started sobbing right in the middle of it. The only blessing I knew was *God is great; God is good,* and I thought that was a little babyish, so I just gave Roy a big hug and said, "Amen." The two of us had a good cry. Roy carved the turkey and I tried to rid the gravy of some of its lumps. Then we sat down to our family Christmas dinner.

We talked about Mama often. I think those talks gave us the strength to carry on. We were careful not to bring up the tragic accident, but limited our conversation to happy times.

Roy did everything a good father should. He took me to church and out to lunch on Sundays. We went grocery shopping together, and we were a terrific housecleaning team. He checked my homework each night, and always reminded me to say my prayers.

By the time school was out for the summer, we were handling things remarkably well, I thought. Roy agreed that I was mature enough to stay alone while he went to the office. He came home for lunch, and I made us sandwiches. If an emergency came up, he could be home within ten minutes.

I did have one traumatic experience that summer: my first period. I was the tallest kid in my class, gawky and sort of rawboned. I knew I would probably begin menstruating during the summer, but I was in no hurry to grow up, so I didn't spend a lot of time thinking about it.

Gloria Jean's cousin, Mary Ann, had come for a visit, and the three of us were at the beach. Roy had bought me a new white swimsuit that showed off my tan. We had finished our picnic lunch and built an elaborate sandcastle. Two boys came over to admire our handiwork. I wasn't supposed to talk to strangers, even if they were kids, so I went to my towel to sunbathe.

The boys started talking to Gloria Jean and her cousin, and before I knew it, they had joined our little group. They added some finishing touches to the sandcastle, laughing and making jokes.

"Hey, sleeping beauty, what's your name?"

I knew he was talking to me, but I didn't answer. He nudged me with his foot.

"I'm not allowed to talk to strangers."

The jeering started immediately. Cruel laughter invaded my ears. Gloria Jean's was the loudest.

"Are you allowed to swim with strangers?"

"Yeah," Mary Ann said. "That's not talking."

The four of them surrounded me. My face was on fire.

"I know what we'll do," Gloria Jean said. "Let's throw her in and then save her. She can't refuse to thank strangers who saved her life."

"Everybody grab an arm or a leg."

I struggled as their hands cuffed my limbs and turned me on my back. The sun was beating down on me as they carried me toward the water.

The tallest of the boys looked down, and he took on a strange expression, one of delight and disgust at once.

"Drop her! She's unclean!" He threw up his hands in mock horror. "She's got the curse!"

They plunked me down on the sand and started backing away. I felt everybody on the beach looking at me.

Gloria Jean and Mary Ann morphed into cheerleaders. "The curse! The curse! The curse!"

My stomach had started to ache, and my lower back hurt. I wondered if they had injured my back when they dropped me. Then I realized what had prompted their hateful teasing: I had started my period. I made myself get up and walk to my towel. Wrapping it around me, I riveted my eyes on the sand and left the beach.

I walked until I reached the trees that fringed the beach. Then I started running and didn't stop until I got home. I filled the tub and sank into the water, crying. I thought I had already suffered more heartbreak than an eleven-year-old should have to endure.

I made do with folded paper towels until Roy came home. As soon as he walked through the door, I told him we needed to go to the store.

"We just went to the store. Whatever you want can surely wait until tomorrow."

"It can't wait."

I guess the tone of my voice convinced him to do my bidding. He drove me to the store and was getting out of the car to go in with me.

"I need to go alone. Just give me some money."

"How much do you need?"

I realized that I had no idea.

"Ten dollars."

"Ten dollars?"

"I'll bring you the change."

He gave me a ten dollar bill and didn't ask any more questions.

There were several choices, and I didn't know which one to buy, so I just grabbed a box and hugged it all the way to the cash register. I paid for it as fast as I could. The clerk seemed awfully slow putting it into a brown paper bag.

"Where's my change?" Roy said, pretending to ignore my red face.

I dug into my pocket and handed him the money.

Roy cooked our dinner and volunteered to set the table and wash the dishes.

"I'm not an invalid, you know," I told him.

He gave me a strange little smile.

When it was time for bed, Roy hugged me goodnight.

"Well, I guess my baby girl's all grown up now." There was sadness in his voice.

I went to bed longing for Mama. I knew she would have turned this tummy-hurting, back-aching experience into something special. She would have made me feel that I had flown over one of life's hurdles and told me to embrace it. So I did my best to accept my newly acquired womanhood.

Roy and I missed Mama so much that we grew closer than ever, but he didn't smother me the way he had right after her death. While he sold insurance, I ran the house, and we both pitched in at nights and on weekends.

When our lease was up, we expected to have to find another place to live, but a turn of events allowed us to stay where we were. Our landlord was relocated to Des Moines, so he continued to rent the house to us.

School started, and I rode the bus to Bluffton with Gloria Jean and some other kids who lived on the island. I made some friends, but I wasn't very popular with the girls. I was nearly a head taller than most of them, and my body was rapidly changing. My gawky, boyish frame was being transformed into curves, and that made the girls jealous. The boys' remarks made things even worse.

Every girl I knew was boy crazy by the time she was twelve, and I didn't understand it. I never gave a fig for boys during my adolescence. Mama Rae was the only true friend I had during that tender time of my life. Of course, she couldn't take my mother's place, but she let me know that I could count on her to listen to my woes. She didn't always impart bits of wisdom when I thought she should, but she was a secret problem solver. After a while, I knew she could do whatever needed doing.

"I apologize for interrupting, Clemmie," Dr. Fitzpatrick said, "I seem to recall other instances when you referred to Mama Rae's mysterious powers. Do you think you could elaborate on those?"

"No. I don't mean to be rude, but I simply can't. I don't have anything concrete to tell you."

"Very well. Our time is up. If you should happen to think of something, anything at all, please record it in your journal."

Chapter Eleven

—

April 18, 1978

Dr. Fitzpatrick wants me to put private things about Mama Rae on paper. I don't understand why that is important. I suppose he wants to study what I write to see if he can make sense of it. I won't put a label on Mama Rae's mysterious nature because I can't. Although I can't prove it, I know that she somehow caused things to happen–things that benefited me.

—

The doctor handed me my journal.

"This is an interesting observation, Clemmie," he said. "That wasn't so bad, was it? Perhaps you'll be able to press yourself a bit more later."

"I'll try to cooperate."

"Good. Now as I recall, you were developing physically, and it was a rather trying time for you."

"That's right."

By the time I was in high school, I was fully developed. I tried to buy clothes that would hide my figure so I wouldn't stand out in a crowd. Boys called the house on a daily basis, and Roy seemed relieved when he heard me turn down their invitations. I had the distinct impression that he would have been happy to see me grow into spinsterhood without having had my first kiss.

On my fourteenth birthday, Roy decided to give me a party. I had attended a few boy-girl parties and hadn't enjoyed them. I didn't know how to dance and wasn't anxious to make a fool of myself. I was basically shy, and the thought of playing kissing games was terrifying. The only reason I went to parties was to try to fit in so the girls would like me. So I always had Roy pick me up early after having spent a couple of hours sloshing down lime sherbet and ginger ale punch off in a dark corner, hoping to be ignored by the boys. Sometimes I was fortunate enough to find an honest-to-goodness wallflower who was willing to talk about most anything and giggle a lot.

"Make a list," Roy urged. "You can invite as many of your friends as you like."

I was hard pressed to come up with a half-dozen people.

Roy looked at the list. "These are all girls." He frowned.

"They're my friends."

"Sweetheart, I'm not real excited about introducing boys into your life, but you can't really have a party without both sexes."

"I don't like any of the boys I know."

I would have given anything to have come up with a reasonable excuse to derail his party plan, but I couldn't think of one. There was no way I could tell him I was afraid of being embarrassed by remarks about my figure.

"Clementine, you can't tell me that you dislike all of those young men who call you nightly. Playing hard-to-get is an admirable quality, but this is going overboard."

"I don't know how to dance," I admitted. "I don't want a party, Roy."

He donned his hurt expression, then forged ahead.

"All kids like parties," he insisted, "and my princess is going to have the best one this island has ever seen."

He sat down at the kitchen table with the list of girls and proceeded to chew the eraser off my pencil.

"Now, let's see," he mumbled to himself. "We'll invite that nice young man who always calls me *sir* on the phone. What's his name?"

"Ted Jeffries."

Actually, Ted would have been my first choice. He was shy, and I had never heard him say anything offensive about my figure or anything else.

"Okay," I agreed.

"Then, there's the preacher's boy, Larry."

I laughed. "Larry's so pious. I don't think he'd be interested in dancing."

"There's nothing wrong with dancing at a properly chaperoned party. Of course, he'll dance."

Roy worked on the list until he managed to come up with a boy for every girl. Then, he appointed himself my dance instructor. He was excellent at slow dancing, and it was easy for me to follow his lead. He admonished me concerning how close to allow the boys to hold me. When I told him that kids didn't slow dance much, he switched gears and started belting out a song with a pretty good beat and dancing like a mad man.

We bought invitations, and I mailed them. Then, I made myself admit to Gloria Jean that I needed a brush-up course on the latest dances. She was delighted with my admission, and promised not to tell a living soul. She showed up after school for five consecutive days to be my instructor. By the end of the week I was enjoying the sessions.

As the night of the party drew near Roy had worked himself into a dither. He wanted to make sure everything was perfect down to the tiniest detail. Ice cream and cupcakes had been ordered, and Roy hired Mrs. Renaker to make a ton of sandwiches. Four cases of soft drinks were stacked on the back porch. And the final touch was the inexpensive tape player he had bought just for my party. He took Gloria Jean and me with him to purchase tapes to make sure the other kids would like the music.

The evening of the party Roy made numerous trips to the store. He was making some rather fancy hors d'oeuvres, and I was afraid he would still be in the kitchen when the guests started arriving.

Just as I walked out of my room, Roy was clapping his hands together in victory.

"Bring on the partiers!"

"I'm ready," I said.

He turned to look at me.

"You're breathtaking, sweetheart. You look for all the world like your mama."

At that precise moment, Mrs. Renaker and Gloria Jean appeared with a huge tray of sandwiches, a bouquet of fresh flowers, and a beautifully wrapped present.

"Come in. Come in," Roy said, taking the tray.

The house quickly filled with teenagers. The table was laden with food, and Roy had the soft drinks in a tub of ice on the back porch. Music blared, and laughter rang out through the house.

Roy had moved most of the furniture out of the living room so there would be plenty of room for dancing. I knew he wasn't wild about our playing kissing games, and I wasn't either, but someone suggested playing *Spin the Bottle* at some point. Roy made sure the kissing didn't last too long when a couple of kids disappeared into my room for privacy. He stood next to the door and banged on it if he thought things were getting too serious.

He had been right to insist on having the party. I danced with every boy there, including the minister's son, and had the time of my life. The kissing wasn't bad, either. I could tell who had some experience and who didn't, and that was rather interesting. Yes, the party added a whole new dimension to my life.

After that night I became more socially active with kids my age. We had lots of impromptu get-togethers like clambakes and wiener roasts on the beach, and on weekends we went to movies as a group.

I still saw Mama Rae at least once a week. She was always interested in what I had been up to, and never failed to sneak in a question about how I was being treated. I thought it was a strange thing to ask.

We were having tea in her living room one afternoon, and I was in need of some womanly advice.

"Mama Rae, do you think I'm old enough to go out with boys?" I asked.

"Depends." She slurped her tea.

"On what?"

"It depends on who the young man is and where you go."

"I think Danny Riley is nice looking and well mannered. He invited me to go to the movies Saturday night, but Roy won't let me go."

"Uh huh."

"I'm not a baby, you know. Roy's been allowing me to socialize with boys for over a year, but only in groups."

"Safety in numbers." Mama Rae grinned.

"Wouldn't you think that double dating would be safe enough? After all, Danny's a real gentleman."

"Some dees young folk not what dey seem." Mama Rae looked thoughtful.

"You're taking Roy's side again. You've been doing that a lot lately."

Mama Rae nodded. "He been showin' good judgment."

Chapter Twelve

—

Hilton Head Island had dramatically changed since 1966. Many families had found their way to our paradise and decided to stay permanently. All kinds of businesses had sprung up; the island was booming. Tourism flourished, and new resorts beckoned to vacationers from near and far. They came in a steady stream for nine months of the year.

In 1971 I turned sixteen. I was lying in bed, having hit the snooze bar on my alarm clock, and luxuriating in a state of half-sleep when Roy burst into my room singing *Happy Birthday* at the top of his lungs.

I pulled myself to a sitting position, hugging my knees and wondering what splendid surprise he had for me.

"What?" I asked in mock horror. "No breakfast in bed?"

He didn't take the bait.

"Stand up," he said. "Here comes the blindfold."

I obeyed, squeezing my eyes shut while Roy tied on the blindfold. He led me through the house and down the front steps, then turned me around and around until I begged for mercy. When he took off the blindfold, I was so dizzy I nearly fell down.

There in the driveway sat a brand new yellow Volkswagen Beetle with an enormous bow taped across the windshield.

"Oh, Roy," I squealed with delight, "you're absolutely the most wonderful father in the world!"

I was the envy of most of my friends.

"It seems you were happy again," Dr. Fitzpatrick said.

"I'm getting a headache, doctor."

"We have plenty of time left. Are you sure you can't continue?"

"I'm sure."

I hurried to my room and crashed. It seemed that sleep was the only respite when one of the headaches attacked.

The next two weeks were wasted time. I couldn't make myself write in my journal, and I was so depressed I couldn't pull my thoughts together during the sessions. Dr. Fitzpatrick had to do most of the talking. He kept asking me questions I couldn't answer. Finally, he dismissed me for a week of rest.

I felt refreshed after a week to myself, and was in a better frame of mind at the next session.

"Hello, Clemmie." Dr. Fitzpatrick stretched thin lips across his front teeth in an ugly rodent's smile.

"Hello."

"Are you ready to talk about your teenage years?"

"I think so."

I was a responsible teenager. Roy complimented me for the attribute often, and that boosted my ego. I was popular with my peers, and it wasn't uncommon for Roy to come home from work and find a few of my friends there, listening to music, or just hanging out. He didn't mind because he knew I put my chores and homework first.

I dated quite a bit, but wasn't allowed to have a steady boyfriend. Roy always wanted to meet the boys and feel them out before he gave me permission to go out with them. He knew most of their parents, and if he didn't care for them, I was wasting my time introducing their sons to Roy.

Sonny Malone was the pick of the litter. My stomach turned flips every time I looked into those October sky blue eyes. Girls waited in line to go out with him, and it was a complete surprise when he asked me for a date.

Roy didn't know Sonny or his parents, so I knew he would give my date the third degree before he let me set foot out the door with him. The only reason he was allowing me to date a total stranger was because we were going to a youth function at our church.

Sonny arrived punctually, wearing a navy sport coat and tie. The sun had bleached his blond hair nearly white, and his gleaming teeth and gorgeous eyes were dramatic against a tanned, handsome face.

I answered the door, and Roy stood to be introduced. I had to take a deep breath before I could speak. The men shook hands, and Roy insisted the three of us have a Coke and get acquainted.

Roy's style of conversation was easy and unassuming, but his thoughts were always a step ahead of the other guy. He had a talent for getting information from the most tight-lipped individual, and he knew how to bring people around to his way of thinking. Everybody liked Roy, and nobody wanted to offend or disappoint him.

I wasn't very interested in Sonny's background or what his father did for a living, but Roy was. Within fifteen minutes he had amassed a wealth of information about the Malone family.

Mr. Malone was an attorney who had joined a prestigious law firm on the island, and his wife was an artist. She taught oil painting, and was about to open her own gallery. The Malones had moved to Hilton Head from Philadelphia. Sonny had a seven-year-old sister named Stephanie. Before Roy was finished with the interview, he also learned that the family was active in the Presbyterian Church.

Sonny seemed to have passed muster with aplomb. Roy sent us out the door with a smile and told us to have a great time. He didn't even remind me to be home by twelve.

We did have a good time, and I practically floated up the steps when Sonny walked me to my door. I stood in the moonlight anxiously awaiting a goodnight kiss, and imagined myself melting in strong arms as our lips met for the first time.

"I had a great time," he said. "I hope you did, too."

"Oh, I did."

He took my hand and brushed it with a kiss. "Well, see you around," he said.

Sonny and I went to a movie on our next date and ran into some of his friends. After the movie, we all went to a pizza place. Sonny made sure I was included in the conversation, and I enjoyed the evening, but I would have much preferred being alone with him. I did receive the goodnight kiss I had dreamed about with the promise of more to come, because he invited me to go to a drive-in movie in Savannah the following Saturday.

"Now, Sonny Malone is the kind of young man I like for you to date," Roy said. "He comes from a good family, and he knows how to treat a lady. I don't worry when you're with him."

I couldn't wait until Saturday. Finally, I would be alone with Sonny, the man of my dreams. I put on every outfit in my closet, trying to decide which one was the most flattering, and chose a pale yellow sundress.

Roy got the door. He and Sonny talked while I pretended to finish getting ready. I stayed in my bedroom, counting to a thousand so I wouldn't appear too anxious.

On the way to Savannah I realized that I had little in common with Sonny Malone. Our backgrounds were very different, and I couldn't think of anything interesting to talk about. He had grown up in a country club environment with two loving parents, whereas my early years were spent in a shabby little apartment with my mother, living hand-to-mouth until we met Roy. I felt self-conscious and inferior when Sonny told amusing tales which could have happened only to the wealthy, and feeling like a big phony, I dropped my jaw and laughed quietly like the movie stars.

We arrived just in time for the show. Sonny drove around until he found the perfect parking place.

"This is a great spot," he said. "It's dark and cozy, and not too close to the concession stand."

I gave him a weak smile.

The movie began, and I focused my eyes on the big screen. I felt uneasy and didn't understand why.

"You don't have to sit all the way over there, sugar." Sonny turned on one of his million dollar smiles.

He slid his arm around me and pulled me toward him. I allowed myself to be pulled across the seat.

"Isn't this better?" He smiled down at me.

I nodded and returned my eyes to the screen.

We watched the movie for a while, and he hadn't made a false move. I was beginning to feel comfortable, and wondered why I had let myself get so worked up. Just because we came from different backgrounds didn't mean we couldn't enjoy one another's company.

As we watched the show, Sonny's arm was draped around my shoulder. Every now and then he would give me a little squeeze, or lightly rub his hand up and down my arm. I couldn't think of any girl I knew who wouldn't haven't given most anything to be in my place.

A double feature was showing, and during the intermission Sonny went to the concession stand and brought back Cokes. I was afraid my inability to engage him in interesting conversation would make my nervousness return, but he was so full of himself I didn't have an opportunity to talk the entire intermission.

The lights dimmed. The second movie was about to start, but I sensed that watching another movie was the farthest thing from Sonny's mind. He drew me close and kissed me. It was the kind of kiss that made me feel beautiful. I let down my guard and settled comfortably in his embrace. My lips were pliable under his kiss, and I had a pleasant feeling inside.

"I think one movie's enough," he whispered hoarsely. "How about you?"

"I guess."

"I want to take you to a place that's nearly as beautiful as you are." He kissed my forehead and gave my nose a tweak.

I felt myself blush at the compliment. I had never dated anyone who affected me this way. Sonny inspired so many different feelings, and I couldn't sort them out. He was undoubtedly the most handsome and best dressed of all the boys I knew. And he was witty and intelligent with a never ending supply of interesting conversation. I was put off by his egomania, but his kisses made me want to forget that flaw in his character.

We were back on the island, and Sonny flipped on a right turn signal. He turned off the main drag onto a graveled road flanked by tall pines. It was a heavily wooded area with a road cut through it, and he seemed to know exactly where he was going.

"This place is really beautiful," he said. "It won't be like this much longer; it's going to be the next big development on Hilton Head."

We came to a clearing, and he parked near a lagoon. The water looked black in the moonlight, and millions of stars paraded across the heavens. I had to agree it was a breathtakingly beautiful sight, and wondered how many other girls he had brought here.

He turned off the radio and rolled down a window.

"Listen," he whispered. "Don't you love the night sounds?"

"Yes, I do. I've never heard so many of them anywhere but on this island."

"These are pretty close quarters," he said, sliding the seat back. He sighed contentedly and held out his hand to me.

"Come over here and keep me company, pretty girl," he said.

He took my hand, and I allowed him to pull me closer. When our lips met, the pleasure was so intense that I tingled. I wanted the moment to last forever. Then the tender kissing changed dramatically. It wasn't sweet, but demanding. Sonny's wonderful, light touch, with just a hint of pressure, was gone. His gentle hands had turned rough, and I knew I was in over my head.

He held me to his chest, pinning my arms under his while he fumbled with the zipper on the back of my sundress. I scratched at his sides, but that only seemed to excite him. The zipper released, and I felt the night air on my bare skin. I tried to scream, but made no sound. Tears leaked from my eyes as Sonny Malone unfastened my strapless bra and yanked it from my breasts.

I knew I was about to be raped unless I could think of something fast. Sonny was much stronger than I. So while he crushed my mouth with kisses so hard that my teeth cut into my lips, and while he ravaged my breasts with his hands and his mouth, I managed to edge myself toward the passenger door.

He was trying to maneuver my body under his. When he gave my hips a tug, my head snapped backward and struck the window encasement. I struggled to sit up, but couldn't. The door handle was digging into my back. Sonny's ragged breathing was nearly as frightening as the things he was doing to me. He started begging me to love him, and began sucking hard on my neck and breasts while forcing his left hand between my legs. I wanted to knee him in the groin, but I couldn't move my leg. Suddenly, I realized my right hand was free. I had been clutching the edge of the seat with it.

This madman was seconds from stealing my virginity when I hit him with all the force I possessed. His head wobbled sideways, and I realized that I was holding my breath. Somebody must have been watching over me, because Sonny stopped cold. He raised himself up and sat behind the wheel.

"What's the matter with you?" His tone was almost scary.

I grabbed my bra from the floor and swiped it across my teary face.

"I'm not the kind of girl you want to date. What made you think you could take me into the woods and ravage my body against my will?"

I put on my bra and wiggled into my dress, but could only get it zipped part of the way.

Sonny started to laugh.

"What's so funny?" My voice trembled with fear and anger.

"You are. You're exactly what I had you pegged for from the beginning: a little tease with a dynamite figure. I was a damn fool to waste my time on you."

"Take me home, Sonny Malone!"

"I'll take you home, bitch. I'll take you home and watch you sit there in your little shack and rot."

"I hate to stop you at this point," Dr. Fitzpatrick said, "but our time is up."

I had been reliving that long-ago hellish event as I told it, and I felt exhausted and humiliated all over again.

The doctor looked at me with something like pity. "It's over, Clemmie. It happened a long time ago. Thank you for sharing it with me."

Chapter Thirteen

—

May 4, 1978

I can still feel myself struggling with Sonny Malone. What a disappointment he turned out to be. And how naïve I was.

I don't see how relating teenage trials to a doctor can solve my problem. Sometimes I think this is how he gets his kicks. Surely, I must be wrong.

———

"Good afternoon, Clemmie. Isn't this a beautiful day?"

"Yes. Sunshine seems to brighten my spirits." I handed him my journal.

I was intrigued by the doctor's facial expressions, especially when he had read a journal entry he disliked. He stiffened and put on a half-smile.

"I assure you, my dear, this is not the way I *get my kicks*. Need I remind you that I am here for the sole purpose of helping my patients return to their normal lives, if at all possible?"

"I apologize. I'm frustrated, and I think I may be paranoid. I don't know why."

"Very well. Now, is there any more pertinent information about Sonny Malone? If there isn't, I suppose we can forget about him?"

"I'm afraid there is more. I intended never to see him again, but that wasn't the way it worked out."

"Hmm."

Sunday morning I played sick. Roy felt my head and brought me a cup of tea. I pulled the bedclothes up to my chin so he couldn't see the bruises Sonny Malone had inflicted. He wanted to stay home and take care of me, but I insisted he go to church.

The phone rang shortly after Roy left for work on Monday. I didn't want to talk to anyone, but answered it, thinking it might be Roy.

"Clementine, please don't hang up," Sonny said.

"How dare you call me?"

"I'm calling to beg for your forgiveness. I don't blame you for being angry; I behaved like an animal. I don't know what came over me. Please, Clementine, let me come over and apologize in person."

"You must be insane. I never want to see you again!" I slammed the phone on its hook.

That afternoon a truck stopped in front of our house. I answered the door, and a delivery man handed me a dozen red roses from Sonny Malone. I trashed his note and kept the flowers.

I did everything I could to cover my bruises so Roy wouldn't see how battered I was. Instead of putting my hair in its usual ponytail, I let it fall loose, and I wore a shirt with a collar.

"Well, well," Roy said, admiring the flowers, "my lovely daughter certainly must have made a hit with someone."

"They're from Sonny. We had a spat, and he wants to make up."

"Oh, you'll have lots of spats." Roy grinned. "That's what dating's all about. I'm sure you'll bury the hatchet in a few days."

I didn't know what Roy might do if I told him about my near rape by the great Sonny Malone. This was something I would have to handle on my own.

Sonny called the house so many times each day it was a chore just to answer the phone. It got to the point that I wouldn't even talk to him to tell him to get lost. He started showing up on my front porch unannounced. I couldn't go anywhere, because he became my shadow. He followed me to the grocery store and to the beach. And when I was out with my friends, he would appear out of nowhere.

Late one night I was awakened by a noise outside my window. I got out of bed and peeked from behind the drapes. Sonny's car was parked on the street, and I caught a glimpse of him as he walked toward it in the pale moonlight. I couldn't imagine what he was doing, stalking me in the wee hours.

I knew I should tell Roy, but I couldn't bring myself to do it. There was only one person I trusted to give me advice, so the following day when I was sure I wasn't being watched, I went to see Mama Rae and told her everything that had transpired.

"He simply won't leave me alone," I said.

"Where dis Sonny Malone live?"

"Somewhere on Forest Beach."

"What his daddy's name?"

"Stuart, I think. Why?"

Mama Rae didn't answer. She told me I would have to leave because she had something important to do, so I went home not feeling a bit better than before I had told her my troubles.

I didn't see Mama Rae again until a week later. I was getting a fill-up at the mom-and- pop station. When I went inside to pay for the gas, she was talking with the proprietor.

"No, I haven't been ailin'," she was saying. "There's just been a big demand for my fried pies on Forest Beach lately. I get more for 'em over there, too. I'll bring you a batch next week."

"Hello, Mama Rae." I smiled .

She nodded curtly, adjusted her slouch hat, and started out the door.

Sonny was still following me, and I was almost at my wit's end. If he didn't stop stalking me, I knew I would have to tell Roy. Then, one day when I came home from running errands, I found Sonny sitting on my front porch steps. He didn't look like much of a threat.

"Sonny Malone, you're a crazy person! Isn't it plain that I want nothing to do with you? Get off my property this minute, or I'll call the police."

Sonny got to his feet, looking like he was about to cry.

"I'm just here to tell you I won't be bothering you anymore."

"It's about time, and you'd better be telling the truth!"

"It's the truth. We're moving to Denver. My dad just received a job offer that he says he can't turn down. I'll be off the island and out of your hair by the end of the week."

He didn't stick around to hear what I might say, but walked slowly to his car. I noticed his signature swagger was missing.

"And was that, indeed, the end of Sonny Malone?" Dr. Fitzpatrick asked.

"Yes. Did that particular chapter of my teenage years bring you any closer to solving my problem? I can answer that myself. It didn't help one bit."

"Try not to be angry, Clemmie. If you can't trust me as your doctor, I can turn your case over to another psychiatrist. This method has been proven to work, and it can work for you."

"It isn't you, Dr. Fitzpatrick. I suppose it's the method that I don't trust. I'm remembering my past, but I don't seem to be getting any closer to the truth. A different doctor won't be necessary; I'll try to cooperate."

Chapter Fourteen

—

"I hope you're feeling better today, Clemmie."

"I am. I remember that right after Sonny Malone left the island, Daniel came to Hilton Head. It was like a miracle."

Dr. Fitzpatrick looked pleased.

"Can you elaborate?"

———

Roy and I always bought our fresh shrimp at the pier behind Hudson's Restaurant. We went there so often that most of the fishermen knew us. One Friday afternoon we went to buy a bucketful, and it turned out to be one of the happiest days of my life.

Roy was gabbing away with one of his acquaintances and told me to buy the shrimp. There were a couple of people ahead of me, and while I waited in line I found myself thinking of Sonny Malone. I was so glad to be rid of him.

I was jolted back to the present when the young man waiting on customers spoke to me.

"May I help you?" he asked.

Neither the voice nor the face registered immediately, but suddenly, he did a double take, and his handsome face broke into a big grin.

I dropped my bucket as Daniel crushed me in a bear hug. We pulled apart and stared at one another in disbelief.

"Oh, Daniel, I can't believe you're really here!"

"Clementine," Roy called, "what's taking so long? I'm famished."

I motioned for him to come down to the pier.

"What's the problem?" he said. Then, a flicker of recognition sparked in his eyes. "Daniel?"

"In the flesh, Mr. Hubbard. It's good to see you."

"What time do you get off work?" I asked.

"Six o'clock. I'll be off in fifteen minutes."

"Come to our house for dinner."

"By all means," Roy said. "We have a lot of catching up to do."

"I'd love to," Daniel said. "Just give me time to shower and change. What's your address?"

Roy scribbled it on one of his business cards and handed it to Daniel.

I was so excited I lost my appetite. We hadn't seen Daniel for so long I wondered if we would have any anxious moments.

"It's hard to believe little Daniel is nearly a man," Roy said. "You two can pick up where you left off."

"I hope so. We were so close when we were kids. I had given up hope of ever seeing him again."

Daniel wore a navy golf shirt and white pants, and he was riding a bicycle.

"Like my wheels?"

"I haven't been on my bike in over a year. Roy gave me a Volkswagen Beetle for my sixteenth birthday."

"Well, I'm sixteen, but I won't be getting a car for a while. I'm staying with my auntie near Bradley Beach, and we can't afford one right now."

We went inside to keep Roy company while he cooked.

"Hey, how are your mama and the baby?" Daniel asked. "Well, I guess he, or she isn't a baby anymore."

Roy and I looked at one another.

"Did I say something wrong?" Daniel said.

Roy wiped his hands on the kitchen towel he was using as an apron.

"Emily was hit by a car not long after we moved here, Daniel. She and the baby both died."

"I had no idea. How awful for you."

"We're doing fine," I said. "Of course, we'll always miss Mama, and we'll never know what the baby would have been like, but the two of us are a great family." I put on my best smile.

"Is your mother here on the island, Daniel?" Roy asked.

"No. She remarried and moved to Greenville. I was there too until my uncle passed away. Then I came to stay with my auntie for a while. I'm not sure how long I'll be here."

We reminisced about old times during dinner, and Daniel and I were still talking long after Roy went to bed.

We saw one another several times a week, and it was as though we had never been apart. I told Daniel all about the boys I dated, and he told me about the two girls he was seeing. Our relationship was strictly platonic, and we were still thick as thieves.

One day I took Daniel to meet Mama Rae. I wasn't sure how she would feel about my bringing a stranger to her little hideaway, but I just knew she would like Daniel. She did, and welcomed him into her home, stuffing us with fresh fruit tarts still warm from the oven while she drew Daniel's life story out of him.

"Mama Rae, I almost forgot to tell you," I said.

"Tell me what?"

"Sonny Malone and his family have left the island. His father took a job in Denver, so he won't be bothering me anymore."

"Dat's good." She smiled.

Daniel was fascinated with Mama Rae. He asked her questions I would never have dared allow to slide from the tip of my tongue, and she answered them. Through Daniel's inquiries, I learned that Mama Rae had never been married and that she had no living relatives.

"You did very well, Clemmie," Dr. Fitzpatrick said. "I'll see you next time."

I could hear one of the volunteers banging on the out-of-tune piano and some earplug singing as I passed the recreation hall. If it weren't for old crazy Emma always trying to run the show, I might have wanted to participate in the sing-alongs.

Dinner was three hours away, and I had nothing to do. I didn't want to look at my pictures or read, and I had nothing to write in my journal. But I was always tired, and had no trouble falling asleep. I could hear the hum of traffic, and my body felt light as a feather as I started to dream.

Daniel was a young man in this dream. He and I were telling secrets, but I didn't know why we were whispering. Red was everywhere, just like it was before: on the wall, in the sink, and the long-legged siren's strappy sandals. It looked like a collage of everything red. Then, everybody was crying: Roy, Daniel, and other people I knew, but couldn't name. Everyone was crying except Mama Rae.

I shook myself awake and went to the desk and opened my journal. Gazing out the window, I tried to form a coherent sentence to describe my jumbled thoughts, but had no luck. That wasn't my only failure. I couldn't remember my session from a few hours ago.

My hand flew to its haven, and I opened the locket to see Daniel's sweet smile. Then, I remembered: Daniel and I had been reunited.

Chapter Fifteen

—

Daniel's coming to Hilton Head wasn't the only unexpected development that summer. Roy truly shocked me with the introduction of his new acquaintance. Her name was Addie Jo Simmons; she was Roy's new secretary.

I was setting the table late on a Friday afternoon when Roy came home. We had planned to grill steaks. I heard him coming up the front steps and went to greet him.

"Sweetheart," he said, "I want you to meet Miss Simmons. She's the newest member of our office staff."

"I'm pleased to meet you, Miss Simmons." I smiled.

"Call me Addie Jo." The redhead gripped my hand.

She towered over me, teetering on stiletto heels. Her skirt was skintight, and the blouse she wore left little to the imagination. She had the emerald eyes and alabaster skin of a true redhead, and showcased her eyes with fake lashes.

"Thank you, Addie Jo," I said, reclaiming my hand.

"I invited Addie Jo to have dinner with us," Roy said. "This is her first day at work. She's staying at the Sea Crest until her belongings arrive."

I smiled at our guest.

"What's in the sack?" I asked.

"Oh, we stopped at the market and bought a steak for Addie Jo. I'm sure there'll be enough salad for the three of us."

I set another place at the table while Roy showed Addie Jo to the powder room to freshen up.

"Why didn't you call me?" I whispered. "We might not have enough food."

"Oh, sure we will. And I didn't have a chance to call you. Everyone was leaving the office, and Addie Jo asked me for the name of a decent restaurant. She doesn't know anyone on the island, and I thought it would be a friendly gesture to invite her to eat with us. It was a spur-of-the-moment decision. You don't mind, do you?"

"Of course not." But I did, and wasn't sure why.

Addie Jo had a proclivity for laughing at nearly everything. She seemed to find humor in anything Roy said. When she chose to favor us with one of her high-pitched gales, she showed every tooth in her mouth and gestured wildly with both hands, flaming nails aflutter. A mouthful of food didn't stop her from talking, and she appeared to choke frequently. I found her to be a singularly unattractive individual, and couldn't help wondering why Roy had brought her home to dinner.

Several times during the meal Addie Jo let it slip that she was a divorcee. I would have bet anything she had her cap set for Roy, and he seemed to be soaking up the attention like a sponge.

When it was time to drive Addie Jo to the office to get her car, I asked Roy if I could go along for the ride.

"Sure," he said. "The more the merrier."

From the moment I met her, Addie Jo Simmons rubbed me the wrong way. She wormed her way into our lives a little at a time. Roy and Addie Jo had business lunches at least twice a week, and had their weekly evening meetings in Savannah each Wednesday. Every now and then, Roy would bring her home for dinner. The insurance business was going strong, and Roy and his secretary frequently spent their evenings working overtime at our kitchen table. I had a strong feeling it wouldn't be long before the spider had Roy caught in her web, and I didn't know any way to prevent it.

Roy called one evening to tell me that he and Addie Jo would be working at our house. He said not to bother making dinner; we'd just get a pizza.

I ran to the bathroom to clean up while he went to pick up our dinner. If I hurried, I could dress and have the table set by the time he got home. I took a quick shower and wrapped a towel around me. As I started to my room, I heard a noise from the kitchen.

"Wow! You get the Mr. Quick award," I said, poking my head around the corner to see Roy's secretary setting the table.

"It's me, Clementine. I let myself in."

"Oh." I didn't try to disguise my displeasure, and went to my room to dress.

Addie Jo had set the table and was arranging a bouquet of fresh flowers in one of Mama's vases when I returned.

"You didn't have to bring flowers," I said.

"Oh, it's the least I can do. I've been here so often this feels like my second home."

The amazon stood in our kitchen, hands on her ample hips, wearing a proprietary expression.

"They certainly do brighten up the table, don't you think?" she said.

"Yes, they do."

"You don't like me, do you, Clementine?"

"Why would you ask such a thing?"

"Here comes the pizza man," Roy called.

He was in high spirits, hustling into the kitchen with a large pizza. He set the cardboard box on the counter, and gave me a peck on the cheek.

"My turn," piped Addie Jo, sticking out her rouged cheek.

Roy choked out a strange little laugh and went to the refrigerator to get Cokes. I glanced at Addie Jo to see her flush right through her heavy makeup.

There was a knock at the door as we were finishing dinner. It was Daniel. He had just gotten off work. I introduced him to Addie Jo. Daniel extended his hand, but she didn't take it.

"I'll take care of the dishes, Clementine," she said, beginning to clear the table. "You go and visit with your friend."

Daniel and I retreated to the front porch.

"That woman is a giant!" he whispered.

"You're telling me. And she's out to catch Roy."

"You're kidding."

"I wish I were. She's been chasing him since the day he hired her."

"You don't sound very happy about it."

"Daniel, I don't like her. I wouldn't mind Roy having a lady friend, but Addie Jo isn't his type. She's loud and stupid."

"Hey, want to go to a movie?"

"How about a rain check? I'm kind of tired."

Daniel knew very well why I didn't take him up on his offer. I didn't want Addie Jo alone in the house with Roy.

"Let's stop here," Dr. Fitzpatrick said. "I sense quite a bit of animosity on your part. Concentrate on Addie Jo this evening. Record all of your feelings in your journal."

"I'll try."

May 16, 1978

When I look back on my late teenage years it's difficult to recall the good times. Everything was fine until Roy hired Addie Jo Simmons. I felt loved and safe with Roy. We had adjusted to Mama's death, and were taking care of one another. Addie Jo came into our lives like a hurricane: gently at first, not much of a threat, while planting seeds of doubt in Roy and me—seeds capable of shattering the trust we shared. As her plan grew, she gathered strength, and her heinous antics became more and more destructive.

Addie Jo was bent on having Roy, and nothing would stop her. His best interest was never an issue. She knew I had no use for her. When Roy was around, she went out of her way to be nice to me, but the minute his back was turned, the charade stopped.

"Shall we begin?" Dr. Fitzpatrick said.

———

I remember the night Addie Jo chose to let me know she was, indeed, in charge. Roy and I were doing the dinner dishes, singing a silly song. Neither of us heard Addie Jo let herself into our home.

Roy hung the dishtowel on the drying rack and pulled me into his arms.

"Sweetheart, you have turned into such a beautiful young lady." He kissed the top of my head.

"You haven't told me how much I look like Mama lately."

"You know you look just like her. It hurts me to see you so grown up." He swallowed hard.

Roy had always been emotional, especially where I was concerned. His eyes filled as he released me.

"I do believe you two have more little intimate chats than anyone I've ever known," Addie Jo said.

She leaned on the frame of our kitchen door, wearing red short shorts and a white halter top. Her hair was pinned up on her head in a tight cluster of curls resembling a nineteen forties hairdo I remembered from old movies.

"Hope I'm not interrupting anything important," she said, bobbing her head just enough to make her dangling earrings catch the light.

"Of course not." Roy blinked away tears. "You know you're always welcome."

Addie Jo stretched red lips across her big teeth.

"I do know that, Roy. You and Clementine have made me feel like part of your family since the first day I came here. You'll never know how much you mean to me. I was sitting in my apartment, watching a stupid television program and getting lonelier by the minute when I realized I didn't have to feel that way because I have you two. So here I am."

"Well, you came to the right place," Roy said. "I know just the thing to cheer you up. We'll go out on the porch and sing."

He went to get his guitar, and Addie Jo and I were alone in the kitchen.

"I'll tell you the truth, Clementine," she said. "Roy's therapeutic for me. Why, he's the best thing that ever happened to me."

The expression on her painted face wasn't wasted. It told me she was here to stay.

"Let's sing *Down in the Valley*," she said.

Roy strummed an introduction, and we began to sing. He and I harmonized perfectly. We had been singing duets since I was a child. Addie Jo couldn't carry a tune, but she was no less shy about her singing than anything else, and drowned us out with her caterwauling.

She asked Roy to accompany her while she whined several country songs. The grand finale was Patsy Cline's *Crazy*. She murdered the song, and her green eyes never left Roy's the entire time she was singing.

"That was real nice, Addie Jo," Roy said, "but it's getting late, so I guess we should call it a night."

I kissed Roy goodnight and went inside. I was in the kitchen by an open window, drinking a glass of water, and I could hear Roy and Addie Jo talking on the back porch.

"Do you have a busy day tomorrow, Roy?"

"Yes ma'am; I certainly do."

"That's too bad. I'm not tired at all."

"Well, I hope you'll forgive this old man because he has to hit the sack." Roy cleared his throat and produced a little laugh.

"How about a goodnight kiss for your little office slave?"

Roy was silent, and I was afraid he was about to oblige her.

"I don't really think that would be appropriate, Addie Jo. You're a real nice person. I hope I haven't given you the wrong impression by inviting you here so often or by taking advantage of your willingness to work overtime."

"Don't be silly. Surely, you didn't think I meant a real kiss."

"Of course not." Roy sounded relieved. "Let me walk you to your car."

"So there was no reason for you to distrust Roy," Dr. Fitzpatrick said.

"I think that, initially, he felt sorry for Addie Jo. He was familiar with the feeling of loneliness, and he was a sensitive person. But Roy leaned toward overkill. It's possible that he did lead her on, but if he did, it was unintentional."

"That seems plausible," the doctor said.

"Addie Jo was out to get Roy. A couple of the insurance agents were interested in her, but she wouldn't even look at them. She was on a mission."

"Be true to your feelings in the journal," Dr. Fitzpatrick said, "but you might try to look at Miss Simmons in a more charitable light. Record the facts as you remember them, but if you can view the secretary from an impartial party's point of view, it might change your impression of her."

"Nothing can change the fact that she ruined our lives."

The doctor removed his glasses and blew out a small sigh.

"We're on the same team, Clemmie. We're trying to get to the truth."

"I know."

Chapter Sixteen

Maybe Dr. Fitzpatrick was right. It was possible that I wasn't being honest with myself. I harbored so much hatred and resentment toward Addie Jo Simmons that I couldn't think clearly. I needed to get myself into the most normal frame of mind possible, and as much as I disliked the idea, that meant being with other people.

As I left the doctor's office, I saw patients lining up to board the bus for the bowling alley. I had never enjoyed bowling, but I ran to the activities director and scribbled my name on the roster. I boarded the bus and took the first available seat.

"Hello," said the man sitting beside me. "Want to hear a joke?"

"I guess so, if it's not risqué."

He ignored my comment and launched into his joke.

"There was this guy who had a flat tire just outside a mental institution. He got out his spare and proceeded to change the tire. He was about to replace the lug nuts, but he was in such a hurry that he accidentally dropped them all down a storm sewer. Well, he was bumfuzzled."

The man appeared to be finished with the joke, but I hadn't heard anything funny.

"Is that it?" I asked.

"Of course not. A patient was sitting on a bench inside the fence, watching the man. So the fruitcake says, 'Why don't you take one lug nut from each of the other wheels and use them to hold on your spare?' 'That's smart thinking,' says the man. 'Say, how come you're in this loony bin?' 'I'm crazy,' says the fruitcake, not stupid.'"

I tried to laugh. "Good one," I said, as the bus came to a halt at the bowling alley.

I had the misfortune of being placed on a team with crazy old Emma.

"I want to be the score keeper," she announced.

"That's fine, Emma," I said. "I'm sure you're a wonderful score keeper."

An elderly gentleman named Ross was on our team. He was a good bowler. Every time it was his turn to bowl, Emma gave him a dirty look.

"Don't gloat about your score," she warned.

"I'm not gloating," Ross said.

"Well, don't start," she said.

I could tell she was itching for a fight.

When all of the scores were tallied, our team came in third.

"Third place is respectable," Emma said, dusting off her hands.

"It's not respectable for me," Ross grumbled. "It's not respectable at all."

Ross and I were sitting on a bench, changing our shoes when Emma came stomping over. She was carrying a bowling ball. I looked up just in time to see her heft the ball over her head. It was obvious that she intended to hit one of us with it. I threw all of my weight into Ross, pushing him off the end of the bench as the ball came crashing down.

I scrambled to my feet, yelling for help. Several of the patients rushed toward me in their stocking feet, but nobody did anything. The activities director was running toward Emma.

"Get out of the way!" she shouted.

I grabbed my shoes and joined the others. Ross was still crouched beside the bench.

"Emma, take a deep breath," the director said.

Emma sucked air into her lungs and grabbed the bowling ball before the director could get close enough to stop her. She knocked Ross off balance with her knee, leaving him flat on his back, and straddled him. Then, she brought the heavy ball down on his chest. He groaned in pain as the director pulled Emma off him.

"Third place is respectable!" Emma screamed.

The manager of the bowling alley called an ambulance and tried to make Ross comfortable until it arrived.

"Emma, you know what this means," the director said.

Emma nodded and started to cry. She wound and unwound a lock of stringy hair around each index finger.

"Do you know why you did it?"

"Yes! I know! I know! Jeez, oh, ack, boo, I shoo, awful, awful, awful!"

Emma wasn't at dinner that evening, and I knew she had been placed in solitary confinement.

May 18, 1978

I don't know how I'll ever get better living in a place like this. Maria seems normal. So did the jokester on the bus, but how can I strive for normalcy in an institution surrounded by people like Emma. I wonder what she is trying to say when she makes those strange sounds—those non-words.

I admit Emma frightens me. I wouldn't want to be alone with her, but I don't hate her. I think I truly do hate Addie Jo Simmons. Emma isn't responsible for the heinous things she does, but Addie Jo knew precisely what she was doing. She planned every move. I can't look upon her with charity. She was nothing but a scheming vixen who wouldn't rest until she had destroyed my life and the people I loved.

Dr. Fitzpatrick pursed his lips and handed me my journal.

"I heard about the episode with Emma," he said. "I'm not sure I understand why you would compare her with Miss Simmons."

"I'm not either."

"Let's resume where we left off. You, Roy and Miss Simmons had spent the evening singing on the porch."

"Yes, I remember."

———————

I didn't see Addie Jo or talk to her on the phone for a couple of weeks, and I didn't let Roy know that I had heard their conversation, because he would have been disappointed that I had eavesdropped.

Roy was working late, and I was bored. I didn't have a date, and there was nothing worth watching on television, so I called Daniel.

"You sound like you're walking on your lower lip," he said. "I'll buy the burgers if you'll be my ride."

Daniel began one of his Johnny Carson monologues the minute he got into the car. He was so smart and funny, and he never failed to buoy my spirits when I was feeling down.

After we stuffed ourselves with junk food, we tooled around the island for a while. As we drove by Roy's office I saw his car and Addie Jo's Mustang parked side by side in the parking lot.

"Let's go in and say hello to Roy," I said.

"Are you sure we won't be disturbing him?"

"We'll be giving him a little break."

I made a U-turn and pulled into the parking lot.

"I might have known she'd be here," I said, nodding at the Mustang. "Don't bother offering her your hand this time."

The front door was unlocked, and the only light in the outer office was the beam from a small lamp in the corner of the room. We walked down the dark corridor to Roy's office. The door was cracked, and we could see the dim glow from his desk lamp.

"Maybe he's asleep," Daniel whispered.

"If that's what he's doing, he might as well be at home," I said.

"Who's there?"

"Just us," I said, pushing the door open. "Are you sleeping on the job?"

"Just a minute," Roy sputtered as we stepped into his office.

I couldn't believe what I was seeing: there on a leather couch were Roy and his secretary, naked as the day they were born. Roy grabbed his shirt and tried to cover them, but there was still a lot of skin showing. I could see pain in his eyes—a father's pain—at having been discovered in a shameful transgression by his adoring daughter.

"We'd better go," Daniel said, taking my hand and leading me out of the office.

We didn't talk on the way home. I parked in front of his aunt's house. He took me by the shoulders and made me look at him.

"Don't judge too quickly," he said, kissing my wet cheek. Then, he got out and disappeared into the house.

Roy was raking a hand through his hair, pacing the living room when I got home. I walked past him to my room and locked the door. The entire scenario seemed surreal. Roy couldn't possibly have fallen for Addie Jo Simmons; she was the antithesis of my mother.

I deliberately stayed in bed the next morning until after I heard Roy leave for work. It was the first time since Mama died that I hadn't made him breakfast.

All morning I tried to fathom a reason for Roy's succumbing to Addie Jo's cheap seduction. I was frustrated from the effort, and each time I thought I had no more tears, a new wave would materialize.

It was noon, and I was sitting at the kitchen table with a box of Kleenex, waiting for the next crying jag when Roy walked in. I was surprised, because he never came home for lunch anymore.

"Have you had lunch?" he asked, not daring to bring his eyes to mine.

"I don't feel like eating."

"Me neither; I want to talk."

"I don't."

"I can't say that I blame you." He sat down heavily. "Would you be willing to listen?"

"I can't imagine what you could have to tell me, Roy. I surely saw the whole story."

"Clementine, I hope you'll believe me when I tell you the look on your face last night hurt me as much as it did the day your mama died. I won't insult you by telling you that nothing happened."

"That's encouraging."

"The fact is, honey, I've been terribly lonely lately. I realize Addie Jo isn't the woman for me. I can't have the woman I want and need; she's gone."

I was so ashamed for Roy that I couldn't bring myself to look at him. Of course, he was lonely. He was still a relatively young man with feelings and natural urges, but Addie Jo Simmons wasn't the answer, and we both knew it.

I stared at my hands while Roy waited for me to say something.

"Addie Jo is a poor substitute for the kind of woman you deserve," I finally said. "She's not a genuinely warm person. She's a big phony on the prowl, and I think she's stupid and pushy beyond words. On top of all that, she looks trashy. She's the direct opposite of Mama, Roy. How can you want her?"

"You're right on all counts, honey, but she and I have something in common: we're both lonely."

He looked like a small boy begging for forgiveness.

"I love you, Roy." I kissed him on the forehead. "You're my dad."

There was relief in his eyes as I turned and walked out the door. I needed to talk to Mama Rae.

Chapter Seventeen

The woods smelled deliciously fragrant, the way they do after a summer shower. I stood in the cool stillness and inhaled deeply, taking in nature's perfume. These woods are an extension of Mama Rae, I thought, and walked the familiar path to her cottage.

I knocked on the frame of the screen door. There was no answer. Mama Rae had to be at home. She never left her cottage without locking the doors.

"Mama Rae, it's me, Clementine."

She didn't answer, and I started to worry. I went around to the back, hoping to find her coming from the outhouse, but there was no sign of her.

Biscuit, her big yellow cat, was on the back step whetting his appetite by tormenting a field mouse. He would allow the mouse the latitude to scurry to the end of the step, then reach out with a paw and swipe it back within glaring distance. After a few attempts to escape, the mouse gave up and sat still. Biscuit became bored with the lack of participation on the mouse's part and began batting the poor creature into the air like a toy.

"You big bully!" I scolded. "Leave that mouse alone. You eat better than most humans."

The cat must have thought I intended to make off with his prize, and he wasn't going to let that happen. He pinned the rodent between his front paws and devoured it on the spot. Such was the way of the woods.

I smacked at him, and he high-tailed it under the cottage.

It occurred to me that Mama Rae might be taking a nap, and I went to look in her bedroom window.

She was lying supine on her bed, dressed in white from head to toe. A gauzy turban covered her hair, and her long robe resembled one a priest might wear. She wore white socks and gloves, leaving no skin exposed except her face. Her ugly, thrown-together doll lay on her chest.

Panic shot through me. Mama Rae just couldn't be dead. I couldn't bear losing her.

Suddenly, she sat up, clutching the doll with both hands. She got up from the bed and began making very deliberate angular motions with her right arm while holding the doll in her left hand. Indistinguishable sounds emanated from her lips; she was chanting in a low, eerie monotone.

Never had I seen such a curious exhibition. Of course, Mama Rae wouldn't welcome company when she was in the midst of one of her strange rituals, and I didn't want her to know I was there. Some of the things she did frightened me, and this was one. I ducked out of sight and ran into the woods.

The house was quiet when I got home. I needed a confidant in the worst way, but there was none.

I set up the ironing board and started pressing Roy's shirts, trying to iron out my frustration when the phone rang.

"Hello."

"Clementine, this is Addie Jo. Please don't hang up."

"Roy's not here, and you and I don't have anything to discuss."

"Roy doesn't know I'm calling you. I left work at noon. I have a migraine headache."

"Why are you telling me? I'm not a doctor."

"Clementine, I have to talk to you, face-to-face. Please give me a half hour of your time. There are some things you need to know."

I never wanted to see her again, but something made me agree to listen to what she had to say.

"Meet me at Coligny Plaza in fifteen minutes," she said.

I hung up and turned off the iron. I had scorched Roy's shirt.

Addie Jo was sitting at an outdoor table beside a duck pond, drinking iced tea. She was wearing dark glasses and a big-brimmed hat.

"Thank you for coming," she said. "Would you like something to drink?"

"I'm not thirsty."

"I don't know where to begin," she said.

"I didn't come all the way down here to listen to you make small talk. You'd better start talking, because this is the last time I plan to see you."

Addie Jo took a deep breath. "Roy has a problem you aren't aware of, Clementine."

"Well, I'm sure he shares his most intimate secrets with the woman he sleeps with. Why don't you enlighten me?"

"Roy's an alcoholic," she blurted.

"That's a lie! I've never seen Roy touch a drop of liquor. He won't even drink a glass of wine with dinner at a nice restaurant."

"I doubt you'll ever see him take a drink. Whenever he gets the urge, he goes to an Alcoholics Anonymous meeting. That's where I met him. You see, I'm an alcoholic, too. Roy and I don't have business meetings in Savannah on Wednesday nights. We go to AA meetings; we have to."

For the very first time I saw sincerity in Addie Jo's face, and I believed what she was telling me. It made sense. I remembered the frequent meetings Roy attended after Mama died. He sometimes went to three a week.

"I don't know what to say," I told her.

"You don't have to say anything. Just don't judge him. He's an alcoholic, and he's lonely. Roy's told me how he adored your mother. I know he'll never love me or anybody else the way he loved her, but I'm willing to settle for less. I'm lonely, too. I've been lonely all my life."

"I'm sorry," I said, trying to feel a shred of sympathy.

"I know you don't like me. You think I'm trying to take your mother's place, but I swear I'm not. I just have to do whatever I can to hang onto my sanity. Roy's been wonderful. He calms me down when I feel like I just can't take it anymore. What you saw last night were two people who happened to be alone together at the right time. It's never happened before. Roy likes me well enough, but he doesn't love me. I love him though. I knew it the first time I heard him speak at an AA meeting."

"I don't understand why you're telling me these things. It doesn't change anything."

"I know that," she said with a little smile. "I just don't want you to hate Roy. He adores you; talks about you all the time."

"Since you know he doesn't love you, how can you want him? There must be other nice men on the island."

"I trust Roy. I've never trusted another man in my life. My daddy was the meanest man who ever walked the face of the earth. He beat Mama and slapped all of us kids around on a regular basis. So when I was eighteen, I ran away from home and married my husband. That was like jumping from the frying pan into the fire. The only good thing about our marriage was that we didn't have children."

"How long were you married?"

"Too long. Sam tried at first, but it didn't do any good. He couldn't hold a job because of his hot temper. He didn't want me to work, but the bills had to be paid. So I had several jobs when he was out of work. It made him mad that I could get a job and he couldn't. Male pride, I guess."

I didn't know why I was letting Addie Jo use me as a sounding board. She may have had a tough past, but that wasn't my concern. I didn't care about the problems she had with her ex, but I couldn't bring myself to say that.

"Sam got real down and started hitting the bottle big time. He was a mean drunk and got a kick out of using yours truly for a punching bag when he was drinking. The only way I could live with him was to drink with him. Then one day I woke up. I realized I had to get away from him to save myself. I knew I couldn't help him; he wouldn't let me. So I left him. He didn't try to stop me from getting a divorce."

"How does Roy fit into this?"

"I started going to AA meetings to get myself straightened out. As soon as I felt strong enough, I took off and left Savannah. The minute I landed on this island, I swore I'd never look back. I lied when I told Roy I didn't know anything about Hilton Head, because I wanted him to take me under his wing. I pretended to be helpless, and that's what he did. I had been here more than a month before Roy hired me."

"I appreciate your telling me the truth. I'm sorry you haven't had a very good life, but you and Roy are not right for one another. Nothing you can say will make me change my mind about that. I'd better be going."

"I'm sorry to interrupt, Clemmie, but I believe our time is up," Dr. Fitzpatrick said.

May 23, 1978

If Addie Jo had left things alone at that point, I think I could have forgiven her. She had most certainly lived a sad life. But in no time at all she was up to her old tricks.

I think Roy was blind to the destructive things Addie Jo was doing to us. He saw only a poor, helpless creature that projected the image of a lost puppy, a woman who had taken more than her share of hard knocks. Roy thought Addie Jo wanted to pull herself up by her bootstraps, but what she really wanted was a free ride at his expense.

"You're a good journalist, Clemmie." Dr. Fitzpatrick handed my spiral notebook across his desk. "You get right to the point."
"Thank you."
The doctor mustered his best excuse for a smile. I wondered if he ever belly laughed. Somehow, I knew he didn't. He didn't wear a wedding ring, but that didn't surprise me. I couldn't imagine a woman who might want to marry him. It seemed strange to me that a person who appeared devoid of feeling would choose psychiatry for a profession.
"Let's resume, shall we?" he said.
I willed my mind to focus.

Roy and I walked on eggshells for the next few days. Neither of us talked about the incident at his office or mentioned Addie Jo.
I had trouble sleeping. Each night when I went to bed I thought about my conversation with Addie Jo. She had seemed so sincere, and I had pitied her. It was easy to see why she wanted to latch onto Roy; he was a good person, and would have been a great catch for her. I prayed she would leave the island and make a new life for herself somewhere else, far away from Hilton Head.
I was concerned about Roy. It amazed me that he had kept his alcoholism a secret from Mama, and I felt naïve at not having found him out myself. Of course, I knew he didn't want to disappoint me, but that would have hurt less than his being deceitful. I had promised Addie Jo that I would continue to play ignorant for Roy's sake, and I wasn't in the habit of breaking promises.
It was Saturday evening, and I didn't have a date. I had been turning down all offers lately because I was stuck in the doldrums. I knew Roy felt guilty since he was responsible for my moodiness. He had tried to lift my spirits all day without success, so that evening he informed me that we were dining out. I didn't want to go, but couldn't make myself refuse him.

The restaurant was well off the main drag, nestled in the trees on one of the plantations, as the resort developers insisted upon referring to them. On the way there we passed a horse boarding stable. Every time I had been down this lovely road, lined with live oaks clasping their leafy fingers overhead, I had seen horses grazing or frolicking in the pasture. I always wondered how it would feel to be astride one of those beautiful animals, racing through the fields with wind in my face.

"Roy, stop the car. There's a horse right by the fence. I want to pet him."

Roy pulled off on the shoulder, looking skeptical.

"Honey, he looks awfully big. What if he isn't friendly?"

"Let's go see," I said, getting out of the car.

Roy got out and followed me.

"Don't get too close," he said. "Some horses bite."

"Come here, boy," I called, reaching over the top slat of the white wooden fence.

The horse looked like a larger version of a carousel pony. His dappled gray coat gleamed in the late afternoon sun. He stuck his head over the fence like a big pet.

"You're gorgeous," I told him.

"I hope you have an apple for him."

"I wish I did," I said, turning to see a truly gorgeous woman.

Her large green eyes danced when she smiled, and her honey-blond hair caught the sun, shining through the trees as she approached. I thought she was probably in her mid-thirties. She wore a white tee shirt and denim cutoffs that showed off her shapely tanned legs. I couldn't help noticing that Roy was openly appreciating her beauty.

"His name's Diablo," she said. "He's spoiled rotten."

"He's magnificent." Roy smiled. "I'm Roy Hubbard, and this is my daughter, Clementine."

"I'm Ava Kingsley," the pretty woman said. "I'm happy to meet you both."

"Clementine was just dying to pet him," Roy explained. "Do you suppose he'll bite her?"

"Give him this." Ava pulled a carrot out of a paper bag. "I was out for my evening walk, and I couldn't pass this way without a treat for my horse."

I held the carrot toward Diablo. He took it gently with his large teeth and munched it quickly.

"Would you like Clementine to scratch your ears?" Ava asked the horse.

I started scratching the velvety spot behind his left ear.

"He sure likes that." Roy grinned and began scratching the other ear.

"He's always been an attention hound," Ava said. "Do you folks live around here, or are you on vacation?"

"We live here," Roy said. "How about you?" Then he laughed at himself. "That was a silly question. Of course you live here. Your horse wouldn't be here if you didn't."

"I've been here for nearly two years," Ava said. "My husband and I first came to Hilton Head on our honeymoon. The island has certainly grown since then."

"What does your husband do?" Roy asked with apparent disappointment.

"My husband's deceased. He was a pilot and ran his own business, flying a commuter plane in the southeast. His small plane crashed three years ago with two passengers aboard. There were no survivors."

"I'm very sorry," Roy said.

"Thank you," the young widow said.

I didn't purposely begin mental matchmaking at that moment, but I knew I was going to like Ava Kingsley, and I thought Roy would, too.

"Do you live on this plantation?" Roy asked.

"Yes. I live back toward the main road, just inside the security gate."

I could tell that Roy would have liked to stay and get to know the pretty lady better, but we were about to be late.

"Roy, I hate to interrupt, but we're about to miss our dinner reservation," I said.

Roy looked at his watch. "You're right. It was awfully nice meeting you, Mrs. Kingsley."

"Same here," Ava said. "Feel free to stop and visit Diablo whenever you happen to be out this way."

"Did you ever see such a pretty woman?" I asked as we got into the car.

"Only two: you and your mama."

Our table was by a window, and the view of the sunset above the shimmering water was beautiful. Roy seemed quiet during dinner, and I wondered if he was thinking about Ava Kingsley. If he had a brain in his head, he would pursue a relationship with her.

"Ava certainly seems like a nice person," I said, breaking the silence.

"What? Oh, yes, she does."

"Maybe you should look her up and get to know her."

"Oh, well, I don't know. I imagine she probably has a significant other."

"What makes you think that? Did you just snatch it from the air?"

Roy laughed. "I guess I did at that."

Sunday came and went without either of us mentioning the lovely Ava Kingsley. I supposed that my discovery of Roy's tryst with Addie Jo had caused him to lose interest in women, at least for the time being.

I told Daniel about meeting Ava and how much I liked her. Then, I solicited his help in a matchmaking scheme. The two of us drove to the boarding stable to see if we could spot Diablo, but there were no horses in sight.

"Drive down the road," Daniel said. "The pasture runs all the way to the intersection, I think."

We finally saw a small herd of horses grazing not far from the fence.

"There they are," he said. "Pull over."

We ran to the fence, and I searched the herd for Diablo.

"He should be real easy to spot," I said, "and I don't see him."

"Don't look so down. We can come back tomorrow afternoon."

We were about to leave when we heard pounding hooves. Out of the trees came Diablo, racing toward the herd. Ava Kingsley sat tall on the horse's back. She rode bareback in jeans and a bright yellow tee shirt, and she was barefoot. Daniel's eyes were glued to the woman and her horse.

"You're right," he said. "She's gorgeous; so is the horse."

"Don't get any ideas. She's Roy's. Besides, she's too old for you."

Ava hugged the horse with her knees as they raced from one end of the pasture to the other. She leaned with the animal as it made a sharp turn to change directions. After doing this a couple of times, she slowed Diablo to a trot and rode over to the fence.

"Well, hello," she said, sounding a bit winded. "I'm glad to see you, Clementine."

"Ava Kingsley, I'd like you to meet Daniel Grover, my best friend."

"Hello, Daniel. I'm happy to meet you." Ava smiled and extended her hand to Daniel.

"You certainly have a beautiful horse," Daniel said, "and that was some pretty fancy bareback riding."

"Do either of you ride?" Ava asked.

"I've never been on a horse," I admitted, "but I've always wanted to try it."

"My uncle used to have an old broken-down nag," Daniel said. "When I was a little kid, my mom would take me to visit, and he'd let me ride the horse."

"How would you like to come out and ride with me this weekend?" Ava said. "I know most of the owners who board their horses here, and I'm sure I can round up a couple of suitable mounts."

Daniel and I looked at one another.

"We'll come riding with you if you'll come to my house for a cookout tomorrow night," I said.

"How can I refuse?" Ava said. "I'll be there."

I wrote our address on a deposit slip along with a sketchy map and handed it to her.

"So you planned something like a blind date for Mrs. Kingsley and Roy," Dr. Fitzpatrick said with a smile.

"Yes, I did."

Chapter Eighteen

—

May 25, 1978

I was so happy that Roy and I had met Ava Kingsley. She was not only beautiful, but genuinely warm and intelligent. I thought she was perfect for Roy. But as the relationship between Roy and Ava began to develop, Addie Jo decided to strike again.

Dr. Fitzpatrick laid down my journal.
"So we're back to Miss Simmons," he said.
"I'm afraid so."

———

Roy was a nervous wreck when he greeted Ava at the door. He had reprimanded me for inviting her to dinner without consulting him, but he didn't sound like he meant it.

Daniel arrived just in time to watch Roy stumble all over himself as he ushered Ava into the living room and backed into an occasional table, causing a lamp to teeter just before righting it. I knew he was hoping I would come to his rescue, but I wanted him to get a grip before I entered the room. He was going to have to learn to relax with Ava, and this was the perfect time to start.

"What may I offer you to drink, Mrs. Kingsley?" he asked.

I came into the room to say hello, and Roy looked a little less panic stricken.

"I'd love a gin and tonic, if you have it. And please call me Ava."

Discomfort returned to Roy's face. "I do apologize, Ava, but I'm afraid we don't keep liquor in the house."

Ava smiled. "That's not a problem. Any kind of soft drink will be fine."

"Daniel?" Roy said.

"A Coke sounds good," Daniel said. "I'll help you with the drinks."

"Please excuse Roy," I said, after the men left the room. "He hasn't had much practice with lady friends since my mother passed away. I suppose you're wondering why I refer to him by his first name. He isn't my real father, but he adopted me after he and Mama married. I was ten, and he's been a wonderful father."

"I see. How long has your mother been gone, Clementine?"

"Seven years. She was struck by a car the summer we moved here."

"I'm so sorry. You must miss her a great deal."

"Yes, I do, but time helps."

Roy lost his case of the jitters when he went to work on our meal. He had bought enough shrimp for the neighborhood and steaks for the grill. I had made a green salad, and Roy had gone to our favorite bakery in Savannah for a loaf of sourdough bread.

As the evening progressed, conversation flowed easily among the four of us, and it was obvious that Roy was having a good time.

"Why don't you go riding with us Saturday, Roy," Ava said. "It'll be fun."

"I'm afraid I don't ride." He laughed. "I hardly know one end of a horse from the other."

"I'll teach you," she said. "There's nothing to it, and I promise you'll have fun."

Come Saturday morning, the three of us met Ava at the stables, and Roy was nervous all over again.

"I have coffee and doughnuts," Ava said. "I hope you don't mind eating in a barn."

The barn was tidy and clean. Ava had a card table set up just inside the big doors. It was covered with a pink tablecloth. A coffeepot was plugged into an extension cord and sat next to a tray of assorted pastries.

"I wouldn't mind living in a barn like this." Daniel grinned.

Ava asked a groom to saddle horses while we ate, and she gave us a few safety tips.

"All of these horses are gentle," she said. "They love people, and they're well behaved."

Roy took one look at his horse, and the color drained from his face.

"He's so tall," he whispered.

"You don't have to whisper, Roy," Ava said. "The horse won't be offended. Come climb aboard the way I showed you."

Roy took a couple of tentative steps toward the horse and froze.

"I'll help you," Ava said.

She led Roy to the horse's left side and placed his hand on the saddle horn.

"I'll hold the stirrup steady, and you put your left foot into it and pull yourself up by the horn."

I could tell Roy wasn't going to be a very good horseman. Daniel and I gave him a boost, and he finally managed to get into the saddle.

"All right," Ava said, "everyone mount up."

She took the lead, and the three of us fell in behind her. The horses seemed good-natured, and didn't appear to take umbrage at having to play follow-the-leader. We rode into the woods and along a meandering creek where the wildflowers were abundant and birdsong filled the air.

Ava had packed a picnic, and when we came to what looked like a perfect spot, we stopped for lunch.

Roy didn't want to get off his horse, but with some teasing and cajoling, we talked him into joining us for our picnic. Ava's fried chicken must have mellowed him, because he managed to get back on his horse without any help.

We were enjoying the ride back to the stables when, all at once, the horses seemed to get excited.

"Rein your horses in a little," Ava said. "They know they're going to get treats when we get to the barn, so they're anxious. You three go ahead, and I'll bring up the rear."

Daniel took the lead. His childhood riding skills seemed to have returned as soon as he got on the horse.

"I'm going to take a chance and let her go," he said, nudging his chestnut mare in the flanks.

She sprang forward, and the other horses followed suit. It startled me when my horse lurched forward, but I managed to hold it to a rough trot that jiggled my insides. I didn't see Ava, but Roy flew past me like a rocket, making keening noises. He was hanging onto the horn with both hands, and one rein was clamped between his teeth while the other flapped in the breeze.

Ava urged Diablo forward until she was almost close enough to catch Roy.

"Grab the other rein, Roy," she shouted.

But Roy had a death grip on the saddle horn, and wasn't about to turn loose. His horse was galloping sideways, but he managed to hang on all the way to the barn. By the time Ava reached him, his horse was walking around in circles.

"You made it, Roy," she said. "Now, let go of the rein before you make the horse dizzy."

When he realized that Ava was holding the horse steady, he climbed down from the saddle.

"Well, that was quite an experience," he said, visibly shaken. "I've done it now, and I don't ever have to do it again."

"That was an amusing anecdote," Dr. Fitzpatrick said. "I must say I've never seen you so upbeat."

"I guess it's because that was such a good time for us. Roy and I were happy again, and we had Ava to thank for it."

"You have a lovely smile, my dear."

"Thank you."

May 30, 1978

Ava was like a tonic for Roy and me. We had a wonderful time with her no matter what we were doing. Sometimes she would show up on our doorstep with a basket containing a home-cooked meal, wearing jeans or shorts and no makeup. There was nothing pretentious about her.

The doctor looked up from my journal and smiled just enough to show his crooked tooth.

"It's a bit unusual for a person to recall the past with such relish," he said. "Let me say that I think it's a good thing, but you must realize that whatever holds the key to your memory loss will, of course, be painful."

"Yes, I know."

"So, will you be able to grace me with a smile during this session?"

"I don't know."

The better we knew Ava, the more she delighted us. In the short time we had known her we learned that she was a good sport, a wonderful cook, and that she was willing to try most any adventure one of us suggested. She went sailing and fishing with us, and taught Roy, Daniel and me to groom horses.

Roy was happier than he had been since Mama died, and I knew it was because of Ava. I realized that she helped fill a void for me, too. I was comfortable with her and found that I wanted to confide in her, so I couldn't wait to tell her I had a potential new love in my life.

"His name's Jimmy Castlebrook," I said into the phone. "He just moved here. His father is a construction contractor, and I don't think his mother works. Oh, Ava, he's my dream come true. I can't wait for you to meet him."

"How did you meet him?" she asked.

"Quite by accident. I was pushing a cart through the parking lot at the supermarket, and he almost drove into me pulling into a parking space. He jumped out of his car and hurried to apologize for nearly running me over."

"That's an interesting way to meet a pretty girl."

I laughed. "After I got over being mad, he helped me load my groceries into the car, and we got acquainted. We have a date for Saturday night."

"Well, I hope your Mr. Wonderful turns out to be worthy of you," she said.

Roy and I invited Ava and Daniel for a cookout Friday evening. They arrived promptly at five o'clock, and were coming up the front walk when Roy snapped a picture of them with his new camera. We played with a Frisbee, had a watermelon seed spitting contest, and horsed around outside until daylight faded. Each of us took a turn playing photographer, and by the end of the evening, we had used a roll of film.

"Excuse me, Clemmie," Dr. Fitzpatrick interrupted. "I thought you were going to tell me about Jimmy Castlebrook."

I felt my hands grip the armrests of the chair, and blood begin to pound in my temples.

"If you don't let me tell you what's fresh in my mind, I'll lose it. I have to tell you about the pictures."

"Very well." The doctor pinched his eyebrows together.

The Monday afternoon following our cookout, Roy called to tell me he had picked up the pictures and that they were hilarious.

I had dinner ready when he came whistling up the front steps.

"Where are the photos?" I asked.

He smacked himself on the forehead.

"I must have left them on my desk. Sometimes my brain just doesn't work. I promise I'll bring them home tomorrow."

He called from work the next morning to tell me that he had forgotten his briefcase.

"I can't believe how absentminded I'm getting," he said. "I don't need the briefcase, but how could I just walk out and leave it sitting by the door? Look in the side pocket, sweetheart, and see if I put the snapshots in it. I can't find them anywhere."

Roy's briefcase was a sight to behold. I couldn't imagine how he ever found anything he'd thrown into its depths, but I searched it thoroughly, and the pictures weren't there.

"They're not here," I said. "Check your desk drawers."

Roy came home empty-handed. He had searched all over his office.

"Well, this is a real mystery," he said. "I guess I'm bound to run across them in a day or two."

The phone rang, and I left Roy to the task of purging unimportant papers from the heap he had dumped on the table.

"Clemmie, this is Daniel."

"So it is," I said. "What's up?"

"I'll tell you what's up. My auntie is about to disown me. A strange woman came to the house and left an interesting envelope taped to the front door."

"What are you talking about?"

"My auntie was in the garden this afternoon when she saw a woman ride up on a bicycle. The stranger ran up the porch steps and taped an envelope to the door, got back on her bike and rode off before my auntie could get to the house."

"Why are you being so mysterious? What was in the envelope?"

"Pictures. Some of the pictures we took at your house the night of the cookout. There was a message printed on the back of the envelope. It said: 'Black boys should know their places. It seems that your son doesn't know his. Maybe he needs to be taught a lesson.'"

"Daniel, I don't understand any of this. It makes no sense."

"Do you remember the shot you took of Ava and me when we were both running to catch the Frisbee? I held out my arms so we wouldn't collide, and we fell down together. Well, it didn't look like an innocent game in the snapshot according to my auntie. It looked a lot like a black man and a white woman rolling around in the grass. My auntie said it looked like we were kissing. Oh, and there was one of me hugging you."

"So what? Simply explain what was really happening to your aunt."

"Humph! I can't talk to her; she's boiling. She won't listen to me, and she burned the pictures."

"Put her on the phone. I'll explain the whole thing to her."

"She won't talk to you. She said that if I see you again, she'll put me on the next flight out. She doesn't know I'm talking to you."

"This is absurd. Did she describe the woman on the bicycle?"

"She said it was a white woman with dark hair. The woman was wearing great big sunglasses."

"I can't imagine who it could have been, but she can't have been anyone who knows you very well. She thought your aunt was your mother."

"You're right. I was so hacked off I didn't think about that."

"Try not to worry, Daniel."

"Clemmie, I'm serious about this. Don't call or come over here. I've never seen my auntie like this."

Dr. Fitzpatrick looked over the top of his glasses.

"Miss Simmons?" he asked.

I nodded.

June 1, 1978

Poor Daniel. His state of confusion turned into a fight to survive. He had somehow ended up with the short end of the stick since the day I met him. The skinny little kid with big brown eyes had grown into a handsome young man. He had matured well: his stutter was gone, and he had tamed his temper and his penchant for revenge. But no matter how hard he tried, he still ended up in hot water.

Chapter Nineteen

"Your journal entry tells me this is not going to be an enjoyable session," Dr. Fitzpatrick said, leaning back in his chair. "Try to relax and stay focused. You're making good progress."

While it was true that Roy was absentminded, he later ran across the photos in one of his desk drawers. Since he had thoroughly searched the desk, he knew someone had tampered with the pictures. All of the prints were accounted for, so he assumed that whoever *borrowed* them had gone to the trouble of having duplicates made to blackmail Daniel.

Daniel dropped out of sight. I didn't call or go to his aunt's house, but I drove down to the pier on two separate occasions in hopes of finding him at work. He wasn't there either time.

Ava and Roy were as upset about Daniel as I was. Ava wanted to talk to his aunt and assure her that what she saw in the pictures was nothing more than innocent fun.

"I'm twice his age," she said. "Surely, his aunt will understand how ridiculous this whole thing is."

Roy agreed with me that none of us should contact Daniel's aunt, but he was so upset that he went to an AA meeting that week. He had been able to put the meetings on hold since he met Ava.

I was watching Johnny Carson rib Doc Severinsen about his gaudy jacket when Roy came home from Savannah.

"You're up late," he said.

"I need to talk to you," I said, turning off the set. "I think Addie Jo is the picture thief."

Roy rubbed the stubble on his chin, and dragged his fingers through his hair.

"That thought crossed my mind, too, but what would she stand to gain?"

"She never liked Daniel simply because of his color. She's the biggest bigot I've ever known."

"I haven't heard her make any bigoted remarks, but I did notice that she was cool toward Daniel."

"She's a mean, sick woman, Roy."

"Daniel's aunt said the woman had dark hair."

"Good grief, Roy! She could have been wearing a wig."

"That's true. But how would she have known about the photos? I didn't show them to her. Our interaction has been strictly business since . . ."

"She's your secretary. She could have seen them on your desk. Doesn't she have access to your office?"

"Everyone does. I never lock my door."

"You look tired. Let's talk about this tomorrow."

The shrill ringing of the phone woke me, and I rushed to answer it, hoping it wouldn't wake Roy.

"Clemmie, it's me," Daniel said. "I'm sorry to call you so late at night. I couldn't sleep."

"Where have you been for the past week?"

"I've been at my auntie's, but I'm at a public phone now."

"I drove down to the pier a couple of times. You weren't there."

"There's a good reason for that. I was fired."

"Why?"

"It seems there have been complaints about me, from women."

"Daniel, this thing has gotten way out of hand. What are we going to do?"

"I hope you won't do anything, and I'm not sure what I'm going to do. My auntie has been plagued with phone calls every day and night since she found those pictures taped to the door. The woman who calls has a vile mouth, and she's made some pretty nasty threats. My auntie is so uptight she's afraid someone is going to burn a cross on the front lawn. Clemmie, she's kicked me out."

"Oh, Daniel, where will you go?"

"She gave me money to go to my mother's, but I'm not going. I have to stay here and figure out who's trying to do me in."

"Stay with us. Roy thinks the world of you."

"I can't, Clemmie. That would just be asking for more trouble. Don't worry about me. I'll be fine."

"But. . ."

"I'll call you later. Gotta go."

The phone clicked in my ear.

Roy was furious when I told him what had happened. He told me he was going to confront Addie Jo.

"You can't do that, Roy. You don't have proof that she was involved."

"Yes, I can. I can say anything I like to her face. I just can't tell anyone else. She'd sue me for slander."

Roy called me as soon as he got to work.

"I've decided to wait," he said. "I'm going to lay low and trap her."

"Be careful, Roy. I'm not sure you're a very good detective."

"We'll see about that," he said, and hung up.

I was tramping through the woods to Mama Rae's house.

"Where you been keepin' yourself?" she said, startling me.

"Oh, Mama Rae, you scared me."

I hadn't seen her because she was crouched by the path, picking herbs. She wore her old slouch hat and clothes that blended with the earth tones of the forest.

"Don't be steppin' in my basket," she scolded. "You got big feet for a girl."

"Oh, sorry." I removed my foot from her herbs. "Mama Rae, I have to talk to you. Something dreadful has happened."

"Uh huh."

"Let's go to your house for a cup of tea."

"Des woods don't have ears," she said, sitting down on a rotting log.

I sat down and told her the bare bones of the awful tale.

"Whew! Lot been goin' on since I saw you."

"I feel so sorry for Daniel, and I don't know how I can help him."

"He a smart young man. He'll work it out."

"He doesn't have a place to stay. His aunt threw him out. I wanted him to stay with Roy and me, but he refused my offer."

"Uh huh."

"Tell me what to do."

"Don't do nothin'. Daniel goin' to be fine. Now, tell me 'bout dis new beau of yours and 'bout Roy's new lady friend."

I told her all about Ava and how much I liked Jimmy. She nodded with approval. Then, she stood and picked up her basket, dismissing me. She hadn't given me any advice except to mind my own business, but I felt better as I started home. Just being with Mama Rae gave me a lift.

It was Friday evening, and Roy and I both had dates. He was going to Ava's for dinner, and I had a date with Jimmy. Roy approved of Jimmy from the time they met, but he made sure that the new young man in my life knew I was his princess.

Jimmy took me to dinner and then for a long drive. We were on a deserted road in the middle of nowhere when he pulled onto the shoulder and killed the engine.

"This area will be developed soon," he said. "I was out here with my dad the other day. He's bidding on a contract to do the job."

"It's really pretty. I love the tall pines."

"Look up there," Jimmy said. "If you look between the branches of those two trees, you'll see the Big Dipper."

"You're right." I smiled.

Jimmy had quickly lost interest in the stars. His face was shadowed, so I couldn't see his expression, but I could feel it.

"Your eyes put the heavens to shame," he whispered.

Then, he kissed me. I returned his kiss as our bodies meshed in a way that felt just right. The kissing continued, and our flesh was afire. I ached for Jimmy Castlebrook. But suddenly, unwanted memories of Sonny Malone came to mind.

Just as I was about to panic, Jimmy pulled away from me and, taking a deep breath, he asked, "May I have this dance, lovely lady?"

"What a wonderful idea."

He turned on the radio and escorted me out of the car and onto the dance floor. Jimmy held me close as we slow-danced on the newly-paved blacktop.

Jimmy Castlebrook made me forget everyone else I had ever dated. He had a heart as big as Roy's, and couldn't seem to do enough for others. Sonny Malone's movie star looks would have been all wrong on him. Jimmy was handsome in a real and wonderful way. His weight and height were average, and his body was well-formed. I loved his laughing eyes, and his slightly crooked smile drove me wild. Everything about him was genuine, and I couldn't get enough of him.

As much as I relished spending time with Jimmy, Daniel was constantly on my mind. I considered telling Jimmy about Daniel and his predicament, but, for some reason, I kept quiet. I wondered if Daniel had tried to call when Roy and I were both away from the house, and hoped he was well and safe.

Roy had tried a few schemes to trap Addie Jo with no luck. The latest was to show the photographs to some of the office staff and make sure she saw them. He wanted to see her reaction when she looked at them, but she didn't take the bait.

"Wow! What a looker!" she said, eyeing a photo of Ava. "Is this your new paramour?"

Roy said he looked Addie Jo square in the face and said, "Yes, she is."

He said Addie Jo showed no flicker of emotion at his admission or when she looked at the snapshots of Daniel.

"This is the young man I met at your home," she said. "He seemed very nice."

She picked up the next photo, the one of Daniel and Ava on the ground in what appeared a compromising position.

"My goodness," she said. "He certainly does like the ladies, doesn't he?"

"How many people were listening to her make those snide remarks, Roy? I hope none of the salesmen believed her veiled accusations."

"They didn't. I was showing the pictures to Addie Jo and a couple of the guys. Don't worry, sweetheart. I explained what was actually happening in the candid shot, and that shut her up."

"Thank goodness."

"Addie Jo put on her *roll-your-eyes face* after hearing my explanation."

"I'm sure she did."

"I told her that Daniel's aunt shared her sentiments, and that was an interesting moment."

"'His aunt?' she asked."

"'Yes,'" I told her. "'Daniel lives with his aunt, you know. She had a fit when she saw that picture.'"

"Addie Jo said she hoped I explained the situation to Daniel's aunt, and I told her that I had."

The following day, there was a report of a Peeping Tom on the local news, and Daniel's description fit that of the voyeur to a tee. The woman who notified the police requested anonymity. She had allegedly been frightened by a young black male looking in her bedroom window while she was undressing.

"I hate to interrupt," Dr. Fitzpatrick said, "but our time is up. I assume I'll hear more about Miss Simmons at our next session."

Chapter Twenty

June 6, 1978

Addie Jo wouldn't rest until she had destroyed Daniel. I couldn't imagine what could have engendered such hatred toward someone she scarcely knew, but it was clear to me that she had made up her mind to get rid of Daniel.

"Can you elaborate?" the doctor asked.

Daniel still hadn't called, and I was worried sick. Finally, a letter with his aunt's return address came in the mail. Daniel had scribbled a note telling me that he would call Thursday evening at nine o'clock. Nothing could make me miss his call, so I concocted a lame excuse and cancelled my date with Jimmy.

The phone rang at exactly nine o'clock.

"Hey, Clemmie."

"Oh, Daniel, I'm so relieved to hear your voice. Can you talk a little louder? We must have a bad connection."

"I can't talk any louder. I'm at my auntie's house. She's asleep in the next room. I picked the lock on the kitchen door so I could get some clean clothes."

"Are you all right? We've all been worried about you."

"I'm fine. Did you see the artist's rendering of me on the news?"

"Yes. Roy saw it, too."

"Roy knows I'm innocent, doesn't he?"

"Of course, he does. Daniel, why don't you go to the police?"

"I'm afraid to. For all I know, there could be a good ol' boy on the police force who might be as insane as that weird female."

"Have you talked to your aunt?"

"No. I'm sure she's glad to be rid of me, though. The phone calls must have stopped, because she's snoozing away. I don't want to make more trouble for her."

"I keep picturing you sleeping under a bridge with snakes and swamp rats, Daniel. Where are you staying?"

"I'm at the safest place on the island—Mama Rae's."

"Oh."

"She's really a nice old girl."

"I know she is."

"I won't be coming back here. I just packed the rest of my clothes. If you want to reach me, I'll be at Mama Rae's place. I'd better go."

"Be safe, Daniel. Good night."

The next day I went to see Daniel and Mama Rae. They were just getting home when I arrived, and they were dressed to the nines.

Mama Rae peered out from under a big-brimmed hat and grinned.

"You show up more than a bad penny," she said.

"Where have you two been all dressed up?" I asked.

"Mama Rae made me put on a coat and tie to go to the police station," Daniel grumbled.

"A little respeck goes a fer piece," Mama Rae said. "Didn't hurt you to get dressed up. You needed to make a good impression."

"You wouldn't consider going to the police when I suggested it," I said hotly.

"She made me go," Daniel said.

"It wuz the right thing to do." Mama Rae wore a look of satisfaction.

"They believe you're innocent, don't they?" I asked.

"'Course they do," Mama Rae answered for Daniel. "I tol' them Daniel wuz here with me. They know I ain't gonna be tellin' no lies."

"I wasn't sure they believed me during the questioning," Daniel said, "but they believed Mama Rae."

"Well, it's wonderful," I said.

I poured lemonade while Daniel and Mama Rae changed into their everyday clothes.

Daniel seemed so at home at Mama Rae's that I felt a twinge of jealousy. I was ashamed of my feeling, but it was definitely there.

"I'm sorry, Dr. Fitzpatrick. I seem to have lost my train of thought."

"Maybe you're rushing. Relax. I'll recap for you."

I took a couple of deep breaths and tried to relax.

"You had gone to see Daniel and Mama Rae. Daniel told you he had been to the police and that everything was fine."

"Now I remember. Daniel had been cleared on the voyeurism charge, but he didn't fare so well with his previous employer. He went to try to reason with his ex boss, but his speech fell on deaf ears. He gave up and took a job sacking groceries at the Piggly Wiggly."

"Very good, Clemmie. Let's call it a day," the doctor said.

I stepped out of the shower refreshed. It seemed that I was recalling my past in larger chunks lately. If I could keep my train of thought during the sessions and stop having the strange dreams, I might feel that I was making progress. I was sure the headaches must be side effects of the medicine. And as for those awful feelings that sometimes took over my mind during the sessions, I assumed the medicine caused them, too.

I was almost giddy as I slipped into a terrycloth robe. My hair would air dry by dinnertime. I picked up my journal and flipped through the pages, wishing for another kernel of hope when my vision started to blur. Blinking hard, I tried to will myself to see clearly, to feel normal, but all I could see was red. Then, two giant hands clasped my temples, and I thought my head might burst. I stumbled to the bed, closed my eyes, and lay very still.

I could see Mama Rae smiling; it wasn't a happy smile. Someone was running, and Roy was strumming his guitar beside a bridge. I was barefoot, and my feet were sore. I didn't know where I was.

It was dark when I awoke. I had missed dinner.

Chapter Twenty-one

━━━

June 8, 1978

My memory appears to be coming back, but I feel totally out of control. My past comes in a jumbled fashion, and nothing makes sense. I'm not sure the new medicine is safe.

———

Dr. Fitzpatrick paced his office, tapping my journal on his palm as if he thought he could beat the truth out of it.

"Clemmie, you must know that the medication you seem to be so afraid of is the agent that is helping you remember. It's all right if your thoughts are disjointed. Everything will come together soon. I've seen it happen many times."

"I knew that was the posture you'd take. You don't seem to care that I have splitting headaches, horrible dreams, and crazy thoughts that make no sense."

"Of course, I care. I know you're unhappy, but we can both see that the medicine is working. You're recalling more each day. Aren't you willing to try it a little while longer?"

"I know you're right. I'm just frustrated. I'll try to stick it out a while longer."

Dr. Fitzpatrick summoned a smile, laid down my journal, and took a seat, looking at me across his desk.

"Can you tell me about Daniel's new job at the Piggly Wiggly?"

Daniel worked Monday through Friday from eight to five. He had stopped dating since he moved out of his aunt's house, and spent his evenings conversing with Mama Rae. She didn't have a television since she considered them to be evil magic machines.

One day while Daniel was sacking groceries, Addie Jo came through his checkout line with a cartload of groceries. He said she treated him like a long lost friend and tried to give him a big tip when he pushed the cart to her car and loaded the groceries into the trunk. He told me he refused to make eye contact with her, and that he turned down the tip.

After that, she bought fewer groceries at one time and came to the store more often. She always made sure to get in the line where Daniel was sacking and never failed to try to talk him up.

I went to Mama Rae's house on Saturday because I knew that Daniel wouldn't be working.

"Come in this house," Mama Rae said. "Maybe you can talk some sense into this young mule."

From her tone I thought she and Daniel must have had some kind of disagreement.

Daniel's bedroom door was open, and I saw him packing a suitcase.

"What are you doing, Daniel?"

"You're not blind, Clemmie. I'm packing."

"Why?"

Daniel wore the tired look of a man who was exhausted from contemplating the task of explaining something to a couple of women whom he knew wouldn't listen . He took my hand and led me into the living room, then sat down heavily in Mama Rae's overstuffed chair. She was so glad he had abandoned his packing that she didn't scold him for taking over her forbidden territory.

"Addie Jo Simmons has made up her mind she's not going to stop dogging me until she runs me out of town," Daniel said. "The woman is a she-devil."

"What else has she done?"

"The clincher came yesterday afternoon. Addie Jo called the pharmacist at the Piggly Wiggly and told him she was sick with a migraine headache. She wondered if he would refill her open prescription and have me deliver it since she knew I came by her apartment on my way home. That told me she thought I still live with my aunt."

"That makes sense, but why would she want you to deliver a prescription?"

"I didn't understand that either, but I couldn't pass up the chance to find out what she was up to. I agreed to make the delivery."

"Oh, Daniel, you didn't!"

"Yes, I did. She was slow coming to the door when I rang the bell, and she really did look sick, dressed in an old seersucker housecoat and no makeup. You wouldn't have recognized her. She invited me inside and offered me some iced tea, but I turned down the drink and left."

"I must be missing something."

Daniel held up a hand. "I'm not through. I had barely gotten down the stairs and climbed on my bike when I heard a woman scream. I looked up, and there was Addie Jo on her balcony, yelling at the top of her lungs. A couple of old guys came outside to see what the commotion was."

"What was it?"

"Addie Jo's hair was a mess, and her robe was torn. It looked like someone had tried to rip it off her. She was pointing an accusing finger at me; said I had attacked her, and begged the old codgers to stop me."

I couldn't believe the despicable stunts Addie Jo was capable of hatching.

"I got away from her apartment building as fast as I could, and took every shortcut I could find to get back here," Daniel said.

"Do you think she's told the police you attacked her?"

"Sure, I do. Why else would she have set me up? She knew those old men who saw me couldn't catch me. They just provided her with witnesses."

"Do you think they can identify you?"

"They'd have to be blind if they can't. It was broad daylight, and I was within spitting distance of them."

"Well, you haven't made the news anymore, or Roy would have told me. He and Ava watched television at our house until late last night."

Mama Rae had been sitting in a little cane-bottomed chair next to the fireplace. She hadn't said a word.

"All you have to do is lay low for a while," she said. "Folks know me, but they don't know where I live. You're safe here."

"I agree with Mama Rae," I said, "but what about your job?"

"I'm not going back; it's not worth it. The best thing for me to do is leave the island."

"Dat's foolishness," Mama Rae fumed.

"No, it isn't," Daniel argued. "If I stay, there's no telling what she'll do next. She might even go after you or Clemmie."

"I ain't skiert of that mean white devil!" Mama Rae spat the words as if she had a bad taste in her mouth. "She don' want to be tanglin' with this old woman."

"Won't you just stay for a few more days and see what happens?" I begged. "Addie Jo doesn't know where you live."

We finally convinced Daniel to stay at least until he found out whether or not Addie Jo had gone to the police.

It lit a fire under Roy when I told him what had happened.

"I'm not playing any more games with her," he said. "I'm firing her."

"Don't you have to have a reason?" I asked.

"I'll make something up. She has to go."

"Let's stop for today," Dr. Fitzpatrick said. "You did quite well. Do you still feel depressed?"

"Yes."

The doctor removed his glasses and rubbed his red eyes. I thought he looked a little like a basset hound without the glasses.

"Have you been attending any of the activities lately?" he asked.

"No."

"Maybe it would help your depression to engage in some of them. Exercise is very good for depression. Why not sign up for tennis? They give lessons for beginners, I believe."

"I don't need lessons. I'm an A player."

"I see. Where did you play?"

"Hilton Head Island and Atlanta."

"Atlanta is a lovely city. When were you there?"

"I don't know."

I left Dr. Fitzpatrick's office and went to the recreation hall to add my name to the tennis roster.

June 13, 1978

I had another breakthrough today. I remembered that I know how to play tennis. Jimmy and I played doubles with several other couples in Atlanta. I don't know why we were there. Dr. Fitzpatrick's irritated eyes reminded me of an asthma attack I had during a tournament. The ragweed had just begun to bloom. Poor Jimmy tried so hard to pretend he wasn't disappointed that we lost the tournament. That's all I remember.

Chapter Twenty-two

The doctor extended a blue-veined hand across the expanse of his desk to return my journal with a look of consternation.

"This is quite a turn of events," he said. "You seem to have skipped ahead. What happened to Daniel?"

"My mind skipped ahead. I don't know how I got to this place in my life."

"Would you like to talk about Jimmy?"

"Yes, I think so."

"Is this the same Jimmy you knew on Hilton Head Island?"

"Yes. We met on the island."

Jimmy was a tennis buff. His family lived in Hilton Head Plantation, but they owned a villa in Palmetto Dunes Resort which they had bought as an investment and put in a rental pool. Ownership in the resort entitled them to play at the Rod Laver Tennis Center. Jimmy was partial to the clay courts. He claimed to be able to play on them all day and never get tired. That tennis center was where he taught me the game.

I was a terrible student at first, because I had a hard time concentrating on the game. I couldn't keep my eyes off Jimmy's gorgeous, tanned body. He always wore white tennis attire and looked like he might have been dressed to play at Wimbledon.

Jimmy was an excellent player. He had a hard, flat serve that could blow most players off the court. But as ruthless as he could be against a male opponent, he backed off his serve for the fairer sex.

After I learned the game, Jimmy took me to the center to play several times each week. I learned to enjoy tennis as much as I did the water and the woods, and became a fairly proficient player. And sometime that summer—I wasn't sure when—I fell in love with Jimmy Castlebrook.

I remember the day Jimmy let me into his world. He came to pick me up to go to the tennis center, and he couldn't seem to stop smiling.

"You have something up your sleeve, Jimmy Castlebrook," I said.

"As a matter of fact, I do have a surprise."

"For me?"

"For us."

"Well, how long are you going to keep me in suspense?"

"Until after our match."

My game was off. I couldn't keep my eye on the ball, and ran through several easy shots because I couldn't manage to plant my feet.

"What's the matter? Don't you feel well?" Jimmy asked.

"I feel fine. I just couldn't concentrate on the game. All I could think about was your big surprise. The match is over. Tell me what it is."

"I'd rather show you."

A lock of damp hair fell over his left eye, and I couldn't keep from smiling. He had no idea how appealing he was.

We got into his car and he drove to the North gate, stopped at the guardhouse, and produced a card for the uniformed gatekeeper.

"Where are we going?" I asked.

"We'll be there in no time," he said, turning left onto Haul Away Road.

Seconds later, we were pulling into a parking space at #30 Hickory Cove.

"Here we are," he said.

"Oh, Jimmy, this is your family's villa."

"Yep. Come on." He got out and came around the car to grab my hand.

"I'm a mess! I can't meet your parents wearing sweaty tennis clothes."

"You look gorgeous. Besides, nobody's here but us. My folks had the villa rented for the week, but the guests cancelled."

The villa was well appointed with comfortable furniture and bright, tasteful prints. From the living room, a sliding glass door led to a deck which looked out on the eighteenth hole of the Robert Trent Jones Golf Course. The deck was flanked on either side by ancient hickory trees.

Jimmy wanted to take me to the beach. He had a key to the owners' closet, and we rounded up swimsuits, beach towels, and a raft, and set out on the five-minute walk.

"Want to stroll down to Possum Point for something cold to drink?" he asked.

"Sure, as soon as I take a quick swim."

I dropped my towel and dashed into the surf. It took me a few minutes to wade out deep enough to swim. The saltwater felt delicious on my skin.

"Be careful," Jimmy shouted. "You'll be out over your head before you know it."

I couldn't imagine why he hadn't come with me, but I didn't question it. I was enjoying the push and pull of the ocean too much to care. I swam farther and farther, until I started to feel the beginnings of fatigue creep into my upper arms. When I finally headed back to shore, Jimmy looked incredibly small. He was standing chest deep in the water, hanging onto the raft. I was breathing hard by the time I reached him.

"Lady, you are one strong swimmer," he said admiringly. "If I ever need a lifeguard, I hope you're around."

"I love to swim," I panted. "I had a good teacher."

"Who was that? Roy?"

"No. It was my friend, Daniel. You haven't met him yet."

"Who's Daniel?" I could hear jealousy in his voice.

"He's my best friend."

We stopped at the foot showers to rinse off the sand before climbing the steps to Possum Point, and found an empty table with an umbrella, looking out on the ocean. While I sensed that Jimmy was ready to drop Daniel as a conversation piece, I knew I wouldn't be comfortable until I explained my relationship with him. I was falling for Jimmy, and that meant no secrets. If he wasn't willing to accept my close relationship with Daniel, I would have to reassess my feelings. I would never let anybody come between Daniel and me.

While we ate hotdogs and sipped lemonade, I told Jimmy all about Daniel and how the two of us had been fast friends since childhood and always would be.

We played in the water and sunbathed all afternoon, then returned to the villa to shower.

"I'd better call Roy," I said. "He doesn't know where I am."

"Tell him you won't be home for dinner. We can eat here."

"That sounds like fun."

Roy's tone projected a pout when he heard my news. He had been counting on a father-daughter evening but hadn't bothered to tell me. I stuck to my guns, but promised not to be late.

Jimmy had definitely planned the evening. He had all the makings of a steak dinner, including two bottles of wine.

"You certainly took a lot for granted," I teased.

"No, I didn't. But I thought it was worth a gamble."

We set the table together, and Jimmy found a couple of slightly used tapers still in candlesticks from a previous dinner. He seemed to know his way around a kitchen pretty well for a young man. The two of us prepared the meal as a team, and he grilled the steaks on the back deck.

We found a radio station with perfect background music for our candlelight dinner.

Jimmy draped a kitchen towel over his arm and produced two bottles of wine for my inspection.

"Which would mademoiselle prefer," he asked in a mock French accent, "the cabernet sauvignon or the Bordeaux?"

Since I had never tasted wine, I didn't have a clue which I preferred.

"You choose," I said.

"All right." He smiled. "Let's try this Mouton Cadet. If you don't like it, we'll open the other bottle."

Candlelight flickered on Jimmy's handsome face as he expertly uncorked the wine and placed the cork beside my plate and waited. I was apparently expected to do something with it.

"Would mademoiselle like to examine the cork?" he asked.

"Whatever for?" I laughed.

Jimmy picked up the cork and sniffed with a pleased expression, then poured a small amount of wine into my glass, gesturing for me to taste it. I took a small sip.

"It tastes fine to me," I said.

He filled our goblets and sat down across from me, lifting his glass in a toast.

"Here's to the most beautiful girl alive," he said, "and to a very special relationship."

"And I will assume that it was a special relationship," Dr. Fitzpatrick said. "I am sorry to interrupt at this point, my dear, but our time is up."

Chapter Twenty-three

—

June 15, 1978

I remember my first taste of wine and my first love, but nothing more. No matter how hard I try, I can't close the gap.

———

Dr. Fitzpatrick was looking out his window at the branch of a maple tree.

"I see the cleaning crew finally showed up," I said. "I can actually see through the window pane."

"Yes, they did. Thank you for noticing, Clemmie. May I see your journal?"

His usual brow-furrow manifested itself.

"I can see that you're frustrated, my dear, but you are progressing continuously. Can't you tell me about the rest of your delightful evening with Jimmy Castlebrook?"

"We went to the beach. Oh, and we took the other bottle of wine with us."

"That sounds romantic."

Every time he interrupted me, blood began to pound in my temples. I started massaging them to make the pounding go away, and told myself to control my temper. I didn't want to ruin the session.

Dr. Fitzpatrick didn't move. His expression was calm as he watched me struggle with my emotions. He seemed to be encouraging me without saying a word.

———

Jimmy opened the bottle of wine.

"I'm not sure I should drink any more wine," I said.

"You don't feel tipsy, do you?"

"No. I feel wonderful."

"Good," he said, getting plastic glasses from a cupboard.

He rummaged in a closet and found an old blanket so we wouldn't have to sit in the sand.

The night sky fairly sparkled as we left the tree-covered footpath and walked onto the beach. There was no light pollution to disturb the star studded heavens, and they stretched to infinity. The ocean looked pitch-black.

Jimmy filled our cups, and we left the blanket and our bottle of wine at the base of a palm tree. We walked down the beach, holding hands and marveling at nature's beauty. Before we knew it, we had walked all the way to the break in the beach where a rock wall marked the separation of the private and public areas.

"Let's go back to our blanket," he said. "My glass is empty."

We spread the blanket and kicked off our shoes. Breakers were crashing rhythmically on the shoreline, adding to the romantic, storybook atmosphere as Jimmy took me in his arms.

I began to feel the strange ache that I couldn't control when he was near, and my muscles tensed pleasantly.

"Would you like more wine?" he asked.

"Just a little."

"Clementine, I know you're not used to drinking. I don't want to alter your thinking, especially tonight."

"I'm fine. You don't think I'm drunk, do you?"

"Um, maybe just a little tipsy."

"What's so important about tonight?"

"You are. There's something I want to tell you."

"Oh?"

"I think I'm falling in love with you."

"And the feeling was mutual?" Dr. Fitzpatrick asked.

I was recalling the night so vividly that nothing the doctor could do or say was going to break into my recollection of that beautiful time of my life. I closed my eyes to continue. My shrink could wait.

"Clementine, I've never felt this way about anyone else. I love everything about you: your laugh, your innocence, and your zest for life. I need to know how you honestly feel about me."

"I've never felt this way. I've had crushes, but those were very different from the way I feel about you."

"Have you ever made love?"

"No," I confessed. I was afraid to ask him the same question; I didn't want to hear his answer.

The beach was deserted, and I didn't attempt to dissuade Jimmy from undressing me. The ocean breeze courted my bare skin and complemented my new-found heady feeling and the pleasant ache that persisted. Any trace of shyness vanished as I slipped my hands under Jimmy's shirt to feel his warm flesh. Together, we tugged off his clothes, then mine, and rolled backward onto the blanket. The first kiss made me tremble with excitement. I had never been kissed, feeling feverish skin next to mine head-to-toe. Jimmy's touch was gentle, his lips were soft, but possessive, and I was experiencing pleasures I had never known. He nibbled my neck and planted tiny kisses on my breasts and down my stomach. His hands were exploring my body, and mine followed suit. Our breathing became ragged, and I ached for him.

"Now's the time to tell me if you have any doubts about this," he whispered.

My eyes stung from sheer happiness. I couldn't wait another second for Jimmy to make love to me.

"I don't have a doubt in the world. I want you more than anything."

The flow of sensations was startling as Jimmy took over my mouth, mind, and body, and I couldn't separate them. They composed the perfect feeling of belonging. His body covered mine, and I could feel the muscles in his back and his toned thighs as he entered me.

The hurt I felt was beautiful, and I arched my body to match his rhythm. Our flesh was on fire, and we seemed a perfect fit. When I experienced the glory of a climax, I couldn't contain my delight, and had to stifle a scream. I had just learned the meaning of fulfillment, and I knew that I wanted to be with Jimmy Castlebrook forever.

"Clemmie, are you with me?" the doctor asked.

I could feel Jimmy's breath on my neck, and the evening breeze coming off the ocean to envelop us, and I had to blink to bring myself back to the present.

"Yes."

"Was the feeling mutual?"

"Yes, it was."

Chapter Twenty-four

"Clemmie, it's good to see you," the athletic director said. "Would you like to play mixed doubles?"

"Yes, I'd like that."

My partner introduced himself as Alex and didn't bother with a last name. I guessed him to be in his late thirties. He was tanned, athletic looking, and prematurely bald. If we had met before, I didn't remember him.

"Which side of the court would you prefer?" he asked.

"I like the backhand court, if you don't mind."

I recalled two things about my game as we warmed up: my backhand crosscourt shot was dynamite, and hitting a hard forehand shot gave me tennis elbow.

Alex and I won the match handily, and I decided Dr. Fitzpatrick had been right to recommend exercise.

June 20, 1978

I'm recalling more of my past in tiny bits. It made me happy to talk about Jimmy. I wonder what happened to him. He's probably married to a beautiful girl and has a family. I hope he's happy.

The night air was warm, and I had left my window open when I went to bed. Lightning and thunder awakened me, and I hurried to close the window. I pulled the drapes and got back into bed to hide from the storm.

I wasn't asleep, but felt as if I were dreaming. I remembered closing the drapes, but I could see the open window. Suddenly, I heard a voice. I was trying to ask who was outside the window, but no words would come. Finally, I screamed, and the utterance was so loud that it drowned out the thunder. I couldn't stop screaming.

I saw Daniel lying on a floor. His head was split open, and blood gushed from the wound, covering his face. He didn't move; just lay there on the mud-covered floor beside his mother's pail of cleaning supplies.

Mama Rae was pouring tea for my mama, but that couldn't be happening because Mama was dead. The teapot was turning into a large darning needle before my eyes, and Mama Rae thrust it deep into the neck of her ugly doll.

Nurse Maude came into my room carrying a candle in one hand and an enormous needle in the other. She set the candle on my bedside table and loomed over me. I think I stopped screaming.

"It's just a thunder storm, Clemmie. The power went off. Thunder storms aren't going to hurt you. My grandma used to tell me the noise was nothing more than the good Lord rolling potatoes."

Suddenly, my arm was cold as ice.

"I'm going to give you something to help you go back to sleep," she said.

Pain ripped through my arm like electricity as the needle pierced my flesh.

"Please don't give me a . . ."

I awoke to the off-key humming of an aide. She was pouring tea into a cup and smiling at me.

"I knew the aroma of a good breakfast would summon the sleeping beauty from her world of dreams," she said in a clipped British accent.

"Good morning," I said. "I don't think we've met. I'm Clemmie."

The young woman must have been six feet tall. Her dishwater-blond hair was done up in a large bun at the nape of a long, elegant neck, and her blue eyes twinkled as she handed me the tea.

"I'm so very glad to make your acquaintance, Miss Clemmie. I'm Bridgette. You're absolutely right; we haven't met. I only just arrived two days ago, you see. How are you feeling, dear?"

"I'm ravenous. Thank you for bringing breakfast."

"You're quite welcome. Let me help you to the bathroom to freshen up a bit."

I swung my legs over the side of the bed, feeling weak. Bridgett held out her arm and steered me to the bathroom.

"I'll wait here to make sure you're well enough to manage," she said.

When I came out of the bathroom, she had placed the breakfast tray on my desk.

"What time is it?" I asked. My clock hadn't been set since the power failure.

Bridgette looked at her watch. "It's exactly ten thirty-eight. Would you like for me to set your clock?"

"Yes. Thank you."

I had slept the entire morning, but felt exhausted.

I wasn't hungry at lunch time, but went to the cafeteria anyway. That feeling of loneliness had returned, and I needed to be with people. I went through the line and got a glass of iced tea and a dish of banana pudding.

Maria waved, and I went to join her. I had just sat down when Alex, my tennis partner, came toward us with a tray loaded with food.

He smiled. "May I join you ladies?"

"Of course," Maria answered.

I introduced the two, and couldn't help noticing that Maria's eyes were fixed on Alex's smile.

"I hate cafeterias," Alex said. "I can never decide what I want and end up taking a little of everything."

"It doesn't show," I said. "You must work it off on the tennis court."

He smiled. The bright overhead lights shone on his bald pate like noonday sun, and I was reminded again how good-looking he was despite his lack of hair.

"Do you play tennis, Maria?" he asked.

"I'm afraid not," she said. "I've never been athletic."

Crazy old Emma was out of solitary confinement. Every time I saw her, she was accompanied by an aide. Bridgett had the honors today, and was seating Emma at the table next to ours.

"Hello, Emma," Maria said.

"Hello," Emma said. Her tone of voice sounded like she would have rather said, "Go to hell."

"Oh, dear," Bridgett said, a little flustered. "You don't have a drink, Emma. What would you prefer? I'll go fetch it."

"What would I prefer?" Emma said thoughtfully. "Bourbon! That's what I'd prefer, you skinny, beanpole twit! Why don't you go and fetch it?"

"Now, Emma," Bridgett soothed, "coffee, tea, lemonade, or milk?"

Emma was in her element. It was apparent that she was rattling the poor aide whose face and neck had turned crimson.

"Maybe you're deaf," Emma shrilled. "I want bourbon, you stupid bitch!"

Bridgett got up from the table, knocking her chair to the floor with a clatter.

Alex put down his knife and fork and turned to face Emma.

"I'll get your drink, Emma," he said.

He went to the drink counter and returned with a glass of lemonade, setting it in front of Emma who regarded it with obvious contempt.

"This is not bourbon, you idiot!" she yelled, picking up the glass and tossing the lemonade into his face.

Alex retrieved his napkin and began wiping the sticky drink from his face.

"No, it isn't bourbon," he said. "Bourbon isn't served in this cafeteria, and you knew that when you requested it. I brought you a drink, and you squandered it. Now you don't have anything to drink. That's the consequence you must pay for throwing your lemonade on me. Do you understand?"

Emma looked down at her plate.

"I'm a terrible, terrible person," she said. "Just terrible."

"I don't know about that," Alex said, "but you're going to be a thirsty one."

"You certainly have a lot of patience," I said.

"I was a teacher," Alex said. "It comes with the territory."

I glanced over at Emma. She was calmly eating her lunch.

Back in my room, I couldn't stop thinking about Alex. I wondered why he was here. He seemed so confident and in control of his emotions. But I didn't have the luxury of ruminating about Alex. It was nearly time for my appointment.

Chapter Twenty-five

⁓

"Good afternoon, Clemmie." Dr. Fitzpatrick donned a concerned expression . "I understand you became somewhat overwrought during last night's thunderstorm. Are you always disturbed by storms?"

"No, not always."

"Was it, indeed, the storm that frightened you?"

"I'm not sure," I lied. I had decided not to mention the nightmare. It was too confusing, and I knew Dr. Fitzpatrick wouldn't be able to make sense of it.

"How do you feel now?" he asked.

"All right."

"Then let's begin. You had spent the day and most of the evening with Mr. Castlebrook at his parents' villa."

I wanted to tell Daniel about Jimmy. I always told him my secrets, so it was important for me to tell him that Jimmy and I had become intimate. But I really didn't want to share that much of myself with Mama Rae; she would not have approved. She didn't have a phone. Otherwise, I would have called Daniel and asked him to meet me in the woods where we could talk. It would never have occurred to Mama Rae that Daniel and I might want to be alone.

I hiked through the woods to Mama Rae's house. When I reached the clearing, I could see her and Daniel sitting on the front porch. Mama Rae saw me and waved.

"Boy, it's hot today," I said.

"Might near hot as it was last night," Mama Rae said.

It wasn't unusually warm last night. Then it hit me. How could she possibly know what happened between Jimmy and me last night?

"How 'bout somethin' cold to drink?" she said.

"That sounds great." I couldn't wait for her to go inside. I knew I would have to talk fast.

"Daniel, I have something to tell you—something private. Can you meet me in the woods ten minutes after I leave here?"

"Sure, but don't ask me to meet you anywhere else; I'm still paranoid. You haven't heard any news have you?"

"No, and I'm sure I won't. Addie Jo didn't report you to the police. She was just trying to frighten you, and she certainly has done a good job of it."

"I can't stay here much longer, Clemmie. Mama Rae's a great old girl, but I'm really beginning to get cabin fever. I have to leave the island."

"But Daniel . . ."

He cut me off in mid-sentence. "Don't try to talk me out of it. I'm going."

"Where will you go?"

"I don't know. But don't worry. I'll be okay, and I'll stay in touch."

Mama Rae came out on the porch with three glasses of ice-cold cider.

"You got rabbit's blood in them feet, Daniel," she said. "Always got to be on the move."

"I didn't mean for you to hear what I said," Daniel said.

"Didn't have to hear; already knew."

"You've been like a mother to me, but I can't stay here forever."

"This cider is delicious, Mama Rae," I said, trying to lighten the conversation.

She nodded, and I had the distinct impression that she wanted me to leave. She had a way of dismissing me without saying a word.

"Well, I just dropped by to say hello," I said, getting up to take my glass inside.

Mama Rae held out a bony hand for the glass. "I'll take it," she said. That meant she didn't want me to go into her house.

I waited in the woods for fifteen minutes, but Daniel didn't show. Maybe he was having a hard time escaping from his benevolent captor. I waited five more minutes, then gave up.

It was five o'clock by the time I clumped up the back steps. I heard Roy talking on the kitchen phone.

"That's what you said last night. You're not upset with me, are you?"

Then I knew he was talking to Ava.

"Well, you could come over here, or we could go out to dinner," he entreated.

It seemed that Roy was being given the cold shoulder.

"I don't give a hang about your neighbors." His voice was rising.

I felt sorry for him.

"I am not yelling. I'm trying to convince you to listen to reason. We're adults; we can be together as often as we like. It's none of their business."

I wondered what was going on between Roy and Ava, but I hated to ask.

"Fine," he said after a long pause. "I won't bother you anymore."

"Hi," I said.

"Hi!" he barked.

"Don't be mad at me because you and Ava are having a disagreement."

"I'm sorry, princess." He looked like a whipped puppy. "I'm not sure I understand women."

"What's the matter?"

"I wish I knew. Everything was just great between Ava and me. But all of a sudden, she's too busy to see me; says she's been neglecting her horse. Then, she says she's worried that her neighbors will say uglies about her because she's spending so much time with me."

"That doesn't sound like Ava."

"No, it doesn't. You don't think she's getting ready to dump me, do you?"

"No, Roy."

"Do you have a date with Jimmy tonight?"

"No. He's playing softball."

"Then it's just the two of us. We'll have a family date. Would you rather eat here or go out?"

"Let's just grill burgers. We have everything we'll need."

No matter what we discussed during dinner, the conversation kept coming back to Ava.

"Sweetheart, I think I'm in love with her," Roy confided. "I didn't think I could ever love anyone else after Emily died, but I think I do."

Ava seemed the perfect match for Roy, and I wanted him to be happy. My mother was gone, and Roy was lonely until he met Ava.

"Well, say something," he said.

"I suppose congratulations are in order. Roy, I think the world of Ava. She's truly a lovely person. I don't know anyone I'd be happier to see you date, or marry, for that matter."

"I can't tell you how happy that makes me."

Roy always looked like a ten-year-old when he found himself asking for my approval. It was gratifying to know that my opinion mattered to him. I had lost both my parents, but I would always have Roy. He couldn't have loved me any more if I had been his flesh and blood.

"Why do you think Ava is refusing to see me?" he said.

"Maybe the relationship is moving too fast for her. You have to remember that you're the only person she's dated since her husband's death. Give her some room."

A week passed, and Ava hadn't called. Roy was determined not to make the first move. He had practically begged her to see him, and she had refused. He had to salvage what little was left of his pride.

I was spending most of my time with Jimmy. We played tennis, spent lazy afternoons at the beach, and made love whenever the opportunity presented itself. I couldn't bear the thought of his leaving for college at the end of the summer.

Roy moped around the house every evening. He was barely able to be civil to Jimmy when he came to pick me up for our dates.

It was Wednesday evening, and Jimmy and I had stayed out much later than we should have. The living room light was still on, so I assumed Roy was watching television. I came into the house ready for battle, knowing he would scold me for staying out so late. The television wasn't turned on, and the house was still.

"Roy?"

His bedroom door was cracked, so I poked my head inside. He wasn't there. I hadn't noticed whether or not his car had been parked in the space under the house. The latticework screen hid it from the street. I went outside and walked around the side of the house. Roy's car wasn't there. It was unlike him not to have left me a note. I decided he must have been feeling so down and out that he had found it necessary to go to an AA meeting.

I didn't hear him when he came home, but he looked terrible the next morning. His face was puffy, and his eyes were bloodshot.

"Roy, are you sick?"

"No, sweetheart; I'm fine. But I don't want any breakfast."

"You always want breakfast. Are you sure you're okay?"

"I'm sure." He tried to smile.

When he came home at dinnertime, he looked even worse. He said he wasn't hungry and went straight to bed without even opening the mail. I followed him to his room, hoping to persuade him to at least let me give him a bowl of soup, but he said he just wanted to sleep.

I called Jimmy and broke our date, telling him that Roy had come down with some sort of bug, and that I didn't want to leave him alone since he felt so rotten.

There was nothing on television but re-runs, so I flopped on the couch with a paperback. I missed Jimmy.

"I'm afraid our time is up," the doctor said.

Chapter Twenty-six

I stopped by the activities center to sign up for tennis and ran into Alex.

"Hello, Alex."

He was pacing back and forth in front of the bulletin board, wearing a scowl.

"Hi," he said, absently.

"I don't see your name on the roster for the next match. I hope you plan to play."

"No. I won't be playing. I've decided to give it up. I'm no good at the sport."

"What do you mean? You're the best player here."

"No. I'm no good at tennis, or swimming, or weight lifting, or anything else. I was a poor excuse for a teacher, too, you know."

Something was terribly wrong. I decided that Alex was having an awfully bad day and could use a friend's ear. He was nothing like the Alex who had calmed Emma in the cafeteria.

"Would you like to get a Coke and talk for a while?" I said.

"Okay," he agreed, "but I'm a lousy conversationalist, too."

We went to the cafeteria for Cokes and took them outside to sit on a bench under one of the beautiful maple trees.

"Maple leaves turn the most gorgeous colors in the fall," I said.

"Yes, they do. I've always loved autumn. I wonder what this one will bring."

I was afraid to ask what he meant by the remark.

"I lived in Chicago until I was ten, and I couldn't wait for the leaves to begin showing their colors. It was really different after we moved."

"Where was that?"

"Hilton Head Island, South Carolina. It's beautiful all the time, but fall isn't any more spectacular than spring and summer."

"Hilton Head is a virtual Garden of Eden," Alex said. "I've played tennis there."

"Oh, really? Where?"

"I've played at Shipyard and at the Rod Laver Tennis Center in Palmetto Dunes. They were both really nice. I actually met Stan Smith at Shipyard. He and his wife were playing in a mixed doubles tournament, some sort of charity thing. He's a great guy."

"The Rod Laver Center is where I learned to play."

"Small world."

Alex took a drink of his Coke. He seemed to be feeling a little better.

"Hilton Head can get cold in the winters, but it's nothing compared to Chicago."

"I've never been to Chicago, but I lived in Denver for a while. The Rockies are fantastic. In the fall the aspen leaves turn gold and quake in the slightest breeze."

"I've heard they're beautiful. I'd like to see them."

"After a heavy snow, the mountains look just like a picture postcard," Alex said. "I was a ski bum for a while, so I got to the point that I took their beauty for granted. As a matter of fact, I took everything for granted."

"Why would you say that?" I asked, fearing I was opening a can of worms.

"Because I was guilty, and I got exactly what I deserved. I lost my wonderful wife and my baby daughter."

"I'm sorry."

"Would you like to see their pictures?"

He whipped out his wallet and flipped it open to a color photo of a pretty blond girl. She was holding a little girl who looked exactly like her.

"They're both beautiful," I said. This is a very nice picture."

"Meghan was a wonderful mother. I'm sure she hasn't changed. And Alexis was the apple of my eye. I miss them terribly."

"Where are they, Alex?"

"They were in Tampa the last I heard. Meghan married a dentist, and they moved there about three years ago."

It was time to change the subject. I didn't want to become privy to Alex's life story. Maybe it had been a mistake to invite him to talk.

"Let's go sign you up for the match," I said. "We'll blow our opponents off the court."

"Not this week. Maybe another time."

Alex got up and started down the path toward the men's dormitory. As he disappeared into the trees, I couldn't help but think that we both belonged here, safe from the outside world.

June 22, 1978

Alex wanted to open up to me today, but I didn't allow him that luxury. Who knows? Maybe I could have helped him just by being a good listener. I've become self-centered since I came here.

Dr. Fitzpatrick handed me my journal.

"I don't find you self-centered," he said. "You're not a doctor; it isn't your job to listen to other patients. You don't need to clutter your mind with other people's problems. Perhaps you feel self-centered because you must talk about yourself during our sessions, but that's the only way to get to the root of your problem."

"I suppose you're right."

"You were disturbed by Roy's behavior."

It didn't take long for me to figure out what was wrong with Roy. He had fallen off the wagon. The first couple of days he had me fooled. I thought he must be suffering from stomach flu, but by the weekend, I knew it was more than that.

On Saturday mornings Roy mowed the lawn. He was always sitting at the kitchen table with the newspaper and a cup of black coffee by the time I dragged myself out of bed, but this morning I didn't smell coffee. I went to the kitchen; it was empty. Then, I knocked on his bedroom door.

"What?" he growled.

"I'm going to make breakfast. What would you like?"

"Go away and leave me alone."

Roy had never raised his voice to me. He sounded like a stranger.

The only time Roy left his room was to go to the bathroom. Each time I could hear him retching behind the closed door. Then, he would stumble back down the hall in his underwear and go back to bed.

I had a date with Jimmy that night, and I hated to leave Roy alone even though he wouldn't talk to me. I made Jello and left a pot of broth on the stove. Surely, he could turn on a burner. I left him a note and waited for Jimmy on the front porch.

"You're much prettier when you smile," Jimmy said.

"Sorry. I guess I was a little distracted."

"Well, cut it out." He grinned. "Look what I have."

He dangled the keys to the villa in front of me, and thoughts of Roy slid to some obscure corner of my mind.

Jimmy had been grocery shopping again, and prepared a fantastic meal for us.

"Who taught you to cook?" I asked, finishing the last bite of flaky fish on my plate.

"Nobody. My mom and the kitchen aren't friendly with one another. A couple of years ago I started experimenting. I enjoy playing around in the kitchen."

I raised an eyebrow.

"Playing around with recipes." He laughed. "Let's take our wine out to the deck and look at the stars for a while."

Just as we got outside, the sky began to cloud over, and we could feel the air freshening. Lightning flashed, and the thunder sounded like it meant business.

"So much for stargazing," Jimmy said as fat raindrops began to pelt us.

We climbed the stairs and went to the bedroom facing the golf course. We could see lights from the villas across the way. Jimmy closed the drapes, and his arms went around me. I could feel the mystery of my body preparing for him. He took his time unbuttoning my blouse, and I knew he could feel my heart pounding at his touch.

"Now that I have you alone," he said in his Bela Lugosi voice, "I shall ravage your lovely body to my heart's content."

"You don't scare me." I grinned.

"I don't? I'm much stronger than you, you know. What if I held both of your hands like this in one of mine? I still have a free hand. You're at my mercy."

Just for an instant I thought of Sonny Malone and how helpless he had made me feel. Then, I began to laugh. I could never be afraid of Jimmy. I trusted him completely, and I wanted him more than my next breath.

"What's so funny?" he asked.

"Your silly game, but I'll play along. I'm at your mercy. Kill me with kisses."

We had left the music on downstairs, and we could barely hear it over the rain. Jimmy drew my nude body to his in a slow dance, and we stumbled over our clothes and onto a chaise lounge. Our flesh burned, and we couldn't wait to complete our love dance. We were slick with perspiration and so impatient that we were clumsy in our consummation.

"Well, that was fun, if comical." He smiled down at me. "Let's see if we're any better at it in bed."

The sheets were cool, and our urgency was slaked, so we delved into the fine art of pure pleasure lovemaking that I never wanted to end.

Birds chirping in the hickory tree beside the upper deck awakened me. I stirred in Jimmy's arms, and the movement roused him.

"This is the way I want to wake up for the rest of my life," he said with a sleepy smile.

"Me, too."

"Have I told you that I absolutely adore you, Clemmie?"

"I don't believe you have."

"I do, you know."

"You've never called me that before."

"What?"

"Clemmie. You've never called me Clemmie. Daniel is the only person who has ever called me that."

Jimmy eased his arm free and cradled his head, staring up at the ceiling.

"Daniel. Daniel. Daniel. He's a pretty lucky guy. Everything I say or do seems to remind you of him."

"That's not true, and it's not fair. Daniel's been my best friend since childhood. There's no reason for you to be jealous of him."

"I'm not jealous."

"Is this a good place to stop?" the doctor asked.

"I suppose."

It irritated me for him to ask that question.

June 27, 1978

*I feel like the author of a soap opera script. How can Dr.
Fitzpatrick ever piece together the scraps from my past to find
a solution to my memory loss? I have told him the most intimate
details of my life, and what have I gained from having done it?
There's nothing left: nobody to love, and no secrets to tell.*

Stretched out on my bed, I stared at my toes. I had painted my
toenails bright coral with polish someone had donated to my weekly
cheer package. Nail polish wasn't high on my list. At least I didn't think
it was. I wiggled my toes, watching them through half-closed eyes and
wondering if the other patients had grown as weary of the tiresome
routine of life in an institution as I had. Had they been compelled to
relate every shred of their private lives to one of the many psychiatrists?
I wondered how many of them had sought help from the institution
of their own volition and how many had been forced to come here by
relatives who simply didn't know what else to do with them.

I don't remember anything about coming here. They told me that I
arrived alone in a taxi and pleaded with them to help me. I supposedly
forked over five thousand dollars in cash. After that, a cashier's check for
the proper amount arrived each month to cover my expenses. I wonder
who still cares enough about me to ensure my safety.

Sunlight shining through the window made me squint. I closed my
eyes and slept.

"It be all right now, chile." Mama Rae's tone was as soothing as her
gravelly voice could possibly sound.

What's all right? What is she talking about?

Then I saw a row of half-pint whiskey bottles lined up on the shelf in
Roy's closet behind two stacks of heavily starched, neatly folded shirts.
The bottles were all empty except one.

"You drink dis," Mama Rae told me. "You'll feel good as new."

I accepted the cup and drank the special tea she had made just for
me. It made me feel warm inside, and I wasn't afraid anymore. I didn't
even feel like crying.

"It's a snakebite wound," the man in the white coat said. "Of course,
I'll have to wait for the lab results before I write the report."

Then, Addie Jo was on our back porch singing *Crazy*, and Ava was
accompanying her on Roy's guitar.

There was a loud knock at the door.

"Clemmie, you're going to miss dinner unless you hurry."

My eyes fluttered open to see Nurse Maude enter my room. She handed me my robe.

"Put this on and wash your face," she said. "I see more naked bodies than I want to. You must hurry and get dressed."

I couldn't imagine what provoked the crazy dream I had just had, but I couldn't think about it with Nurse Maude urging me to hurry.

"Would you mind taking John over?" she said. "I parked him at the elevators. His aide is already in the cafeteria."

"No, I don't mind."

John was counting aloud.

"Why are you counting, John?" I asked.

"Just counting 'til you got here."

"Are you hungry?"

"Yeah. Hurry," he urged as the elevator door opened.

"We're fine, John. The door won't close on us."

"Whew!" he said.

John's aide met us in the cafeteria. She had already brought his food to the table.

"I'll be back with my tray in a few minutes," I said.

When I returned, John and his aide were in the middle of a standoff.

"More!" he demanded. "More 'roni and cheese!"

"Only if you promise to eat your other food as well," the aide countered.

I couldn't help overhearing snatches of conversation between two women at the next table. The younger woman was obviously paying her dining companion a duty visit.

"Thank goodness, you'll be leaving this place soon, Grace," she said. "I don't know how you stand it. That man-child at the next table is making me nauseous, slobbering like a big bulldog."

I didn't catch Grace's comment. Unsure whether John had heard, or processed the insulting remark, I began telling him that he'd better start eating his meat and vegetables before the aide returned.

John looked anxious as he prepared to follow my instruction. He grabbed a plastic squeeze bottle of mustard and began decorating his hamburger. It was clear that he enjoyed playing with the mustard and making bright, yellow, squiggly designs on the meat. Suddenly, as though possessed, he gripped the bottle firmly in both hands and began squirting mustard in what seemed all directions, splattering every diner within reach, including me.

"No, John," I said, reaching for his weapon.

"Well, I never!" the visitor screeched.

I turned to see her dabbing at the yellow stains on her Chanel suit. Her face and hair were also splotched with mustard, and she looked as though she could kill.

"You're disgusting!" she spat at John who promptly began to cry.

"Don't speak to him in that tone," I said.

"Mind your own business," she said through clenched teeth, and threw her glass of water at John.

When the water hit John, he started laughing. Everyone was watching as he loaded his straw with English peas. He puffed out his cheeks like a trumpet player and shot peas at the angry woman, missing her entirely, but blasting the man sitting at the table behind her.

"What the devil?" the startled man said.

Then, he saw that John was laughing with glee at the sight.

"Two can play this game," he growled. "You want to act like a kid; I'll show you some real kid stuff."

He scooped up a gob of mashed potatoes on his teaspoon, drew it back, and let it fly. John's aide caught it in the face and had to remove her glasses.

"Do it again!" John shouted. "Again!"

Seconds later, the entire room seemed to be in on the free-for-all. Someone sounded an alarm, and several attendants dashed in to put an end to the mayhem. I wheeled John out while his aide cleaned her glasses. Then, I started toward my dorm thinking that what I had just witnessed wasn't so out of character for those of us who lived here.

Chapter Twenty-seven

The doctor frowned as he read my journal.

"Shall we begin?" he said.

Roy was in the bathroom when I got home. I could hear the shower running, so I knew he wasn't still hugging the commode. After a few minutes, he came into the kitchen in a terry cloth robe, clean-shaven and bearing a striking resemblance to the real Roy.

"I'll make coffee," I said.

"I've already made it. I'll whip up some pancakes and bacon while you shower. You'd better get a move on, or we'll be late for church."

He knew that I hadn't come home last night, and I wasn't looking forward to our breakfast conversation.

I got ready as fast as I could and went to join him in the kitchen. He was buttering my pancakes.

"Sit down and eat, princess," he said.

I sat down and stared at him.

"Eat," he repeated, sitting down and drowning my pancakes in a river of maple syrup.

We ate in silence, then stacked our dishes in the sink, and drove to church. I didn't hear a word the minister said.

We went to lunch in Savannah at a restaurant on Factor's Walk—one we hadn't visited since my mother's death.

"Clementine, I owe you an apology," Roy said, looking uncomfortable. "I've behaved horribly."

"It's all right, Roy."

"No, it's not all right. I've been weak. There's something I've never told you, and you deserve to know the truth. Sweetheart, I'm an alcoholic."

So Addie Jo had told me the truth. It saddened me that she had beaten Roy to the punch.

"I suffered from alcohol addiction before I met you and your mama. I could never bring myself to tell Emily, because I was afraid she wouldn't want me. Can you understand that?"

"I'm not sure that I can. Mama was broadminded and understanding. She wasn't judgmental."

"I just couldn't take a chance that she might reject me. I adored her; I simply had to have her."

"She would forgive you if she were here right now."

"How about you?"

"I love you, Roy. You're the only dad I've really known. I'll do anything I can to help you."

"I managed pretty well with my AA meetings for a while. That's where I was all those nights I told you I was at business meetings."

"I see."

"Whenever I felt myself weakening, I'd go to a meeting. It always helped me get back on track until this thing with Ava."

"So Ava doesn't know?"

"I never got around to telling her."

"She deserves to know, Roy."

"She won't even see me. I don't know what to do."

Roy seemed to have aged ten years in the past week. His temples were beginning to gray, and his eyes held a sad expression. There were deepening lines in his face that I had more than likely chosen to ignore until now.

"Call Ava this afternoon."

"Maybe I will. By the way, is there anything you'd like to tell me?"

"Like what?"

"Well, for starters, I thought you might like to tell me where you spent last night."

I couldn't lie to those blue eyes. He had been straight with me. Besides, I was certain he knew the answer before he asked.

"I was with Jimmy at his family's villa."

"Just the two of you?"

"Yes."

"Clementine, you're my baby girl. You always will be. I'm not going to lecture you, but you need to know that if you play with fire, you usually get burned."

I felt better on the drive home. Neither of us approved of the other's indiscretions, but we had been honest with one another, and that was liberating.

"Come with me," Roy said, and led me into his bedroom. He opened the closet door. "Hold these," he said, handing me two stacks of folded dress shirts. "This will show you what a slave I am to the stuff."

I stared at a row of whiskey bottles that lined the wall. They were all empty but one. Roy loaded his arms with the bottles, including the one that was untouched.

"I'm counting on you to help me be strong. Put the shirts back, and we'll get rid of these."

We went to the kitchen where Roy dumped the empty bottles in the trash. He opened the full half-pint, and poured its contents down the sink.

"I'm afraid our time is up," Dr. Fitzpatrick said.

June 29, 1978

My poor Roy. He must have been destined to lead a lonely life. It seemed unfair that every time he was fortunate enough to find happiness, fate stepped in and snuffed it out. In addition to losing the two loves of his life, he was constantly at war with alcohol addiction. Its hold on him was far greater than that of any woman.

———

Maria and I were having dinner together. She was a very private individual and never told me anything about her personal life. We usually engaged in small talk, but this evening she was the back fence gossip of the neighborhood. She told me that Emma was back in solitary confinement. She didn't know the particulars.

Maria always seemed to be the picture of serenity, but tonight she appeared very nervous. She was wearing out a cheap paper napkin by constantly dabbing at the corner of her mouth, and her hand trembled each time she lifted her knife or fork. In an attempt to cut her meat, she dropped her knife, and it went clattering to the floor.

"Are you all right?" I asked.

"I'm fine," she said. "Just clumsy. I'll be right back."

She returned to the table with a clean knife.

"Just call me butterfingers." She laughed, making light of the situation.

I smiled.

"Did you hear that old Mr. Jenkins left us?" she said.

I shook my head.

"His children checked him out and put him in a nursing home. I heard it was because he wasn't improving and this place was costing them a fortune. I liked him; I'll miss him."

"I didn't know him very well."

Maria dabbed at her mouth again. "And that new aide, the British woman, was fired for stealing."

I wasn't in the habit of keeping up with the institutional gossip. All I wanted to do was figure out my own problems and get out of this place.

"Have you seen Alex lately?" I asked, hoping to lighten the table talk.

"Alex? I assume you mean loony Alex. We won't be seeing him anymore."

"Why not?"

"Because he's dead, Clemmie. Where have you been? That's the biggest news flash of the year. He managed to sneak into the kitchen and steal a butcher knife and smuggle it back to his room where he slashed his wrists, sitting in a tub of hot water. He even left a note."

I felt sick. I couldn't believe Alex would do such a thing. He had to have been a very disturbed man.

Alone in my room I grieved for a man I hardly knew. I felt that death was always near me. It must have followed me to Still Waters where I was supposed to be safe from all harm. I had a gripping feeling that I attracted the dreaded culprit—the thing for which there is no cure.

I had to force myself to show up for the next session with Dr. Fitzpatrick. He flipped through his notes.

"It seems that you and Roy were on good terms after having confessed your transgressions to one another. You had just witnessed his getting rid of the whiskey."

I talked Roy into going to see Ava. While he was gone, I decided to go to Mama Rae's. I found her sitting on the porch. She cradled Biscuit in her arms, and she was sobbing.

"Mama Rae, what's the matter?"

"He gone," she said.

"Daniel?"

She nodded. "I was pickin' herbs, and when I got home, he was gone; took his valise and all his clothes."

It hurt me to see Mama Rae cry. It seemed an unnatural thing for her to do.

"He'll let us know where he is, Mama Rae. Daniel wouldn't just walk out without telling you unless he had a good reason."

"He left his bicycle," she said.

No matter what I said, Mama Rae wouldn't be consoled, so I left her to cry out her frustration.

Roy was stretched out in his recliner, looking like a broken man.

"What happened, Roy? Did you talk to Ava?"

"No. She's left the island supposedly to visit friends. She didn't say where, but she knew I'd come crawling to her."

"How do you know?"

"Because she left this for me. It was taped on her front door with my name on it."

He handed me the envelope, and I read the letter.

"What do you think?" he said.

"I don't know what to think. It's easy enough to believe that Addie Jo discovered where Ava lives and went to see her. And I have no trouble believing that she told her a pack of lies, but how could Ava have been taken in by them?"

"Beats me."

In Ava's letter she told Roy that life was too short to be involved in a love triangle. She wasn't willing to go through the pain of having to fight for a man at this stage in her life.

Roy couldn't stand to think that Ava believed he was having an affair with Addie Jo while pretending to be falling in love with her. And what was even more maddening was Addie Jo's insistence that Ava question me about it. She had told Ava that I witnessed the two of them making love in Roy's office.

"Ava's not the only one who has disappeared," I said. "Daniel left while Mama Rae was gathering herbs. She has no idea where he is."

"That's probably more of Addie Jo's doing."

"I don't see how she could be involved. She didn't know that Daniel was staying with Mama Rae, and she doesn't know where Mama Rae lives."

"I wouldn't bet on it," Roy said.

We made sandwiches and watched the Sunday night movie on T.V. It was a hokey horror film about a scientist who was searching for a combination of rare plants. He was working on a formula that he thought would restore youth in human beings.

His search took him to an African village. He lived there with his assistant, an elderly gentleman who became acquainted with an old woman who was a member of the peaceful village tribe. She had learned a smattering of English from previous visitors and seemed to enjoy trying it out on the assistant.

Through his friendship with the old woman, the assistant learned a great deal about the jungle and its plant life. Although the woman wasn't aware of the names of many of the plants, she could recognize them on sight and knew many of their uses.

The assistant showed the old woman pictures of the plants he sought, and she led him deep into the jungle where some of the rarities appeared to thrive. Eventually, the two found their way to the final coveted prize which completed the formula.

Instead of rushing back to the scientist with the good news, the assistant decided to keep the secret to himself. Why should he turn it over to a man of great acclaim who was already wealthy? He, a nobody, had searched diligently for the plants; he should get credit and reap the reward.

Each evening after the scientist fell asleep, the able assistant worked in the makeshift lab until he had perfected the formula. He tested it on monkeys which the old woman had captured and caged in her hut.

When he was satisfied that the formula worked, it was time to do away with the scientist. The assistant had never resorted to foul play before, and spent days thinking of the perfect plan. Finally, it hit him: he would use the old woman. He knew that she practiced voodoo; he also knew that she would help him.

When he explained what he wanted her to do, the old woman instructed him to furnish her with a lock of the scientist's hair, or some of his nail clippings. That would be easy. The scientist was out like a light before darkness fell over the village each evening.

The day after he had snipped a lock of his mentor's hair, the assistant put it into an envelope and took it to the woman's hut. Two days later, when he went to wake the scientist for breakfast, he found him dead.

Upon returning to the States, the assistant accepted the award for his wonder drug. He smiled broadly as flashbulbs blinded him. He was a rich man, and very soon, he would be young enough to enjoy his good fortune.

"I'm sorry to interrupt, Clemmie," the doctor said. "I'm afraid I don't understand how this movie is relevant."

"I don't either."

"Well, I must say that your recall of intricate details is impressive. I feel as though I just viewed the film."

I felt ridiculous. Why had I told him about an old movie?

July 4, 1978

I can't recall ever celebrating this holiday, but I must have. Red, white, and blue are everywhere I look, but the colors are meaningless to me. Instead, I remember every little detail of an old movie. If I don't have a breakthrough soon, I know that Dr. Fitzpatrick will up the dosage of my medicine. I don't want to be a walking zombie like some of the others. Poor Alex is dead, and Maria has turned into a nervous wreck. I want to get out of here.

Chapter Twenty-eight

—

I steered clear of the activities center for the most part, but on this particular morning I stopped there after breakfast. Nobody was in the common area. I went to the piano and sat down on the padded bench, then limbered up with a few scales. It all seemed familiar. *Moonlight Sonata* began playing in my head, and my fingers moved over the keys. It was a joyous feeling, and so effortless. I changed keys and began playing *Clair de Lune.*

"Clemmie, I didn't know you played the piano; beautifully, I might add," the activities director said.

"I thought I was alone."

"You were. I was just passing through and heard your wonderful music. Play as long as you like. We don't have anything scheduled in this area until after lunch."

I waited for her to leave and tried to remember anything about my playing ability, but it was useless. Maybe I could find a clue hidden in my box of photographs. I had been through the pictures with Dr. Fitzpatrick during one of my initial sessions, and it hadn't proved helpful. But it couldn't hurt to try again.

I shuffled through the photos until I located a picture of my father with a big fish. And holding it over my heart, I fell asleep. I dreamed about fish. I could see Papa diving into the murky creek and reaching under the cleft of a ledge of rock where the big ones fed. My muscles relaxed as he broke the surface, keeping himself afloat while hanging onto his prize.

My thoughts turned to Jonah in the belly of the whale. But it wasn't Jonah who was spewed from the mouth of the enormous fish. It was Daniel, the same skinny little nine-year-old who stripped naked and dove fearlessly into Horse Pen Creek to catch a fish. The whale had swallowed him, putting the fear of God in his rheumy, brown eyes. I found him on the beach, and Mr. Slocum from the general store drove us to the hospital in Savannah.

Finally, I dreamed about my own fishing experiences. Daniel called me a mama's baby because I wanted him to bait my hook. I wasn't a baby; I was a year older than he was.

I gritted my teeth and stuck my hand into the nest of squirming worms as they tried to escape from the can of dirt. They felt cold and horrible, but I intended to capture one and bait my hook without any help from Daniel. I forced myself to grasp one of the slimy creatures between my thumb and index finger and pull it out of the can. Then, while it wiggled and twisted for its life, I plunged the hook into its flesh. In and out, in and out, I wove the shiny hook until the deed was done.

Guilt from having inflicted such pain on a living creature tormented me, but I refused to let it show. I casually tossed my line into the water and smiled at Daniel.

Sunlight glistening on the ripples of the creek's surface made me sleepy, but I had to keep watching my line in case a fish started to nibble at the bait. As I watched, the ripples turned to colored leaves—thousands of them. At first, I thought I was at the thoroughbred races at Keeneland Race Track in Lexington, Kentucky, hurrying to the clubhouse under a long line of maple trees, their leaves fluttering to the ground under an October sky. Jimmy and I were holding hands, and we were walking as fast as we could; we wanted to get inside and find our seats to study the racing form before the first race.

I was digging in my purse for a pen to cross off the scratched horses on my program when the scene changed. Jimmy and I were driving around the University of Kentucky campus in his MGB. We had the top down and had on jeans and sweaters. Maple leaves blanketed the ground, and we jumped and rolled in them like frisky puppies at the first cool nip in the fall air.

Then, the leaves were gone, and we were in our apartment, making love. This apartment was our first home together, and I recalled every detail: the courtyard below our living room window, the windowless kitchen, and the sparse traffic on Virginia Avenue that lulled us to sleep each night.

Dr. Fitzpatrick had been right. My memory was returning. Jimmy and I were married. I remember the day we moved into the apartment, and I could see his neat printing on the tiny piece of white cardboard when he slid it into the name slot of the mailbox: Mr. and Mrs. James Castlebrook.

I knew that Jimmy and I were married. I began to recall more and more things about our married life, but I couldn't remember our wedding. My wedding gown and bridal bouquet were missing. I couldn't see myself walking down the aisle on Roy's arm, or Jimmy's smile as he turned to watch me march toward him to become his bride.

July 6, 1978

Jimmy and I were married. I remember smatterings of our married life with clarity, but I can't recall our wedding. I don't know where we were married, and I don't know the circumstances of our leaving Hilton Head Island. I know that we lived in Lexington, Kentucky where we both went to college, but I don't know where my husband is. I don't even know if we're still married.

"Well, my dear, this is quite a revelation," Dr. Fitzpatrick said, looking self-satisfied. "Things are beginning to come together just as I told you they would."

"But it's all still so disjointed."

"Trust me, Clemmie. You're getting there. It won't be long now."

"You said that my last name is Hubbard."

"That's what our records indicate, but you were alone when you checked yourself into Still Waters. You were distraught. I submit that you simply misplaced your married name."

"I don't see how I could have done that. I loved my husband."

"Your loss of memory probably has nothing to do with love."

"I've told you everything I remember. I'm at a dead end."

"Let's go back to Hilton Head and take it from where you and Roy watched the strange movie. Maybe you've skipped over something of import."

I was so tired of rehashing little details to find missing pieces that I felt like giving up, but if I did that, I'd never know what happened.

I called Addie Jo and asked her to meet me for lunch. Roy wasn't going to confront her regardless of his grumbling about the nasty things she had been doing, so I would have to do it.

"Well, a voice from the past," she said. "What a pleasant surprise."

"It's been a while since we talked," I said, trying to keep my tone even.

I arrived at the restaurant first to get a table where we could carry on a conversation. I had only been there a couple of minutes when Addie Jo breezed in like she owned the place and greeted me with a big, fake smile. She sat down and crossed her legs.

"Clementine, I can't tell you how surprised I was to hear from you. It's nice to know you don't hold a grudge the way Roy does. He's been positively hateful to me since he's been dating Miss America. I told him that I wished him the best, but I guess he'd already made up his mind not to believe me. He barely speaks to me."

"Let's order lunch," I said. "The crab salad is supposed to be good."

"Oh, it is!" she enthused. "Roy and I used to get it all the time, before he took up with his beauty queen."

We ordered, and I got right to the point.

"I want to ask you some questions, and I hope you'll answer them truthfully."

"Of course, I will," she said. She was the picture of innocence.

"Have you ever met Ava, the woman Roy's been dating?"

"No, and I don't want to meet her. I did see a snapshot of her that Roy was showing around the office. There were some cute pictures of you and your friend, too, the young black man."

"Daniel."

"Yes, Daniel. I'd forgotten his name."

"The photos you saw were taken at my house."

Addie Jo nodded.

"I guess I don't blame Roy for dumping me for his new squeeze. She's really pretty."

"He didn't dump you for anybody, Addie Jo. He hadn't even met her when the two of you broke up."

"What's this all about, Clementine?"

"You know very well what it's about. You've met Ava, and you didn't forget Daniel's name."

"I don't know what you're talking about. What have I done?"

"Here's what you did, and lose the dumb act: you set Daniel up, making your neighbors think he had attacked you. You caused him to get fired. Then, you paid Ava a visit and told her a pack of lies about Roy. What do you think you have to gain from that kind of behavior?"

Addie Jo deserved an award for her acting ability. Her expression was one of utter dismay.

"This truly hurts me, Clementine. How in the world can you think I would do such things? You must see me as some kind of monster."

Her eyes welled with tears, and she dabbed at them with her napkin. I couldn't believe how crushed she looked.

"I think you're a very sick woman," I said.

Addie Jo's face stretched into an amazing mask of pain. She opened her purse and tossed too much money on the table, then fled the restaurant.

I went home more frustrated than ever. Addie Jo wasn't going to come clean, and I had no way to prove her guilt. I couldn't go to the police; they would think I was a fool. I would go to my most reliable source for help: Mama Rae.

I just knew Mama Rae practiced witchcraft. I'd seen her do too many strange things to think otherwise. What was she up to when she mumbled those weird chants in Gullah? What was in the terrible-smelling boiling pots? And why did she play dress up in those outfits that were so foreign to her everyday clothes?

She might get mad at me, but I was going to have to ask her point blank about her powers. Maybe she could exert some control over Addie Jo Simmons.

I knocked on the frame of the screen door, and Mama Rae appeared. She was dressed in her normal attire, so I knew she wasn't in the middle of a ritual.

"I ain't heard a word from Daniel," she said.

"I haven't either," I said, taking my usual seat in the rocking chair.

I knew she thought I had come to commiserate about our mutual friend, but I was on a mission, and I was determined to see it through.

"Mama Rae, I have to ask you something personal. I hope you won't think I'm prying into your private affairs, but this is important."

Her deep-set eyes were unblinking, and I steeled myself for a reprimand and mustered the courage to ask my question.

"Mama Rae, do you have special powers?"

"Special powers," she mused. "I can cure some folks' ills with my herbs. That ain't no secret."

"I know that," I said, forging ahead, "but what I meant to ask is, well, do you practice voodoo?"

She looked at me as if I had two heads.

"What make you ask such a question?"

"I want to know if you can do anything to put a stop to the things Addie Jo Simmons is doing. She's frightened both Daniel and Ava off the island with her evil deeds, and I don't know anything to do about it."

"Uh huh."

"Can you help me, Mama Rae?"

"Would if I could. You sure got you a big 'magination, chile. I got to res now."

She was dismissing me, and I knew that any special powers she possessed and her willingness to use them would remain her secret. I went home to fume alone.

Roy raced up the porch steps two at a time and burst into the house with news that couldn't wait.

"Princess, you'll never guess what happened this afternoon!"

"What?"

"Addie Jo came into my office at the end of the day and handed me her resignation."

"Really? Did she say why?"

"She didn't give a reason. The letter was very professional and quite complimentary to the company."

"What a shock!"

"You're telling me. She offered to stay and help train someone to take her place, but I told her that wouldn't be necessary. She's gone, sweetheart."

"Do you think she'll leave the island?"

"I have my fingers crossed. Now it'll be easier to talk to Ava when she comes home. I feel like an albatross has been lifted from my neck."

"I'm afraid our time is up just as the plot thickens," Dr. Fitzpatrick said. "By the way, I neglected to mention it earlier, but I hear you're something of a pianist."

"I'm afraid the compliment isn't justified, but I did take lessons when I lived in Lexington."

I hadn't remembered the lessons until that very moment.

Chapter Twenty-nine

For the first time since I began therapy I felt that I was truly making progress. Remembering that Jimmy and I were married was a real breakthrough. As much as it hurt to think it might be true, I tried to recall whether we had split up. Maybe our marriage had gone sour, and the memory of it was so horrible that it had caused me to suffer a mental breakdown.

Why didn't I have a single memento of our life together? The institution hadn't taken anything away from me. I had the box of photos. Why didn't I have any pictures of my husband? I would never have been able to part with anything so dear.

Dr. Fitzpatrick had told me not to expect too much recall at one time. He said it could be days, or even weeks between recollections. He was proven right at my next session and seemed disappointed at my inability to continue the saga.

He prompted me by reading from his notes, but it didn't help. I had hit a brick wall. My head was beginning to throb, and I felt panicky, like a newly trapped animal. I had to escape this small room.

"I have to go now," I said, feeling tears on my face.

My fingers were white, gripping the arms of the chair. I saw Dr. Fitzpatrick coming toward me. His slight frame grew to gigantic proportions as he came closer.

"Get away!" I screamed. "Don't come a step closer!"

"You're going to be fine, Clemmie. You're just experiencing a bit of anxiety."

"Please don't touch me," I whimpered.

I awoke in a sterile-looking room in a hospital bed. The walls were painted institutional green, and there was no furniture except the bed, a portable meal tray, and an armchair.

"Well, you're awake," a nurse said. She was seated in the chair with a magazine.

"Where am I?"

"You're in the infirmary. Would you like some dinner?"

"No. Why am I here?"

"The doctor will be in to see you shortly. He'll be able to answer your questions. In the meantime, you must eat something; it's nearly time for your medication."

She pushed a call button and ordered a dinner tray.

"I don't think I can eat," I said. "Just smelling food makes me nauseous."

"It really looks good," she said. "You have chicken and dumplings with green beans and fruit cobbler for dessert."

I shook my head. "I can't."

"You must eat, dear. You can't take your medicine on an empty stomach. You'll feel better after we get a few bites down you. I promise."

She picked up the fork and force-fed me several bites. I thought I would surely upchuck, but I began to feel a little better. She gave me the fork, and I finished feeding myself.

"Good girl. " She smiled. "Now, I'll give you your medication."

She handed me a tiny paper cup containing three pills.

"This must be someone else's medicine," I said. "I only take one pill, and it's orange. There's been a mix-up."

She walked to the foot of the bed and examined my chart.

"No," she assured me, "there's no mix-up. This is what Dr. Fitzpatrick ordered for you."

"I don't want to take any medicine until I talk to my doctor."

"But, dear, you must. You're on a schedule, and if you don't take your pills now, you'll have to start back at square one. You do want to get well quickly, don't you?"

I sighed, tossed the pills into my mouth, and washed them down as fast as I could. Yes, I wanted nothing more than to get well quickly.

I must have fallen asleep, and when I awoke, I saw Dr. Fitzpatrick's familiar face peering down at me.

"How are you feeling, Clemmie?" His voice sounded as though it were coming from an echo chamber.

"Terrible. Those pills made me sick, and I'm so sleepy I can't keep my eyes open."

"That's a normal reaction. When you get used to the medicine, you'll feel better. You need to rest a while. Things were moving too fast for you."

"No, they weren't," I argued. "I've been able to handle everything I've remembered. I want to go back to my room."

"You'll be back soon, but you need to stay here and rest for a few days. You're going to be fine."

I tried to protest, but sleep overtook me.

I lost all track of time and hadn't any idea how many days I had spent in the infirmary. All I did was eat, sleep, and take pills. I was so lethargic that I couldn't get out of bed. I was vaguely aware of sponge baths, and I had the presence of mind to buzz for a bedpan when I needed it.

Dr. Fitzpatrick came to check on my progress frequently. Each time I tried to explain that the medication was too strong, but he wouldn't listen. He would pat my hand and tell me that everything was fine.

I knew I would lose all control if I kept taking the medication, so one morning when the aide was refilling my water pitcher, I hid the pills in my leftover oatmeal.

"Okay, sweetie," the aide said, "here's your fresh water. You can take your pills now."

"I already took them with my juice."

"Didn't you like the oatmeal?"

"I just wasn't hungry."

If I could manage to avoid taking the pills, I knew that I could convince Dr. Fitzpatrick to release me from this hell hole. I couldn't keep hiding the pills in leftover food. That was too risky. I spent the rest of the morning trying to find hiding places to stash them. Finally, I discovered the perfect place: one of the hollow metal bars on the bed railing was loose. If I pulled it toward myself, I could drop the pills into it one at a time.

The pills were supposed to keep me sedated. Dr. Fitzpatrick wanted me to rest as much as possible, so when a nurse came to check on me before lunch, I pretended to be asleep.

When my lunch tray arrived, I stirred faintly. The aide had become accustomed to having to wake me for meals. She raised the head of my bed in order to feed me.

"How are we feeling?" she asked.

I wanted to tell her that I was feeling like shit and to stop referring to me as *we*.

"I think I'm a little stronger. I'll feed myself."

"Good." She smiled, pleased.

I ate everything on the tray and obediently popped the pills into my mouth, hoping they wouldn't be washed out from their hiding place, and swallowed.

As soon as the aide left, I ran my tongue between my lower teeth and the soft flesh of my cheek to dislodge the soggy pills. Then, I dropped them one by one into my secret receptacle and pushed it back into place.

I had to get out of this awful place, so when Dr. Fitzpatrick came to check on me before dinner, I surprised him by greeting him from the armchair.

Purple lips stretched across his rodent's teeth in a thin line that was his smile.

"Well, Clemmie, I see you've finally reached the plateau."

"I don't understand."

"In layman's terms it means that your medication has kicked in. You're calm and you appear rested, but you're not lethargic. This is what we've been waiting for."

"Oh."

Nothing could have made me argue with him. I knew that the only reason I was feeling human again was that I had missed two doses of the dastardly medicine, but I certainly wasn't going to share that with him. I didn't know what kind of miracle drugs he thought he was giving me, or what they were supposed to do, but they had rendered me nearly unconscious for days.

"If you're still doing well in the morning, I can release you from the infirmary," he said.

"That's wonderful news."

The aide arrived with my dinner tray. I could tell she was surprised to see me sitting in the armchair.

"All better, I see," she said, lowering the dining tray to a comfortable height.

The doctor left, and the aide sat on the foot of the bed while I consumed what Roy would have called a blue plate special. She looked on happily as I shoveled in meatloaf, mashed potatoes, and peas.

"I truly enjoy watching a hungry person eat," she said. "If you keep up the good work, you'll be leaving here before you know it."

"Dr. Fitzpatrick's releasing me in the morning."

"That's good news. I was beginning to wonder if you were ever going to get used to your new medicine."

"What is this medicine?" I ventured to ask.

"It's just something to keep you calm so you'll rest well. I understand that the patients who take it never become hostile. They're happy and relaxed all the time."

I'll bet they are, I thought.

"Here's your little cup of goodies," she said, handing it to me.

I tossed the pills into my mouth and turned my head slightly as I reached for my water glass. The pills were barely tucked into place when the aide came to remove the dinner tray. Taking a gulp of water, I got up and headed for the bathroom. My muscles had been idle for so long that I felt weak. I felt myself sway toward the wall.

"Where are you going?" she asked.

"To the bathroom."

"You're not supposed to go alone."

"Yes, I am. Dr. Fitzpatrick said it was all right."

I had talked too much; one of the pills had crept out of its niche.

"All right," she said, "but I'll stay to make sure you're okay."

I forced myself to walk a straight line to the bathroom and closed the door behind me. Dislodging the pills with my finger, I dropped them into the commode and sat down.

"You have to pee," I told myself over and over, but I couldn't do it.

There was a deep crack between the bottom of the door and the floor. The aide would hear the slightest noise emanating from the bathroom. I thought about turning on the water. Maybe that would help. Then, I decided to just brazen it out. I flushed the toilet, washed my hands, and opened the door.

"False alarm," I said.

The aide smiled.

I got back into bed with the knowledge that I would soon be back in my own room with nobody to give me orders. The solitude of the green room was somehow soothing now that I knew we would be parting company. It was quiet as a graveyard, and my mind was tabula rasa.

My body clock awakened me just as breakfast arrived. I ate and took the pills in my newly acquired manner, finishing just before Dr. Fitzpatrick arrived.

"Good morning, Clemmie." Dr. Fitzpatrick said. "I assume you slept well."

"Yes, I did."

He looked at the breakfast tray.

"You seem to have a good appetite. I see no reason for you to remain in the infirmary. You may get dressed and return to your regular routine."

"That's great."

"Oh, and Clemmie, I'll have the nurse bring you a month's supply of your new medicine. You seem to have adjusted to it very well."

I nodded. All I wanted to do was escape from the infirmary. I didn't tell him that there was no way on earth I would ever swallow another of those pills.

"It's very important for you to stick to a rigid schedule with these pills," the nurse warned. "Be sure to take all three pills immediately after each meal. Throw your old medicine away. We wouldn't want to mix it with these."

I took the pills and went to my room. I couldn't wait to take a shower. Stripping off my clothes, I stepped under the spray. It was wonderful to be alone. I almost felt free.

I opened the bathroom door to let some of the steam escape. As I toweled myself dry, I saw my journal lying on the corner of the desk. That's strange, I thought. How did it get here? I must have taken it to my last session. If I hadn't, Dr. Fitzpatrick would have reprimanded me. I didn't recall a dressing down by the doctor; I always remembered when he did that. It was one of the things I disliked about him, and I couldn't let it go for days.

I picked up the journal. The last entry was dated July 6. Dr. Fitzpatrick had mentioned today's date in passing this morning, otherwise, I wouldn't have realized how many days I had wasted in the infirmary, popping pills that reduced my brainpower to that of a slug.

Leafing back through the pages, I read the last few entries. The most recent referred to my marriage to Jimmy. Then I remembered my visit with Mama Rae and lunch with Addie Jo. Yes, and Addie Jo had quit her job. I was back on track. I could prove to the good doctor that I was capable of recalling everything from my past, and I didn't need his high-powered pills to do it.

July 20, 1978

I'm happy to be back in familiar surroundings. Like Dr. Fitzpatrick said, I simply had a little setback. I'm focused, and my mind is clear.

Roy was overjoyed that Addie Jo had resigned. Having her out of the picture would let us put our lives back in order. Ava would return to the island, and Roy would smooth things out with her. I would spend as much time with my darling Jimmy as I could, and Daniel would surely get in touch with us and put our minds at ease.

"Good afternoon, Clemmie," Dr. Fitzpatrick said. "I must say you're looking exceptionally lovely today."

He never failed to compliment me when I wore blue. Everything was back to normal.

"Thank you."

I handed him the spiral notebook to share my entry.

"Very well. Let's begin."

———

Roy and I spent more time together the next week than we had all summer. Ava hadn't returned from her trip, so Roy was home every evening. When I had a date with Jimmy, I asked him to pick me up after dinner so I could cook for Roy and talk to him while we ate. I wanted to give him all the love and support that a good daughter should. It was obvious he missed his whiskey. He seemed restless all the time, but he never mentioned his drinking problem. I knew he wanted me to think he was miserable just because he missed Ava, so I played his game.

"I can't lose her, Clementine," he said. "When she comes home, I'm going to do whatever it takes to win her back."

"Don't worry, Roy. Ava's just confused and hurt."

"I hope you're right, honey."

Roy was always ready to talk about Ava, but he hadn't mentioned Jimmy's name since he discovered how intimate our relationship had become. I knew he would have liked nothing better than for me to tell him Jimmy and I had broken up.

We were at a drive-in movie, and Jimmy was clearly distracted. It was nearly time for him to leave the island to begin his college career.

"I can't leave you," he said. "There's no way I'll be able to study. We'll be apart for weeks."

"It'll be hard for me, too. I probably won't know what to do with myself, but what choice do we have?"

"We could get married."

"Your parents expect you to go college and make something of yourself, and I still have another year of high school. We'd be a couple of dropouts."

"No, we wouldn't. You could take the GED test. We could get married, and you could go with me. Lots of married couples live on campus. It would be perfect."

"I don't know, Jimmy. I'll have to think about this."

I loved Jimmy more than I had thought I could love anyone. I had dreamed of the moment when he would get down on one knee and propose to me, but I pictured it happening in some romantic setting under the stars. Jimmy's words sounded desperate—almost surreal. What if he awoke in the morning with a change of heart?

"Clementine, tell me you love me and that you'll be my wife. I can't live without you."

"Oh, I do love you. You can't imagine how I adore you, but this is the biggest step we'll ever take. We have to think it through."

"All right. We'll both think about it tonight. I'll come over in the morning, and we'll discuss it rationally, but I want you to know it's a waste of time on my part."

I thought his last statements sounded like a business deal, but that was my fault. He took me straight home, and when we kissed goodnight, I knew I wouldn't sleep a wink.

"I seem to have a proclivity for calling our sessions to a halt at crucial moments," Dr. Fitzpatrick said. "I do apologize, Clemmie."

I wanted more than anything to continue because I was remembering it all so vividly, but I would be a model patient. Never again would I allow myself to become emotional. If I appeared anxious, Dr. Fitzpatrick would put me back in the infirmary. I was through being his guinea pig.

"Good afternoon," I said, and smiled.

Chapter Thirty

⌒

July 25, 1978

I still can't recall taking my wedding vows, but I know I will soon recapture that special moment. I do remember the devastation I felt at Jimmy's parents' reaction when they learned he wanted to marry me. And Roy—my care-giver and protector who loved me as if I were his blood and had sworn that he wanted nothing but my happiness, made me want to weep.

Dr. Fitzpatrick was shuffling papers into a neat pile. I had never seen his desk so messy. He took my journal, and I watched him as he read. I couldn't help wondering if he sometimes felt like God, experimenting with the minds of his patients. Konrad Witz's fifteenth century painting came to mind: Jesus is standing on the shore, telling his disciples who are in a boat, to trust him, and let down their nets; they will need the help of other fishermen to lift their haul. I could easily picture my doctor wearing that red robe with its tubular folds and the fancy halo, handing out orders to his patients, telling them to trust him because he was all-knowing.

"Very interesting," he said. "Can you elaborate on your entry?"

————

Jimmy came to the house early the next morning. He told me that he hadn't slept all night. I couldn't sleep, either, worrying about how Roy would take it if we decided to go through with our plan. Jimmy's parents and Roy would have to agree to sign for us because we were minors. It would hurt Roy if I went against his wishes, but the thought of living each day without Jimmy was unbearable.

"Yes," I said, looking into his dark eyes.

"Yes, what?"

"Yes, I'll marry you."

He crushed me to his chest. I listened to his heart pound, and felt more loved than I thought possible, safe and warm in his embrace.

"I swear you won't be sorry." His voice was hoarse. "I'll make sure you never regret this decision, no matter what it takes."

I believed him.

"I'll come over this evening and ask Roy for your hand in marriage," he said. "He's kind of an old fashioned guy; I think he'll expect that."

"Maybe I should talk to him first. The idea of his baby girl getting married is going to throw him for a loop."

Reluctantly, Jimmy agreed. He would tell his parents during dinner, and I could talk to Roy.

I spent the day planning how to approach Roy. Nothing I could think of seemed like a good idea. No matter how I presented it, he was going to have to hear the cut and dried fact that Jimmy and I wanted to get married. I didn't know whether to beat around the bush, or slap him in the face with it.

"Whoa!" Roy did a double take when he saw the table set with flowers and candles. "Am I at the right address?"

"You are, indeed."

"What's the occasion?" He kissed my cheek.

"I thought you deserved to dine in style for a change."

Roy beamed at me from across the table and ate like a starved animal. It was really tough to engage in polite conversation with every bite feeling like a boulder in my throat, and it only got worse when I thought about how to drop my bomb. Roy raved over the beef stroganoff until I thought I would scream, and when I served the chocolate pie I had made from scratch, he couldn't contain his praise.

"I'm glad you enjoyed the meal, Roy." I felt my heart begin to race. "I have something to tell you."

"What's that, sweetheart?"

I wished he hadn't said *sweetheart*; it made me feel so young. He called me that when he was telling me how much he loved me, and how proud of me he was.

"Jimmy and I are in love. We want to get married."

It wasn't supposed to have come out like that. What I had said was the simple truth. Why had it sounded so harsh and rebellious?

Roy put down his dessert fork, and looked at me with an expression so sad and shocked I might have told him I was dying.

"Clementine, you can't mean that. Why, you haven't finished high school. You're not old enough to vote."

"It's true that I'm young," I admitted, "but Jimmy and I are in love; we can't be apart. I'll take a GED test, and we'll get married. I'll be able to go with him when he goes away to school."

"You're pregnant!"

I shook my head in denial, but Roy wasn't looking at me.

"Oh, my poor baby! I told you what would happen if you continued those little rendezvous, but you didn't listen. Now, look where it's gotten you." His hand flew to his head to rake through his hair. "Don't worry. I'll take you to a doctor first thing in the morning. Old Roy'll never desert his baby girl."

"I'm not pregnant, Roy. I'm in love. You know what that's like. It makes you want to spend every minute of every day with the person you love. Please give us your blessing."

"I can't do that, Clementine. You're the only child I have, and I can't allow you to do something you'll regret for the rest of your life."

"You haven't listened to a word I've said."

"Yes, I have. I understand that you think you're in love. Sweetheart, you're just infatuated. It won't last."

"You're treating me like a child!"

"I'm sorry, Clementine, but sometimes a father has to do what's best for everyone concerned. I'm going to talk to the boy's father. I can't let you go through with this."

He was out the front door before I had a chance to say anything else.

I ran to the phone to call Jimmy. He answered on the extension in his room and told me he had just had a terrible fight with his parents. They wouldn't listen to reason, and refused to give their permission for us to marry. They even threatened to cut off his funds if he went against their wishes. He was ordered to stop seeing me.

"Oh, Jimmy, what'll we do?"

"Don't worry, sweetheart. We can work it out."

"How can we?"

"I'll come over in the morning and explain. Good night, sweetheart."

I cleaned the kitchen and went to bed. Roy tapped on my door when he came home, but I ignored him. The last thing I wanted to do was listen to him tell me what a big favor he had done for me.

He left a note for me on the kitchen table the next morning:

My Dearest Clementine,

I realize you believe I've done you a terrible injustice. Young love can be awfully painful. Every adult has been injured by it.

The Castlebrooks agree with me that you and Jimmy are deeply infatuated with one another, and with the idea of marriage. They also agree that if we allowed the marriage to take place, it would be a terrible mistake.

We believe the most expedient way to end the pain for you and Jimmy is to call a halt to your dating, at least for the time being. When Jimmy comes home after having been away at school for a while, you'll both more than likely be dating other people.

I hope you'll mull this over and give yourself a chance to digest it. I also hope you can find it in your heart to forgive me. I love you.

Roy

"Is this a good stopping place, Clemmie?" Dr. Fitzpatrick asked.

"It's fine."

"You seem to be thinking so clearly, Clemmie, and you don't seem restless. I wish I had changed your medication earlier."

I felt sad every time I walked by the tennis courts. Since Alex's death I hadn't signed up to play, but my body craved exercise, especially since I ditched the drugs.

I changed into shorts and tennis shoes to go for a jog. A shady path leading into the trees called to me, and I broke into a run. I ran through the trees and across a wide, manicured expanse of lawn. Flowers and shrubs were a blur as I ran past them. When I was finally winded, I dropped to the ground to catch my breath. As my breathing became easier, I began rolling in the grass. I rolled down an incline like I had done as a small child, and when I was on level ground, I closed my eyes against the sunlight. The sun was hot, and I could see tinges of red through my lids.

The last time I remembered rolling on the grass I wasn't alone. Jimmy and I were rolling in what was left of the autumn leaves. The trees were nearly bare, and Thanksgiving was just around the corner.

I was crying, shedding tears of joy. I remembered my wedding day. I jumped up from my imaginary bed of leaves, and raced to the dorm to grab my journal.

July 26, 1978

Jimmy and I were married in Chattanooga, Tennessee by a justice of the peace. I recall that we lived with friends in Atlanta, Georgia, but I'm not sure it was right after we married. We also lived in Lexington, Kentucky.

Dr. Fitzpatrick looked pleased as he read what I had written.

"Clemmie, you're definitely getting closer. You have dredged up a wealth of lost information already."

"There are still gaps, but I am recalling a lot."

"Let's begin."

The day Roy wrote the note turned out to be most fortuitous for Jimmy and me. Roy came home early. He was really agitated. I was in no mood to listen to his problems, but he looked so distressed that I asked him what was troubling him. He told me he had to go to New York for a conference. His boss had been scheduled to go, but developed a last minute conflict, and Roy was taking his place. He would be gone for a week.

"Here's the phone number in case you need to reach me," he said, handing me a slip of paper.

He had a frightened look in his blue eyes when he told me goodbye.

"Keep that number by the phone, sweetheart. And don't forget to lock up at night."

Jimmy came over after he knew Roy had left the house. He couldn't believe our good fortune when I told him Roy would be gone for a week.

"What a gift!" he said.

"Yes, we can be together without fear of Roy's coming home unexpectedly."

Jimmy was planning more than a week of mad, passionate love. He made me sit down while he laid out the plan step-by-step. He would tell his folks he wanted to spend a week with his friend in Atlanta. The two of us would drive to Atlanta where we would spend the night. The following morning, we would get up early and drive to Chattanooga, Tennessee.

"Why would we want to go there?"

"Because we can get married there without our folks' consent."

"Oh, Jimmy, I don't know if I can go through with that. What if Roy calls?"

"We'll think of something. Sweetheart, this is our only chance."

I knew Roy was going to be devastated. But Jimmy and I were in love, and this was the only way we could be together. I agreed to elope.

We reached Atlanta after eight o'clock that night and checked into a modest hotel. After a quick supper in the coffee shop, we went to bed and asked for an early wake-up call.

I don't remember what we talked about on our way to Chattanooga, and I couldn't believe that I was actually married even after I heard myself say, "I do." My linen suit wasn't the white satin gown I had envisioned for my wedding day, but Jimmy told me that I was the most beautiful bride he had ever seen.

We drove back to Atlanta where we spent our wedding night, and the next morning we headed back to the island. We had planned for Jimmy to stay at my house the rest of the week, but that didn't work out. Roy called the night after we returned to tell me he would be home earlier than planned.

"Well, exactly when will you be home?" I asked.

"Just in time to take my princess out to dinner tomorrow night," he said.

Jimmy and I decided to keep our marriage a secret until the last minute. Roy and the Castlebrooks would surely be more reasonable when they learned that we were already married. But I dreaded facing Roy. I had never kept anything from him.

Jimmy told his folks he had come home early because his friend had a family emergency.

Roy took me out to dinner, and our conversation wasn't nearly as painful as I had anticipated. He was so engrossed in telling me all about New York that he did most of the talking. When he got around to asking me how things had gone on the home front, I told him that I still hadn't heard from Daniel. Neither of us mentioned Jimmy.

Jimmy and I wanted to be together more than ever since our wedding. A few stolen hours during the day only whetted our appetites. We wanted to look into one another's eyes, to snatch a quick hug or kiss in the middle of conversations, and to make our plans for the future.

Every night he came to my bedroom window after his parents were asleep. My window wasn't high, so it was easy for him to climb in and spend the night. Each morning he left before dawn.

Roy kept encouraging me to go out with my friends. He accused me of moping around, and I knew he assumed my attitude was due to his insistence that I not see Jimmy. He told me to go out with my girlfriends if I didn't feel up to dating yet.

It was Sunday afternoon. Roy was reading the paper, and I was lounging on the couch, longing for Jimmy.

"Want part of the paper?" he asked.

"No, thanks. I think I'll go see Mama Rae."

I found her by the front porch. When I called her name, she turned to face me, and I couldn't believe my eyes. She held a huge snake by its middle as it crawled up the front of her shirt, its head just inches from her neck.

I stood stock still. "What are you doing with that snake?" I said.

"Pettin' it."

She grasped the snake behind its head and pulled it away from her neck.

"That thing's going to bite you," I said. "Put it down!"

"Ain't no snake goin' bite me."

The reptile had twisted itself around her arm. She disentangled it and gently dumped it into the tall grass at the edge of her yard.

"You heard from Daniel?" she asked, wiping her hands on the folds of her skirt.

"Not a word."

"He never comin' back," she said.

"You don't know that, Mama Rae. I feel sure he'll get in touch with us soon."

I had come to tell her that I was a married woman, but changed my mind. She couldn't get Daniel off her mind, and I wasn't sure how she would feel about what I had done. I did give her the news that Addie Jo had resigned.

"I hope she's off the island and that we never see, or hear from her again," I said.

"Don't 'spec you will."

Dr. Fitzpatrick looked at the wall clock and put the cap on his pen.

"I'm afraid it's that time again," he said.

July 27, 1978

This is an addendum to today's session. The remainder of my visit with Mama Rae was inconsequential, but what happened later that evening was a blockbuster. I don't know how I could have buried it in my mind. Roy and I were watching the late news. We were both half asleep, but came to attention when we heard that a local woman had driven her car to a bridge and parked sideways at the entrance, blocking oncoming traffic. Then for reasons unknown, she had leaped to her death. That woman was Addie Jo Simmons.

I closed my journal and began crying. It's coming back. It's all coming back, I thought. I'm going to make it this time. I just know it.

I deliberately waited until the last minute to go to dinner. I didn't want to run into Maria or anyone else. How I longed to share what I had just recalled with someone who cared about me. But there was nobody to tell but my doctor. I ate a piece of soggy fish and some coleslaw, then went to my room feeling happy and sad at the same time. I would be leaving Still Waters soon. I could tell I was about to unearth the final culprit that had stolen the last four years of my life. Freedom couldn't be far away.

"So the infamous Miss Simmons met her demise." Dr. Fitzpatrick's brows squeezed together in a bridge over his glasses.

"I don't know how I could have forgotten such a tragic incident. Roy and I wanted to be rid of Addie Jo, but we were both devastated by the news of her death."

"Let's begin."

Addie Jo's death did something to Roy. He felt responsible, because he had given her the cold shoulder at work, and he was so depressed that I was worried about him. Addie Jo's suicide coupled with Ava's absence was more than he could take. I could tell he had broken his vow never to drink again.

"I'm sorry, doctor. I've lost my train of thought."

"Take a couple of deep breaths."

I closed my eyes, tried to relax, and breathed deeply.

"I'm sorry."

"There's no need to apologize. You've just come to a snag—an obstacle you subconsciously choose not to remember"

"I can't imagine what it could be."

"Do you think you can skip over it and tell me about your married life?"

"I don't know.

My temples were beginning to throb, and I was afraid I would go berserk again. I won't let it happen, I thought. It can't happen.

"Clemmie?"

I don't know how long it took me to gain control of my thoughts.

"Jimmy and I were in Atlanta. I don't know how we ended up there because we were supposed to go to Macon where he would attend school."

"Good. Good. Continue, my dear."

We had hardly any money. Jimmy didn't go to school. Both of us had jobs, but they paid next to nothing. We lived in a large house with people Jimmy knew. It was located on the south side of town, close to the airport and the zoo. The house was a big, rambling affair with noisy pipes that seemed to clang constantly. There was an overabundance of shade trees and a wrap-around porch that I loved. The house wasn't air conditioned, but we didn't need it, because there was always a wonderful breeze. We kept the doors and windows open until the weather turned chilly.

Our home was something of a commune. Jimmy and I had an upstairs apartment consisting of two rooms and a tiny bath. Six other people lived in the house. Jimmy knew the four guys; they were childhood friends when the Castlebrooks lived in Atlanta. He hadn't met the two gay women who lived across the hall from us, but they seemed nice enough.

The old-fashioned kitchen and the high-ceilinged living room on the ground floor were common areas. We all contributed to the monthly grocery fund, the rent, and utilities. I volunteered to cook the evening meals for the entire household, so our part of the rent was less than what the others paid.

We managed with one car. I don't know what happened to my Volkswagen, but we had Jimmy's car. I landed a job in a card shop a few blocks from the house, so I walked to work. Jimmy drove a school bus twice each day and worked at a dry cleaning shop during his off hours.

There were public tennis courts not far from the house, and Jimmy and I joined a group of regulars who showed up to play on Friday nights. The courts were hard-surfaced and in disrepair, a far cry from the manicured clay courts on Hilton Head Island.

I took the GED test and passed it easily. We were broke, but neither of us had lost sight of going to college. I don't remember why it seemed so important, but we wanted to save enough money to move into a place of our own before we began our college careers.

"Our time is up, Clemmie. You did very well."

Chapter Thirty-one

My head throbbed. I soaked a washcloth with cold water and laid it on my forehead, trying to make my mind go blank. Finally I fell asleep and dreamed.

I was in my bedroom. Roy had come home stinking drunk, and I was disgusted with him. He was sobbing and calling Mama's name— not Ava's. Addie Jo was standing on the bridge where she had taken her life, singing a country song while Mama Rae watched her from the shadows of a thicket by the roadside. I thought I could see Jimmy climbing through my bedroom window, but it wasn't him. I tried to scream, but couldn't. Fumes from my cup of herb tea made everything look wavy before my eyes, and I could hear Daniel moaning.

I knew I should record the dream in my journal, but I couldn't make myself do it. It was too bizarre.

"Good afternoon, Clemmie," Dr. Fitzpatrick said.

"Hello."

"Could I see your journal?"

"I didn't make an entry."

"Let me see." The doctor flipped through his notes. "You and Jimmy were living in Atlanta in a sort of commune. You were saving money to move into a place of your own."

We had saved enough to move out of the house and into our own place. But about a week before we were to move, Jimmy received a letter from his uncle who lived in Lexington, Kentucky. I don't recall what the letter said, but I remember that the uncle enclosed a check for five thousand dollars. We had found a small apartment in Atlanta, but we moved to Lexington instead.

Our new home was in the Garden Court apartment complex on Virginia Avenue. We both found full-time jobs. Jimmy drove a UPS truck, and I was a receptionist for a dentist. Jimmy could have gone to school the first semester, because he had already taken the SAT test, but he decided to work that term and save as much money as he could.

I took my SAT, and we were ready to enroll at the University of Kentucky for the second semester. Jimmy's uncle suggested we use his address so we would be exempt from having to pay out-of-state tuition. We both felt guilty about doing it, but decided to take his suggestion since we would have to pinch our pennies.

We quit our jobs the week before Christmas. I was giddy because it was going to be our first Christmas alone together as man and wife. We bought a little tree from the local Jaycees and decorated it with ornaments we found at a discount store. It was so tiny that it only required one string of lights. We put it on the coffee table in front of our living room window so it could be seen from outside.

Every day we took turns making excuses to use the car so we could sneak out to shop for one another. We had promised not to spend much, and we didn't. But every evening there would be a package for each of us that hadn't been there that morning.

On Christmas Eve, we went to an early candlelight service, then out to dinner. It was snowing when we got home, and we went for a walk. Our faces were frozen from catching snowflakes on our tongues, and we were as happy as children waiting for Santa.

The apartment was toasty when we stomped the snow from our boots. We hurried inside and each of us ripped the paper off one of our gifts. Then we were rolling around on the ugly shag carpet, making love by the lone string of lights on our Charlie Brown tree. I was the richest woman alive.

Christmas morning we sipped coffee and opened the rest of our presents, so happy to be together. Jimmy cooked a late breakfast of bacon and eggs which we inhaled. While families packed up their children to go to grandma's house, we went to a matinee then came home to make a prime rib dinner. The apartment filled with smoke as we baked the Yorkshire pudding, and set off the smoke alarm.

We were lying in bed. Jimmy was caressing my hair, and I was counting my blessings.

"I have one more gift for you," he said.

"You do?"

"Remember when you told me that you'd always wanted to play the piano?"

"Yes, I remember. Oh, Jimmy, we can't afford a piano. I won't hear of it. Our education has to come first."

"You're right. We can't afford a piano, but we can afford piano lessons. I've signed you up to begin this semester. You'll take lessons in the music building on campus. There are several rooms with good pianos where students can practice."

"What a terrific gift!"

"One day I'll buy you a baby grand," he promised.

"Let's stop on that happy note." The doctor smiled at his pun.

I lay in bed trying to figure out what had caused me to draw a blank at my afternoon session. It had to have been something that transpired on Hilton Head Island, because I remembered living in Atlanta and Lexington.

A whippoorwill was delivering its relentless call over and over. I couldn't remember hearing one since I came here. Roy loved whippoorwills. He used to sing about them in an old song: *My Blue Heaven*. We would sit on the porch and listen to the whippoorwills and cicadas after dinner when we were happy on the island.

I massaged my temples and tried to focus on Hilton Head. I had so many good and bad memories of that Garden of Eden. The beach was so wide, the plant life so lush, the forest so dark and cool. Roy and Mama Rae were my constants then, because Mama was gone. It seemed that everyone else came into my life, then left: Daniel, Addie Jo, and Ava. Even Gloria Jean got lost in the shuffle; I don't know what happened to her.

I went to my next session ill prepared. I hadn't been able to make any journal entries.

"It's all right, Clemmie." Dr. Fitzpatrick tried to smile, but I could tell he wasn't happy.

"I've come to another dead end."

"You'll get back on track. Now, if I recall correctly, you and Jimmy were about to embark upon your college careers."

"That's right."

"I assume your husband had a student deferment from his military obligation."

"Yes, he did."

"Can you take it from here, Clemmie?"

"I'll try."

Our class schedules left a lot to be desired. Jimmy was in class when I was home and vice versa. We shared the household chores. He cooked most of the time since he was good at it, and I did the laundry. We played the rest by ear.

Both of us studied hard that semester. Neither of us took on jobs because we wanted to do our best in school. We had to be frugal, because Jimmy's parents had followed through on their threat to cut him off. He wrote to them several times, but never received a reply. His uncle had been uncommonly generous, but it wasn't enough. We took full-time summer jobs, and Jimmy found a part-time job two nights a week so we could replenish our bank account.

"Excuse me," Dr. Fitzpatrick said. "Did you stay in touch with Roy?"

"No."

"I thought you might have since the two of you were so close."

I was suddenly confused. Why had he interrupted me when I was on a roll?

"Why did you do that?" My voice sounded angry, even to me.

"I'm sorry, Clemmie. What did I do?"

"What did I do?" I mimicked. "You interrupted me! You do it constantly! I'm sick of it!"

I slammed my journal down on his desk and leaped up to pace the room. My body felt overheated, and I could feel tears gathering in my eyes, blurring my vision. I couldn't stand looking at Dr. Fitzpatrick in his baggy pants and ugly tie. And those thick-lensed glasses made him look like a frightened owl. I wanted to snatch them off his face and smash them into a thousand pieces! I glared at him as he got up from his leather chair.

"Now, Clemmie, I do apologize for the interruption." His voice was velvet. "If you'll just take your seat, we can continue. I promise I won't interrupt again."

"You're damn right, you won't!"

He was growing as he inched his way toward me. I knew I would die if he touched me. Backing away from him, I grabbed a book from his bookcase and hurled it at him.

"I'm warning you, stay away from me. I mean it."

He kept his distance, dodging the barrage of books I was aiming at him. As he reached for the phone, I threw a volume that knocked it off his desk.

"Oh, look, doctor. I'm afraid our time is up." I pointed to the wall clock. "It's three o'clock."

"So it is." He sounded so calm—not like someone who had been the target of a mad, missile-throwing woman.

"Well, guess what? We're going to continue this session and mess up your precious schedule. How do you like that?"

"Clemmie, try to calm down. You'll feel better in just a moment."

"You calm down, asshole!"

I sailed another book at the owl. It smashed into his face, breaking his glasses neatly in half. A bright spray of blood spurted from his nose. Miss Yantz opened the door, and in rushed two beefy attendants. I laughed while they hauled me out of the office. Then, I felt a needle stab into my arm.

I was disoriented when I awoke. The light was dim, and it was deadly quiet. I couldn't seem to move my hands, and my arms felt tired and useless. This didn't look like the infirmary, and I wasn't in a hospital bed. I was huddled in the corner of a padded cell, and someone had put me in a straight jacket. My life was over.

Sticky tears wet my face, and I needed to blow my nose. I looked down at the coarse canvas of the straight jacket. The more I thought of being trapped in it, the more furious I became. I had my wits about me now, so I knew that attempting to fight the restraint was futile. Sinking deeper into the padding of the cell wall, I wondered how long they would leave me here in the quiet. The stillness was killing me. I wanted to scream, but I knew that wouldn't be smart. If I made trouble, they might send me into oblivion with more of their wonder drugs.

My nose itched. Maneuvering myself sideways, I rubbed my face up and down on the cell wall. I was being treated like an animal. Finally, I slept.

I was stiff all over when I awoke. My shoulders were tired from having my arms in the same position for so long. The constraint had allowed me no freedom above the waist. I had slept with my knees bent and my feet tucked under my buttocks. I simply had to move, so I braced my forehead against the wall in order to get to my knees. There wasn't a commode in the cell, and I had to pee so badly that I ached. What would I do? Then, it didn't matter. I lost all control; urine ran down my thighs, and I started to sob.

"Let me out of here!" I screamed. "Somebody let me out!"

Moments later a key rattled in the lock, and the door swung open against intense light. A giant of a woman stood there. She wore no makeup, and her hair was cut butch short. Her face showed no emotion as she looked down at me.

"What's the trouble here?"

"I had to go to the bathroom."

"Okay, let's go. The next time you have the urge, you might just want to step on the buzzer in the corner instead of waking everybody in the building."

"I didn't see the buzzer."

"Well, you see it now, don't you?"

"Yes. Yes, I see it."

"You got to go, or don't you? I don't have time to stand around and chat."

I was embarrassed. "I'm afraid it's too late. I've ruined my clothes."

She looked down at my skirt. "So I see."

"Do you think you might have something dry for me to put on?"

"You don't have to whine. I expect I can round up something."

I struggled to get to my feet, assuming she would bring the clothes to the cell and dress me.

She helped me stand. "Well, come on. I don't have all night."

I followed her past several other cells that looked exactly like mine into a room which I thought must be a lounge for the attendants. She headed for a closet, and kept looking over her shoulder to make sure I was following.

"Looks like these'll do," she said, holding up a pair of white, baggy pants.

"They'll be fine."

"That's what I said. Now, don't take this personal."

She reached under the straight jacket and unbuttoned my skirt, sliding it down over my hips. Then, she pulled my soggy panties down to my feet.

"Step out of them. You through bein' mad?"

"I'm not mad; I'm humiliated."

"Come with me," she ordered.

I felt ridiculous, running around in the middle of the night in nothing but shoes and a straight jacket.

"I got to come in with you," she said, flipping the light on in a small bathroom.

I went in, and she stepped in behind me. I stood there, not knowing what to do next. She gave me another piercing stare that made me think she was looking right through my eyes and into my mind.

"I'm gonna take this restraint off so you can clean yourself up, and you're not gonna tell anybody."

I nodded.

It didn't take her long to free me from the jacket, and nothing had ever felt so good. I stretched my arms over my head and shrugged my stiff shoulders.

"Thank you," I said.

I slapped cold water on my face to wash off the salt.

"Maybe you'd like a bubble bath."

"I'm sorry."

I turned my attention to more important matters, then pulled on the baggy pants. They fell to the floor.

"They're too big. Do you have a safety pin?"

"Girl, I can't be givin' you no safety pin. Stay here, and be quiet."

If I had intended to make a break for it, this would have been the time to do it. She was gone for several minutes, and returned with two long shoelaces tied together. Threading the makeshift belt through the loops on the pants, she tied it in a big bow.

"You have any supper?" she asked.

"No. I had lunch."

"Hungry?"

"Yes."

I followed her back to the lounge and waited while she scrounged around in a refrigerator and the cupboards. She found two slices of cheese and some stale soda crackers. I washed them down with a cup of tap water.

"Okay," she said, "break's over."

"Thank you for being so kind to me."

"Yeah. Yeah. Get on up, now. You know I got to put you back in your tux. What'd you do to be put in this thing, anyway?"

"I hit my doctor in the nose with a book."

The big woman grinned, and I did, too.

Chapter Thirty-two

Settling in the corner of the padded cell, close to the buzzer, I went to sleep. I dreamed I was in the woods with Mama Rae. We were picking wild raspberries. The scene was very familiar, because we had picked the lush red berries together many times. Nothing in the world was tastier than Mama Rae's raspberry tarts.

"For ever berry you put in the bucket, two goes in your mouth."

I heard my old friend's gentle reprimand as though she were standing right beside me. She put on her sly grin, and the twinkle in her eye peeked out from under the brim of her old, floppy slouch hat.

"I can't help myself. They're so good."

I popped another fat one into my mouth and crushed it between my teeth, sending its rich juice to every taste bud on my tongue. Savoring its goodness like a sip of fine wine, I swished it around in my mouth before swallowing it.

When our pails were full, we returned to Mama Rae's cottage and dumped our haul into a large bowl of cold water. We rinsed them in the bowl, then strained them in a colander and poured more water over them.

While Mama Rae readied her baking paraphernalia, I stared down at the deep red of the fruit, glistening wet in the colander. Bright daylight shone in through the window above the sink. Suddenly, the berries began to liquefy under my steady gaze. They turned into a thick, sticky substance.

I couldn't tear my eyes away; I was mesmerized. Mama Rae was sifting flour. I tried to call her to come and see the strange transformation, but I couldn't make a sound. With my eyes still transfixed on the scarlet liquid, I saw Daniel's face. His eyes stared up at me, and his gaze seemed to go right through me to the low ceiling of the kitchen. I could hear Mama Rae mumbling her strange Gullah as the liquid filled Daniel's mouth, and rivulets of it poured from his nostrils.

I awoke with a start. My eyes adjusted to the dim light, and I remembered where I was and why I was here. The straight jacket held my arms in a tight wrap around my sides. I inched myself down until I was supine on the floor. Then I swiveled my hips from side to side, and banged my numb legs on the cell floor.

When the feeling in my legs was restored, I bent my knees, and pounded the bottoms of my feet until they tingled. Finally, I was able to guide my right foot and push the buzzer with my heel. It was still sounding when the attendant opened the cell door. She bent down and removed my heel to silence it.

"What you want, baggy britches? You need to go potty again?"

"No."

"Then what's the matter? Maybe you want a down pillow and a blanket."

"You've been awfully lenient with me, but could you bend the rules one more time?"

"Depends. What you want?"

"I need to record something. I'm afraid I'll lose my train of thought if I don't do it right now."

"What you talkin' about, girl?"

"I'm supposed to write things that I remember from my past in a journal. Then I share it with my psychiatrist."

"I can't turn you loose again. Think you can dictate?"

"I've never done it, but I'll try."

She left me lying on the floor and returned a few minutes later with a folding chair, a pen, and a steno pad. She pulled me to a sitting position in the corner and sat down, ready to write.

"Don't talk too fast; I don't take shorthand."

"You do realize that everything I say is privileged information."

"Yes, I know that. We gonna do this, or not?"

"Write today's date at the top," I instructed.

I waited while she scribbled the date.

"Okay, shoot," she said.

My voice was calm and clear as I told this woman whose name I didn't know that I had witnessed a murder. I went on to tell her exactly how it had happened, and at whose hand. Using as few words as possible, and sounding devoid of emotion, I minimized the event as I told the tale. There was no reason to burden this good woman with details. It was all clear as a bell to me, and I knew that nothing could ever erase it from my mind. Finally, I could fill in all the blanks.

As I finished the revelation, the tears came, and I let them roll freely, washing away the terrible weight that had kept me imprisoned for the last four years.

"You poor child," the attendant whispered.

She reached into the pocket of her uniform, and pulled out a crumpled tissue.

"Blow," she said, placing the tissue over my nose. Then she dried my eyes and face.

"Thank you for being so kind," I said.

"I'll be back in a minute."

She left the cell, taking the folding chair with her, but leaving the notebook and pen beside me on the floor. I looked at her childlike scrawl on the sheet. She had written my exact words, and put the entire text in quotation marks.

A few minutes later, she returned with a plain, white envelope.

"Come on," she said, helping me up. "You're gettin' out of here."

She unfastened the straight jacket, and took it off me.

"Where am I going?"

"I called Dr. Fitzpatrick; got him out of bed." She grinned. "I'm takin' you to the infirmary. He'll meet you there right after breakfast."

"I'd rather stay here. The last time I was in the infirmary, they pumped me so full of drugs that I didn't know where I was."

"Don't you worry. It's after seven o'clock, and I'm off duty now. I'll stay with you 'til the doctor comes. You gonna be all right now."

She tore the pages of my dictation from the notebook, folded them, and stuffed them into the envelope. Then, she licked the glue, and ran a thumb and forefinger from one end to the other.

"Wouldn't be no safer in a bank," she said, sliding it inside the front of her shirt.

"What's your name?" I asked.

"Madeline. Maddie, for short."

"That's a nice name. I'm Clementine. My friends call me Clemmie."

Maddie checked me in at the infirmary and watched me devour a large breakfast while she sipped coffee from a Styrofoam cup. She stayed with me until the doctor arrived.

"Well, Clemmie," Dr. Fitzpatrick said, "I see you've been in capable hands. This place would shut down without Maddie."

"She's been wonderful."

Maddie pulled the envelope out of her shirt and handed it to the doctor.

"Clemmie's journal entry," she said. "Be seein' you both around."

Maddie left the room, and I was embarrassed to look at my doctor. His face was bruised, and he had fastened his glasses together with adhesive tape.

"Dr. Fitzpatrick, I sincerely apologize for my outrageous behavior. I truly don't know what came over me."

"Apology accepted, Clemmie. Do you want to have our session here, or would you prefer going to my office?"

"I prefer your office. Do you think I could change clothes first?"

"Certainly. I'll check you out, and you can meet me in a half hour."

I went to my room and threw on a pair of jeans and a blue shirt just for my doctor. It felt strange going to my session at eight-thirty in the morning, but I couldn't wait to begin.

"Good afternoon, Clemmie," Dr. Fitzpatrick said.

"It's morning." I smiled.

"So it is. I must say that you look lovely in blue, my dear."

"Thank you."

"I've read your journal entry. If you can flesh out what you have written, I think you'll be almost there. You've been carrying an enormous burden."

"I'm anxious to tell you everything."

"Let's begin."

Jimmy and I still hadn't told anyone we were married. We planned to give his folks and Roy the news the day before we left the island. By that time, there wouldn't be anything they could do about it.

Roy's drinking problem had gotten steadily worse since Addie Jo's death. It had such a hold on him that he didn't bother hiding it from me. I tried to talk to him about it, but he wasn't interested. He seemed bent on self-destruction, and didn't want anyone to stop him.

Sometimes he went to work, but there were days when he didn't get out of bed. He lounged around in his underwear most of the time when he was home, and didn't bother to shave. My dear, sweet Roy had turned into a drunken bum.

Although I knew there was nobody to blame for his pitiful state but himself, I secretly blamed Addie Jo. I also blamed Ava. She should have trusted him. And even if she hadn't, she could have let him down more easily.

Since Roy was home most of the time, it wasn't easy for Jimmy and me to be together. I would have to tell Roy that I was going out with friends so I could meet my husband away from the house and we could spend a couple of hours alone.

Late one afternoon Roy told me that he was hungry. He had lost so much weight that he looked gaunt. I was so glad he was hungry, and made one of his favorite dinners, but he had changed his mind by the time I called him to the table.

I went to my room to read, but couldn't concentrate, so I abandoned the book and started cleaning out my chest of drawers. It was something I would have to do before leaving the island, so I decided to get it out of the way. I separated my lingerie into a pile to keep and another to throw away.

Just as I headed to the kitchen for a trash bag, I heard Roy start his car. I looked out the window to see him backing into the street. It was too late to stop him. I didn't know anything to do but pray that he would be spared an accident, and that he wouldn't hurt anyone else.

I finished cleaning out the chest and went to bed, wondering what would become of Roy when I left Hilton Head Island. Who would take care of him? He would surely lose his job if he didn't clean up his act. I hoped that Ava would come to his rescue, but I doubted that she would. Roy wasn't the man she had thought he was.

I must have dozed off, because when I looked at the dial on the clock, it was after twelve. Jimmy was usually in bed with me by eleven, and I wondered why he was so late. I was too tired to think about it. I thought I heard a car, and assumed it was Roy's. One less thing for me to worry about, I thought. Jimmy would wake me when he came to bed.

Later, I thought I heard him outside my window. I didn't bother to look at the clock. I just slid over and waited for him to climb through the window and come to bed.

Suddenly, I was wide awake. Instinctively I knew that the person outside my window wasn't my husband. I heard myself scream, but I couldn't move. Surely, Roy would come to see what was going on, even if he was drunk. But he didn't come, and I screamed again.

"Clemmie. Clemmie. It's me, Daniel."

He hurtled through the window, and his long legs bounded across the room toward me just as Roy crashed through the door, wielding his old Louisville Slugger. He was weaving and yelling like a wild man as he slammed the bat down hard, hitting its mark, and crushing Daniel's skull.

Roy fumbled for the light switch and flipped it on, thinking that he had saved his princess from being raped, or killed by some sinister intruder. He was breathing hard as he hoisted the bat high in the air to deliver another blow, but he stumbled and fell backward into the wall.

I looked down at Daniel. He had fallen on his back and didn't move. Blood gushed from his nose and mouth, and a steady crimson stream ran from the wound on his forehead and down his temple. His eyes rolled up under the lids. I was afraid to touch him—afraid to know for a fact that he was dead.

Roy couldn't have been remotely aware of what he had done or who his victim was. He hugged his baseball bat, and slid down the wall to the floor. His eyes were closed, and he wore a contented smile.

My throat was dry, and so were my eyes. I scooted backward across the bed, unable to pull my eyes away from Daniel. The entire scene was surreal as I climbed out the open window and ran blindly through the darkness. Barefoot and wearing nothing but my nightgown, I raced through backyards. I crossed a vacant lot with its tall grass and weeds that put me at the edge of the woods.

It was strange that I didn't run to my husband in my panicked state. The soles of my feet were tender, and I knew they were cut and bleeding from my trek, but I made myself keep running. I had to get to Mama Rae. She would know what to do.

I saw the outline of her cabin when I reached the clearing. It was dark and still as I made my way to the porch steps. I was feeling my way up when I stumbled on Biscuit. He hissed at me. I kept moving forward in the darkness, and found the front door. I pounded on it as hard as I could.

Mama Rae padded to the door with a candle. She was barefoot, and dressed in a long nightshirt with a turban on her head.

"Come in dis house," she said, unhooking the screen door. She didn't seem surprised by my late-night visit.

"Oh, Mama Rae," I sobbed, embracing her.

"You goin' make me drop dis candle."

"Mama Rae, the most horrible thing has happened!"

She nodded.

"Come on in the kitchen. I 'spec you need a cup of tea."

The night air was warm, but I felt myself shiver as I waited for her to brew the tea. She went about her business silently. I wanted to blurt out the unspeakable thing that I had just witnessed, but I knew she wouldn't allow me that luxury until she was ready to listen.

Finally, she shuffled toward me with the cup of steaming, dark liquid. She put it before me and sat down, rubbing her eyes. Folding her arms across her chest, she looked at me.

"Drink it 'fore it gets cold. Everthing gonna be all right."

"Mama Rae . . ."

"Drink."

I took a sip of the tea. Then, I couldn't wait any longer.

"Daniel's dead! He's been killed!"

A peculiar expression crept over the old woman's face. She got up from the table and poured herself a cup of tea.

"We'll drink our tea, then you tell me the res'."

Mama Rae had always been able to make me do her bidding. I wasn't afraid of her, exactly, but I would never have done anything to incur her wrath. There was no doubt that she possessed strange powers that I didn't understand. I had seen evidence of them too many times, but I couldn't imagine what she could do for Daniel.

We sipped our tea in silence. When our cups were empty, Mama Rae put them in the sink. She picked up the candle, and we went into the living room. We sat in our respective chairs, and she heaved a deep sigh.

"Go on," she said.

She had made me wait so long I wasn't sure how to begin. I hadn't told her that I was married. How could I tell her that I had been lying in bed, waiting for my husband when the atrocity occurred?

"Daniel must have heard about Addie Jo Simmons's death. He must have thought it would be safe to return to Hilton Head."

The old woman sat motionless in the big chair as I told her how drunk Roy had been. I told her how Daniel had climbed in through the open window and frightened me. The brutal truth spilled out of me quickly, unvarnished.

Mama Rae gazed at the flickering candle, taking her time to digest what I had told her. I wanted a quick response to calm my fear and ease my pain, but none was forthcoming.

Slowly, she got up and walked to the fireplace. I rocked in silence, waiting for her to speak. She was staring at her doll collection. Calm began to spread through my loins, and I could feel my muscles relax. My eyelids were so heavy that I could hardly stay awake, but I kept rocking. I was in a dream world. Mama Rae was chanting, but I couldn't make out what she was saying. She kept studying her dolls and finally, she reached up and lifted the ugly hodgepodge doll from the mantelpiece.

Her singsong mumbo jumbo sounded so silly it made me want to giggle. I tried to ask her why she was playing with dolls and mumbling those ridiculous non-words when I had just told her about the horrible thing that had happened, but my mouth couldn't seem to form the words. My eyes kept closing, and it was all I could do to open them.

Mama Rae reached for something else on the mantelpiece. I couldn't tell what it was. Through flickering eyelashes I watched as she plunged what appeared to be a long, sharp hatpin into the neck of her ugly doll. What a strange thing for her to do, I thought, as she repeated the act.

I simply couldn't stay awake any longer. My heavy lids closed. I could faintly hear something that sounded like sirens in the distance, but I slept.

When I awoke, I recognized the patchwork quilt; I was in Mama Rae's bed. The shade was up, and sunlight poured in, illuminating tiny dust mites in the air. I could hear Mama Rae bustling around in the kitchen, and a delightful aroma filled my nostrils.

I limped to the kitchen on sore, swollen feet and dropped into a chair. The awful truth of last night's heinous drama came back in a rush, and I began to cry. Mama Rae hadn't greeted me and showed no sign that she intended to do so. She dusted flour from her hands on the large piece of cheesecloth she had tied around her waist to serve as an apron, and picked up a fork to turn whatever she was frying before sitting down across from me.

"I have to go see about Roy," I said. "The police must have locked him up by now."

"Not 'til you eat."

"I'm not hungry."

"Yes, you are. You jes' don't know it."

She went to the stove, forked the crispy meat out of a spattering skillet, and put it on a platter. Then, she took a pan of biscuits from the oven and proceeded to make gravy.

"We'll eat, and I'll go with you to the police station," she said.

She brought the food to the table and helped herself. I watched as she picked up a piece of meat with her fingers and began eating hungrily.

"Better have some," she said, digging into the biscuits and gravy.

Suddenly, I was starved. I took helpings of everything and started to eat.

"What kind of meat is this? It's delicious."

"Squirrel."

"You killed it?" I asked, horrified.

"It didn't jes' jump out of a tree and into my fryin' pan. Caught it with a snare. Squirrel didn't know nothin' about it."

I lost my appetite.

"I'll have to go home to dress," I said.

Mama Rae nodded.

As we washed the breakfast dishes, it hit me: I would have to go into a room where a murder had been committed to get my clothes. Maybe the police had cordoned off my room and wouldn't let me inside. Maybe...

"Mama Rae, what if the police want to interrogate me?"

"Don't worry, chile. I'll be with you."

Chapter Thirty-three

⌒

I was so worried and confused that I didn't know what to do. My best friend was dead, and my father had killed him. I was sure the police had Roy in custody. And my poor Jimmy had to be beside himself wondering what had become of me.

"Mama Rae, there's something I haven't told you."

"Somethin' I need to know, or somethin' you want to get off your ches'?"

"Both, actually. I'm sorry I didn't tell you earlier."

"Go on; tell it."

"I'm married."

Mama Rae showed no surprise; just nodded. She went to her bedroom and came back with a plain looking house dress and her purple sandals along with a washcloth and towel that appeared never to have been used.

"You clean up here at the sink while I get ready," she said.

I was buckling the sandals when she came into the kitchen wearing the same blue crepe dress she had worn when she and Daniel had gone to the police station.

Mama Rae's grandma dress and purple sandals made me look like a kid playing dress up, but it was better than walking through the woods in my nightgown barefoot. When we reached the far edge of the forest, she decided we should cut through to the highway and go directly to the police station instead of going to my house. I didn't want to be seen in public dressed the way I was, but I wasn't going to argue with my mentor.

Jimmy was the first person I saw when we walked into the police station. He was pacing back and forth in front of the sergeant's desk, and he looked terrible.

"Jimmy," I said.

He jerked around at the sound of my voice.

"Dear God, you're safe. Oh, sweetheart, you're safe. I've been so worried. Where have you been?"

"It was so late, and you hadn't come to the house. Roy was really drunk, and…"

"Shhh. It's all right, baby. Now that I know you're safe, everything's all right."

"I was so frightened. You weren't there, so I went to my friend's house to spend the night. I didn't know what else to do."

Jimmy was in such a hurry to tell me what had happened that I wasn't sure he had listened to me.

"I had a big blowout with my folks," he said. "We got into a heated discussion during dinner, and I told them about us. They've cut me off, and that's fine with me. We don't need their money. Oh, sweetheart, I'm so awfully sorry."

I didn't know if he was talking about Daniel and Roy or the money.

"Have the police let you see Roy? Do you know if he's sober?"

Suddenly, there was pain in my husband's eyes.

"You don't know, do you?" His voice was a hoarse whisper.

Mama Rae cleared her throat.

"Oh, Mama Rae, forgive me. This is my husband, James Castlebrook. Jimmy, Mama Rae is a dear friend of mine."

"Hello, Mama Rae." Jimmy took my old friend's hand in both of his. "I'm very glad to meet you."

Mama Rae nodded.

I turned back to Jimmy. "I don't know what?"

"There isn't an easy way to tell you this, sweetheart. I think I just have to say it outright: Roy's dead."

"Dead? You can't mean that. When I left Roy, he was smiling. He can't be dead."

I felt like I was having a nightmare. I saw Roy hugging his baseball bat and smiling. He was definitely alive.

"I know it's a horrible shock, and I know how much you loved him. It breaks my heart to have to tell you that it's true. It was so freaky, dying from a snakebite."

"A snakebite?"

"That's what the coroner wrote in his report, and I saw the fang marks on Roy's neck. Honey, it's true."

"Where is he? I have to see him."

"His body is at the hospital morgue. Are you sure you want to do this?"

I felt like my life was over. Losing my father and best friend in the same night was too much to take.

Jimmy looked at the sergeant who was sitting at his desk shuffling paper while taking in all the excitement.

"Is there somewhere my wife and I can talk?" he asked.

The sergeant looked confused. "This is your wife?"

"Yes. This is my wife. You can call off the search."

"In there." The sergeant gestured toward a door by the water cooler.

"Come with us, Mama Rae. I want you to know everything," I said.

The three of us went into the small conference room. The look in Mama Rae's eyes told me to be quiet and listen. Then, my husband proceeded to explain what had transpired the previous evening.

Jimmy held my hand as he told me how he had fought with his folks before leaving the house in a huff. He parked his car a couple of blocks from my house where he usually left it. He said that he was hesitant to come to the house because there seemed to be some sort of commotion on my street. He was afraid Roy had been awakened by the flashing lights and that he might be outside rubbernecking to see what was happening. As Jimmy came closer, he realized that the police cruisers and ambulance were parked in front of my house.

He ran toward the scene, fearing that something had happened to me. He was afraid that Roy might have gotten stinking drunk and actually harmed me in some way. Jimmy reached the driveway just in time to see someone being loaded into the ambulance on a stretcher, and he was terrified, thinking it was me. The police wouldn't talk to him, or allow him to come any closer, so he ran back to his car and followed the ambulance to the hospital. He watched while the EMTs wheeled not one, but two gurneys into the emergency room.

Jimmy got into the reception area as fast as he could. He couldn't see the face of the person being wheeled through the double doors toward the exam rooms, but the second stretcher was left in the hallway where a doctor rushed out to examine the patient. My husband watched horrified as the doctor pulled the sheet over Roy's face.

Roy was taken away promptly, and Jimmy was allowed to talk to a harried nurse through a glass window. He asked the identity of the person on the first stretcher, explaining that it might possibly be his wife. The only information he received was that the patient wasn't a woman.

Jimmy went to the police station to solicit their help in locating me only to be told that I couldn't be considered a missing person for forty-eight hours. When he told them that my father had been pronounced dead on arrival at the emergency room, they decided to bend the rules. They wouldn't actually put out an APB on a missing person, but they would send out a couple of cruisers to look for me.

Jimmy went back to the hospital and explained that he was Roy's son-in-law. He was then taken to the morgue to identify the body.

My mind was racing so fast that I wasn't sure what I was hearing. If Jimmy was right, that meant that Daniel was alive. But that couldn't be true; I saw him lying dead on my bedroom floor. None of this made sense. When I fled from the house, Roy was very much alive.

Mama Rae wore a glazed expression, like she was in one of her trances when she wore the strange clothes.

"We have to go to the hospital," I said.

"Sweetheart, there's no need to do that. I told you, I've already identified him. It'll just hurt you more."

"You don't understand. The person on the other stretcher had to be Daniel."

"Daniel?"

I told Jimmy everything that had transpired in detail, and Mama Rae didn't try to stop me. She sat very still, wearing that far-away expression.

"My poor baby," Jimmy said. "No wonder you ran away."

Dr. Fitzpatrick cut his eyes to the wall clock over my head. "Would you like to take a break, Clemmie?"

"Yes, I think I would."

I spent the twenty-minute break walking around the grounds of Still Waters. The institution had kept me safe, and my doctor must have helped me uncover a great deal from my past. I felt a sort of freedom after unearthing these last revelations, but I had a nagging feeling that I hadn't come to the hard part. It didn't matter. Learning that my mother and Roy were both gone had wrenched at my heart to the point that I thought I might want to join them, but I knew that wasn't true. I had gone through hell to get this far. There would be no turning back.

"Your recall is amazing, Clemmie," Dr. Fitzpatrick said. "I can't help but wonder what finally struck your memory button."

"Neither can I, but you were right; this system does work."

"Shall we continue?"

I nodded.

———

If I closed my eyes, I could see a younger Roy, right after Mama and I met him. He had his eye on Mama, and showed up unannounced most everywhere we went. We saw him in church, at the post office, and even at the Laundromat. That was before he convinced my mother to allow him to court her. He was so smitten with her that he was clumsy. Then, when Mama finally relented and married him, he turned us into a perfect loving family.

Everything had been so hectic that I don't think I had actually digested the undeniable fact that Roy was dead. I didn't feel grief, and the shock had lessened. I felt only remorse for what he had allowed himself to become the last few weeks of his life.

Jimmy and I took Mama Rae with us to the hospital. When we arrived, we were amazed to learn that Daniel had already been moved from the ICU to a private room. The blow from the baseball bat had only caused a minor concussion. His nurse told us that he looked terrible, but that he was going to be fine.

Daniel's eyes were closed when we tiptoed into his room, but they opened wide when he heard me call his name. It reminded me of another visit I had made to a hospital to see him when we were children.

"Clemmie?" he said weakly.

"Yes, Daniel. It's me. I'm tired of visiting you in hospitals."

He tried to grin. "Boy, do I have a headache."

I introduced Jimmy to Daniel, and Mama Rae came forward. She looked down at Daniel and patted his hand.

"I knew you'd come back to the islan'," she said.

"I can't say I was very happy about my greeting. Roy sure does swing a mean baseball bat." He looked at me and saw the pain in my eyes.

"Oh, Clemmie, I know he didn't realize it was me he was clobbering. He was just protecting his baby. Tell him not to worry; the doctor says I'll be good as new in no time."

I don't know what kept my tears at bay, but I managed something resembling a smile.

"I'll tell him."

Chapter Thirty-four

My house was quiet by the time Jimmy and I got there. The police and detectives were gone, and the driveway was empty. We packed my clothes and box of photographs and checked into a hotel.

While I was supposed to be resting, Jimmy drove to his parents' house and told them everything that had happened. He packed his clothes and walked out. They didn't try to stop him.

I had Roy cremated which he had long ago told me was his wish, and had a memorial service for him at the church he had attended for so many years. Among the mourners was the beautiful Ava. I hadn't known she was there until I saw her get into her car and leave immediately after the service.

That afternoon Jimmy and I visited Daniel in the hospital. It was one of the most difficult things I had ever had to do, but I told him the truth about Roy. He was devastated.

"Jimmy and I are leaving Hilton Head in the morning, Daniel. I want to stay in touch. You've been elusive since the day we met. Where will you go when you leave the hospital?"

"My auntie came to see me this morning. I'll be staying with her, at least for a while."

"I'm glad, but don't forget Mama Rae. She loves you like a son."

"She won't be able to keep me away."

I dropped Jimmy off at the hotel and went to tell Mama Rae goodbye. Leaving the car at the mom-and-pop store, I went into the familiar woods. It made me feel sad to know that I wouldn't be coming here

Bili Morrow Shelburne

whenever I felt the need to talk to my old friend. I tiptoed past two setting hens and climbed the porch steps. Just as I was about to knock, Mama Rae appeared at the door dressed in mourning clothes.

"What you doin' in that pink dress?" she said. "You need to be showin' some respec' for the dead."

"Roy didn't like black."

She donned a mask of disapproval, and held the door for me.

"Here are your things," I said, handing her a paper sack containing her dress and sandals. "Thanks for the loan."

The aroma of apples and cinnamon filled the cottage. I hadn't left the island, but I already missed the sweet smells coming from Mama Rae's kitchen.

My eyes traveled to the lineup of dolls on the mantle. The ugly one was missing again. Over the years, I never knew whether to expect to see it or not.

"Where's your *put together* doll?"

"Gone."

"Gone where?" I wouldn't have been surprised if she had told me I was asking too many questions.

"Burnt up in the wood stove."

"Why would you burn it? You've had it forever."

"How 'bout some apple pie?"

"I'd love it."

We went to the kitchen, and Mama Rae sliced the pie and brought it to the table. I couldn't count the times I had sat at this table sharing the gifts of her labors of love. While we ate, I told her Jimmy's and my plans. She didn't seem saddened by my news that we were leaving Hilton Head.

"I have something for you, Mama Rae." Opening my purse, I took out a little velvet box. "I hope you'll think of me when you wear them."

"What in dis world?"

"Open it."

Her fingers trembled as she lifted the lid to see Mama's diamond stud earrings—the ones Roy had given her the Christmas before he proposed marriage.

"Land sakes," she whispered.

"Try them on. They were my mama's."

Expertly punching the broom straws through the holes in her earlobes, she slipped in the studs and carefully slid on the backs. She didn't even need a mirror.

I smiled. "I love you, Mama Rae; I'll never forget you."

My old friend appeared to glow in the dim light. I've pleased her, I thought. My gift really made her happy. It would have been a pipe dream to think she would break down and give me a warm hug.

I turned, and walked out the door and down the steps.

"Don't you be scarin' my settin' hens," she said.

Dr. Fitzpatrick rolled his eyes up to see the time. "Shall we call it a day, Clemmie?"

"Yes. I'm pretty exhausted."

I went to my room and fell into the twin bed that had been mine for too long. Soon I would be leaving this room, my doctor, and all of Still Waters. I wondered where I would go. I would have to get some kind of job, but I didn't know what my capabilities were. Dr. Fitzpatrick had told me there was a placement service for patients who were leaving the institution. Somehow, I would figure it out.

My mind still hadn't let me go to the worst hurdle, or hurdles that challenged me. I was excited to be leaving Still Waters, but afraid of finding the elusive event from my past that was keeping me here until I faced it. I knew it had to be something beyond merciless.

I went to the desk and opened my journal to a clean page.

August 4, 1978

Everybody has rough spots in their lives, but it seems that I have had more than my share. I know there are more I have to come face-to-face with before I can be free; before I can go out into the real world.

I put my journal aside along with my self-pity and took a long, hot shower. The truth was rushing to the surface of my mind since my stint in the padded cell. I was aware that too much at once might make me regress, so I tried to focus on nothing but pleasant things, no matter how trivial. The grounds at Still Waters were beautiful with flowering shrubs, old shade trees, and even a rose garden. My bed was comfortable, and my skin felt refreshed from the shower.

Because I was exhausted, I was able to sleep like a stone. If I dreamed, I had no recollection of it, and awoke rested and famished. I dressed and went to the cafeteria for breakfast. Even the green scrambled eggs looked appetizing.

I wondered how to spend the weekend without obsessing about the revelation that I both needed and dreaded. Playing the piano worked for a couple of hours, followed by a long walk. I ran into Maria at lunch.

She had lost her nervousness and seemed totally lethargic. It was clear to me that she had been medicated to the point of oblivion.

I was on my way to the dorm when I saw Maddie coming toward me.

"How's it going, baggy britches?" She smiled.

"Pretty well. I'm getting closer. Dr. Fitzpatrick thinks I'll soon be well."

"That's great. What are you up to on this fine day?"

"There isn't a lot to do around here on weekends. No activities are offered except during the week."

"Why don't you go to the library and look at some magazines? I'll bet you'd like to take a look at the latest fashions and such."

"What a good idea. That's exactly how I'll spend my afternoon."

I had visited the library lots of times, but only to check out books that I couldn't seem to finish because my mind was so muddled.

Fall Fashions littered the pages of every magazine I opened. Belted coats, tall leather boots with heels, gaucho pants, tweed suits, and cable knit sweaters were all favorites. Afro hairdos and wire-rimmed glasses were different. I didn't know whether I liked the new fashions or not. At least, I had an idea of what was in style.

I abandoned the periodicals and checked out a romance novel. Granted, it wasn't literature, but it would keep me busy for the remainder of the weekend. I could try to lose myself in it, and pretend I was on the other side of the fence. And that was exactly what I did until the next Tuesday afternoon when I met Dr. Fitzpatrick for my session.

"Good afternoon, Clemmie. I hope you had a restful weekend. Are you anxious to get started with our session?"

"Yes, and no. I want to get well, but I know that entails facing another terrible event that I've experienced."

"You've been exceptionally brave thus far. Just think of all the traumatic experiences you've endured. I firmly believe that your mental block was caused by not one incident, but layers of horrendous pain: your mother's death, Roy's alcoholism, prompting his abominable behavior and ensuing death, Miss Simmons's conniving practices, and even her demise."

"I'm sure you're right, doctor. I even lost my two best friends. I don't know if Mama Rae is still living, and I have no idea where Daniel is. That's heartbreaking enough, but I'm more concerned about my husband, if he still is my husband. I don't know if there is anyone outside Still Waters who cares whether I live or die."

"There's only one way to complete the puzzle, Clemmie. You do realize that."

I nodded.

"You and Jimmy were preparing to leave the island. You had said your goodbyes to Mama Rae."

The next morning Jimmy and I sold my Volkswagen to a used car dealer. With our bags packed, we loaded everything into Jimmy's car and headed for Atlanta, leaving our past behind us.

I've already told you that we lived in Lexington. We both completed our undergraduate degrees. Jimmy received his degree in Political Science; he wanted to go to law school. My B.A. was in Elementary Education, and I had a minor in Art.

I wanted to go to graduate school, but I needed to work for a while first. Even though we had full-time jobs during the summer, our expenses seemed to keep growing. We tried to buy used text books, but that wasn't always possible. Tuition might have seemed like a bargain for some people, but it was a fortune for us.

I was fortunate to land a teaching position the fall semester after graduation, and Jimmy enrolled in law school. We worked like our lives depended on it. Jimmy took a full course load. Somehow, he managed to schedule all of his classes on Mondays, Wednesdays, and Fridays, so he could work on a survey crew Tuesdays, Thursdays, and Saturdays. I taught in an elementary school during the days and had a temporary secondary school certificate which enabled me to teach an Adult Education art class two nights a week.

Whoever got home first did the grocery shopping and started dinner. We both did housework whenever we had a few free minutes. I usually had papers to grade, so Jimmy did most of the laundry. Youth had its advantages.

"Clemmie, are you with me?" asked Dr. Fitzpatrick.

I realized that I had fallen silent and that I was staring down at my hands in my lap. I was clasping and unclasping my fingers.

"I'm sorry, doctor. I can't think. I don't know what I was telling you."

"You were painting a lovely portrait of your young married life with Jimmy. You lived in Lexington, and you were very busy."

"I'm sorry. I want to go to my room."

"Very well. Write in your journal as soon as you can."

I started hyperventilating as I traversed the grounds. Stop looking ahead, I thought; look down at the bricked path. What is it that John does when he's restless? He counts. I started counting, and my breathing became easier.

In my room I dropped the journal on the desk and rushed to my bed. Don't get a headache, I told myself. Please don't get another headache. You don't need pills. You're almost ready to get out of this place. You're not crazy.

I closed my eyes and tried not to think. My mind was blank, I thought, but then, my tenth birthday was as vivid as it was all of those years ago.

———

I was excited because Mama had taken me to a restaurant not far from our apartment building. She hadn't made a fuss because I had insisted that a sweater was a warm enough wrap even in December. Mama understood my feelings; she knew I was ashamed to be seen in my too-short coat with the pilling wool.

It wasn't a fancy restaurant, of course, because we barely had enough money to get by. I had no idea what Mama had sacrificed so we could dine out to celebrate my birthday. We sat facing one another at a table by a window which allowed us to watch pedestrians hustle by, bundled up against the Chicago winter air.

I could see Roy Hubbard eating his dinner over my mother's left shoulder. His ice-blue eyes rolled toward the ceiling with every bite he took. He seemed to be thoroughly enjoying his meal. I couldn't tear my eyes away from him. Finally, Mama nudged me under the table with the toe of her shoe.

Roy watched as I blew out the candle on my slice of lemon meringue pie, and he wished me a *Happy Birthday* as we left the restaurant. That would have been the end of the man with the friendly smile and pretty eyes if Mama hadn't broken a heel of her navy pump. But as fate would have it, Roy happened to witness her misfortune. He introduced himself, and offered to drive us home. Mama turned down the kind gesture, but only after she had introduced us to him.

That introduction was all the encouragement Roy needed. He looked up our address, and we found one of his business cards wedged into our front door when we returned from church the next day. The rest was history. Roy Hubbard had fallen in love at first sight, not only with Mama, but with me. He wanted the three of us to be a family, and he pursued his goal until he made it happen.

I had loved my mother dearly, and I recalled everything about her. She had a beautiful smile and wonderful laugh lines at the corners of her eyes. Nobody had a sweeter disposition, and she loved me fiercely. I still missed my mother, but I was young when she died, and time had dulled the pain of losing her.

Roy was the parent I missed the most, maybe because he was there for me after Mama was killed. He nearly smothered me with his love and protection. During my adolescent years he was both mother and father, and no one could have done a more superb job. I loved Roy's infectious laugh and his big-kid personality. He loved me as though I were his own.

Alcoholism ruled Roy's life. He simply wasn't strong enough to keep it at bay. It was his crutch as well as his enemy. I'll never understand how such a strong father figure and self-possessed man could be so weak in the face of temptation. Roy truly broke my heart.

I had to let go of the past if I wanted to face the real world. Lying in bed reminiscing was only making me miserable. I told myself to shake it off and do something productive.

There were no decent summer clothes in my closet. I supposed that was because it hadn't been warm weather when I came here. The only light weight clothes I had looked as though they had come from a bargain basement. Someone at Still Waters must have bought them for me with the money my benefactor sent each month.

I found a pair of cutoff jeans and an ugly knit top, then put on my sneakers and went out into the fresh air determined to clear my head and think straight.

Sitting on a bench by the wrought iron fence, I watched people on the other side, walking down the street as free as birds. A group of teenagers joked and laughed as they passed by, and I wondered if they were telling loony bin jokes. After all, they were walking past such a place, and one of the crazy people was kind enough to perch on a bench by the fence for their inspection.

Cars passed by, and I wondered if I would remember how to drive. I thought of the yellow Volkswagen Roy gave me for my sixteenth birthday. It was the perfect gift for a teenager. I wondered what had become of my driver's license. It wasn't in my belongings, such as they were. Maybe I would have to take a driving test to get a new one.

Chapter Thirty-five

—

"Were you able to write in your journal, Clemmie?"

"I could have, but I didn't see the point. My head is clear now."

"I'm glad to hear that. We could be close enough to the last bit of the block that you won't need the journal any longer."

"I realize I've resisted putting my thoughts on paper. That's natural, isn't it?"

"In most cases, yes."

"I want to tell you that I think it has helped me. It's just not something I like to do. It opens wounds."

"Yes, it does. That's why it's necessary. Now, if I recall, you and Jimmy lived in Lexington."

———

We looked forward to our weekends even though Jimmy worked on Saturdays. All day Sunday was ours to do whatever we pleased, and many times we did nothing at all. We found fun in engaging in everyday things that weren't expensive: building a snowman in the courtyard, going to the music building so I could play a piano for Jimmy to see how much I had improved in a week, and watching movies on T.V.; just silly things.

Since Jimmy worked on Saturdays, I always made a new recipe for our dinner. It was a joke between us, because we never knew if it was going to be mouthwatering or unfit for human consumption. When it turned out to be the latter, we simply dumped it into the garbage disposal and forgot about it.

Making love with one another always made everything bothersome cease to exist. We forgot missing dinner, unpaid bills, piles of ungraded papers, and dirty laundry. It was simply the cure-all for whatever ailed us.

I had depleted our food budget for the week to buy ingredients for pork fried rice. Jimmy would be home at about the same time as the dish was finished cooking. I hurried to freshen up so I would look pretty when he came through the door.

"What's burning?" He sounded truly concerned.

I flew from the bathroom to see what was going on. Smoke filled the kitchen, and Jimmy was running around, raising windows. He opened the front door to let out more smoke and turned off the stove. I stood in the doorway in my underwear and started to cry.

"Oh, Jimmy, I've ruined our dinner. Our food allowance is gone. I might as well have thrown it away."

"Don't cry, sweetheart. By the way, what was dinner?"

"Pork fried rice."I cried harder.

"Maybe we can salvage some of it."

He lifted the lid and spooned some of the rice into a bowl, careful to avoid what was stuck to the skillet. He held the spoon for me to taste.

"We can't eat it. It tastes burned even though it isn't."

"Hey, sweetie, it's just dinner. We'll leave the windows open while we run down the street for a burger. It won't smell like the place is on fire by the time we get back."

He dumped the burned rice into the disposal, put a lid on the skillet, and took a shower while I fumed.

The apartment smelled fine when we came home. We closed the drapes, turned down the lights, and made everything right with the world.

"So you and your young husband were very happy," Dr. Fitzpatrick said.

"Ecstatically so."

For some reason, it didn't bother me that he had interrupted me. It was only a short time ago that it had prompted my throwing books.

Miss Yantz's nasal voice came over the intercom.

"I'm very sorry to interrupt, doctor, but you're needed at the infirmary. There's some sort of emergency."

"Thank you, Miss Yantz." He switched off the intercom.

"Clemmie, I do apologize. I'm afraid we'll have to pick up here next time."

"It's all right. If I recall, you dropped everything when I was in the infirmary and needed you."

I felt almost lighthearted as I left the doctor's office. The sun was shining, and there was a slight breeze that caused my hair to blow across my cheek. Suddenly, I had an urge to play the piano. I went to the activities center to see if it was in use. Doris, the director was sitting at a table scribbling notes.

"Oh, I'm sorry, Doris."

"Don't be. I'm just working on my schedule for next week. If you'd like to play the piano, it would be a treat for me."

"As a matter of fact, that's why I came by."

"Do you happen to know any hymns?"

"Why, yes. It's been a while, but I remember lots of them. My father took me to church every Sunday. Do you have a favorite?"

"No. No favorite. I love them all."

I played hymn after hymn for over an hour, and Doris stayed for the entire recital.

"That was wonderful, Clemmie. Let me return the favor by taking you to an early dinner."

"I don't think the cafeteria is open for dinner yet, but thank you."

"I'm not talking about going to the cafeteria. I'll sign you out, and we can go to a real restaurant."

"I didn't know I was allowed to leave the grounds."

"You are if a staff member signs you out."

"I don't have any nice outfits. Could we go someplace where I can wear jeans?"

"Sure. There's a cute little place just down the street. It's casual; you can wear pretty much whatever you want. Lots of college kids frequent it. They serve sandwiches, burgers, homemade soup, and wonderful desserts."

"That sounds great. It won't take me but a few minutes to change."

The activities director began apologizing for her messy car before we got to the parking lot. The back seat was covered with folders, books, a raincoat and a couple of umbrellas, and the front floorboard was home to a host of fast food wrappers.

I honestly couldn't remember the last time I was in a car as I slid into the passenger seat of Doris's blue Plymouth Duster. As the gates of Still Waters opened, and we drove onto the street, I tasted freedom. It was foreign to me, and I liked the feel of it.

The restaurant was just as Doris had described it. The food was good, and the atmosphere casual. Young families were there, feeding their small children. Senior citizens had come for the early bird specials, and a horde of college students inhaled burgers and fries.

I found the ladies' room before we left the restaurant. It was the first time I had been to a public restroom off Still Waters grounds in four years. There was toilet tissue on the floor, and the facility could have been cleaner, but that's how the public left a restroom that wasn't their own. They didn't have to clean it. Anyone could walk in, make a mess, and leave without a care. I wasn't particularly proud to have embraced that line of thinking, but it was freedom—the thing I craved.

Back in my room I undressed and imagined myself as a member of society, away from the institution where I had no responsibilities except to show up for my sessions. I wondered how I would support myself. Perhaps I would work in an office, or a restaurant, or the postal service. The possibilities were endless. There must be tests I could take to discover my strengths and weaknesses. Whatever I did to earn my bread and butter, one thing was certain: I would make time to volunteer for some sort of public service.

August 10, 1978

I hadn't intended to put my thoughts on paper again, but tonight I feel the need. Looking ahead without a map and uncertain of the terrain is more than a little frightening, even though it has been my goal. I'm very close to starting that journey, and I'm afraid of doing it alone. My fantasies of a strong hand to lead me through the transition from total dependence to living on my own have long since disappeared. Whatever has been keeping me from stepping over the thin line into the real world will soon be met with all of my courage and determination. I will face it in the light of day, and I will be the victor.

"Hello, Clemmie." Dr. Fitzpatrick sat on a corner of his desk and dangled a foot.

I supposed he was trying to strike a casual pose to put me at ease, but he just looked silly to me. His striped sock had slipped down, exposing stark white skin. It showcased his elevated shoe.

"I see you've brought your journal." That seemed to please him.

"Yes." I handed it to him.

"You sound like a warrior, my dear."

"I have to be one."

"Sometimes even warriors take small steps. You needn't feel compelled to charge into battle. It could be overwhelming."

"I know that. How many times have I come to a standstill because I've remembered something crushing? The problem is that I don't know any other way to get there."

"I realize you're anxious to climb this mountain, Clemmie. You want to leave here and face the world. I've seen you come such a long way, and I'm confident you'll finish the course soon. You're almost there. Take your time and be surefooted."

I had walked into this room bold as brass. Why was my doctor trying to dissuade me? I was David with his slingshot, ready to slay Goliath, and he wanted me to slow down to find the perfect stone.

"I'll go slowly, and if I feel afraid, I'll back off."

"Good. You and Jimmy were living in Lexington. Do you remember?"

"Yes."

———

It was late on a Friday afternoon. I had stayed late at school to make lesson plans for the following week, and Jimmy beat me home. He went to the dry cleaners to pick up our clothes while I changed for dinner.

Fridays were special, because we always ate out. Each week we chose a different restaurant; it was a game we played. One Friday we might spend most of our weekly food allowance at an expensive restaurant, and the next week we could be found in a hamburger joint. We never went to the same place twice.

This particular evening we planned to dine at Stanley Demos's Coach House. The restaurant had gotten rave reviews in the Lexington Herald. A local food critic had sung its praises and listed some of the specialties on the menu. Just reading about them made our mouths water. We couldn't wait to try it.

I redid my makeup and put on the dress I had been saving for a special occasion. The price tag still dangled from its sleeve. As soon as I dabbed on a little Chanel No 5, I'd be ready to go.

Our reservation was for seven o'clock. It was six-thirty already, and Jimmy wasn't home. I knew traffic was bad because it had been cold and rainy all day. There were always several fender benders every time it rained, and it was cold enough that the rain could turn into sleet any minute. I turned on the local news to see if I could catch a weather report, but a domestic violence item was being described in vivid detail.

I looked out on Virginia Avenue. It was raining so hard I could barely make out the crawling line of traffic as it snaked off the bridge. If Jimmy was stuck in that mess, there was no telling what time he would get home. Maybe he had already made it to the parking lot. I went to the living room window, hoping to see him dashing up the stairs from the courtyard, taking the steps two at a time, but there was no sign of him. He'd be soaked to the skin when he got here, and he'd have to change before we went to dinner.

I was about to call the restaurant to see if I could change our reservation to a later time when there was a loud knock at the door. I smiled; he had forgotten his key again. I ran to let him in.

"You did it again, didn't you, Boy Scout? I thought you guys were always prepared." I laughed as I opened the door.

"Clemmie? Are you all right?"

I could hear my doctor's voice, but it sounded like it was coming from an echo chamber. My hands were cold, but clammy. My entire body felt numb as if it were asleep. I tried to speak, but couldn't.

"Is this it, Clemmie—the last giant step?"

Noise filled my head like a rushing mountain stream, and my temples pounded like a drum. I was being carried along with the rest of the debris the swift flood had picked up and swept down the mountain to places unknown.

A familiar face was staring at me when I awoke. I was in my bed, wearing one of my nightgowns, blinking at Maddie.

"It's about time you woke up, Rip van Winkle," she said.

"Why are you here, Maddie? What's happened?"

"Your doc thinks you've come nose-to-nose with your worst enemy. You're just scared, girl. Somethin' real mean's smacked you down. You're strong enough to get up; you just don't know it."

"Is he going to prescribe more medicine? Please tell me that's not going to happen. I can't stand feeling like a zombie."

"He didn't say nothin' about no pills, and he's not gonna put you in crazy jail neither. You're lookin' at what he prescribed: me."

"I don't understand."

"He knows you trust me. You do, don't you?"

"Yes, of course. But how are you going to help me face the awful thing that's holding me hostage?"

"All I plan to do is be your friend. You'll have to do the rest. We'll just carry on normal conversations. We'll talk about the weather, the shitty cafeteria food, doctors who think they know everything. Then when you least expect it, you'll talk about what really matters. I know what I'm talking about, baggy britches; just ask the shrinks. I'm good."

Chapter Thirty-six

Maddie moved into my room with a cot. Surprisingly, she didn't seem to get in my way. She didn't push me to talk, but she was always willing to chat when I was in the mood. I wasn't expected to change any of my habits for her. She always made sure I had my shower before she took hers. We went for long walks, shared meals in the cafeteria, and could have been described as hermits, because we only engaged in activity with one another.

Maddie kept a log. She never shared it with me, but I knew it had something to do with me.

"I know those notes you're taking are about me. What did you just write? I have a right to know."

"I don't nose around in your journal; you don't have a right to know what's in mine. It's private."

Her attitude was so reminiscent of Mama Rae's that it almost filled a hole in my heart. What good people they both were.

I enjoyed Maddie's company, but as far as I could tell, we weren't accomplishing anything. She never asked questions about my past, so how was I ever going to be able to break through my last barrier? Whatever it was had happened at least four years ago, and I would have to let it hurt me one more time before I would be free.

Crossword puzzles were among Maddie's favorite pastimes, and she got me hooked on them. She was most certainly wise, and I liked her a great deal, but I didn't consider her to be overly intelligent. Her grammar was pretty atrocious. I couldn't understand how she could be such a whiz at puzzles.

"What's a six-letter word for *beautiful*?" I asked.

Maddie looked up from her own puzzle and massaged her chin between her thumb and forefinger.

"Comely."

"Oh, sure. Thanks. I don't know why I couldn't come up with it."

"Your mind's just on a different track. If you'd asked me yesterday, I probably couldn't have thought of it."

"What are we doing, Maddie?"

"Puzzles. What you think?"

"You've been here for nearly a week, and nothing's changed."

"Things have too changed. You ain't tense; you're relaxed. You're gonna be spittin' that bad boy out for old Maddie real soon. Stop worryin'."

I wanted to believe her, to trust her enough to let my mind travel back in time to the place that had crushed my soul, then leave it forever.

Thunder cracked like a loud gunshot next to my ear, and I sat up in my bed wide awake. I could see Maddie in the semidarkness. How could she sleep through such noise? I wanted her awake; she would somehow protect me.

"Maddie?"

"Huh? What?"

"I'm afraid of storms."

"Well, ain't that somethin'? I'm not. Storm's not gonna hurt you. Go back to sleep."

"Please stay awake until it's over."

The big woman got up off her cot and came across the room. She grabbed my hand and pulled me out of bed.

"Come on," she said. "I'm gonna show you there's nothin' to be afraid of."

She led me to the window and opened the drape. I shut my eyes against the bright lightning, and put my hands over my ears to keep out the storm. My mentor pulled my hands away and rested her arm around my shoulders.

"This buildin's grounded. The lightnin' can't strike you, and that loud-mouthed thunder ain't nothin' but noise. Open them eyes and look out there. Maddie ain't gonna let nothin' hurt you."

I made myself open my eyes. Rain was gushing off the eave and splashing on the windowsill. It was hard for me to breathe, and my vision started to blur. The rain seemed to be hitting shiny black discs that looked familiar. I could feel Maddie's strength pouring into me as she hugged my shoulders. The two of us watched the storm in silence.

We stood at the window until the storm passed. I had perspired so much that my gown clung to my body, and my face was wet with tears. Maddie hadn't said a word; she had simply been my protective friend.

"You want to talk?" she said.

I couldn't answer.

"That's what I thought. You can put it in your journal. That's just as good."

She went to the bathroom and brought me a cold washcloth.

"Here. Wash your face. You can take a shower after a while."

I sat down at the desk and opened my dog-eared notebook.

August 23, 1978

Here at last. I'd lost faith that I would ever make it. Thank God for Maddie, her patience, wisdom, and kind heart. I guess she's my guardian angel. It's mindboggling to me that she can be in cahoots with Dr. Fitzpatrick. Two people couldn't be more different, but they're an amazing team.

Maddie gave me the courage to let the monster in and crack the code. I feel tremendous pain coupled with relief. Now I can leave Still Waters knowing that I can do whatever I have to do to reclaim my life.

"Feel better?" Maddie asked.

"Yes. I'm so sad that I almost want to die, but a tremendous burden has been lifted. I can laugh, cry, turn somersaults, or curse the world. I can do whatever I please, and I don't have to ask anyone's permission to do it."

"That's right."

"Maddie?"

"Yeah."

"Do you want me to tell you what the monster was?"

"Not just yet. Tell your doc first. He's been real worried about you. I'll go downstairs and call him first thing in the mornin'."

I took a shower and tried to go back to sleep because Maddie was softly snoring on her cot. How could she spend half the night watching me watch a storm, have a revelation, and go right back to sleep?

I was too excited to eat breakfast. A cup of coffee was all I could manage. I raced to Dr. Fitzpatrick's office and smiled at Miss Yantz.

"Dr. Fitzpatrick has cancelled his morning appointments for your convenience," she said, sounding like a recording.

"Good morning, Clemmie." His smile actually showed in his eyes.

"Good morning."

"I understand you made an important journal entry last night."

"I did, but I only hinted at what I have to tell you." I handed him the journal.

"I see what you mean." He returned it with a raised eyebrow and flipped through his notes.

"You and your husband were going to one of your Friday night dinners. It was raining. He was late getting home, and had forgotten his key."

———

I opened the door to see two grim-faced policemen standing in the rain, looking uncomfortable.

"Mrs. Castlebrook?"

I nodded.

"Ma'am, I afraid we have some unsettling news."

Fear shot through me as I stood in the doorway watching rain spatter on the shiny bills of the policemen's hats.

"Come in," I finally managed.

The two stepped into the living room. They removed their hats and stood just inside the door.

"What's happened?" I asked, afraid to hear the answer.

"There's been an accident."

"What kind of accident?"

Before either of them could answer, I began screaming. "My husband! What's happened to my husband?"

"Please sit down for a minute, Mrs. Castlebrook."

"I don't want to sit down. I want to go to dinner. I want my husband. What have you done with him?"

"Mrs. Castlebrook, I'm sorry to inform you that your husband has been in an automobile accident." The policeman looked truly pained. "It was fatal."

"No! No! That just can't be; not my Jimmy. You've made a mistake."

"There's no mistake, Mrs. Castlebrook. Your husband's car stalled on the railroad tracks. We haven't been able to ascertain why he failed to get out of the car, but the conductor couldn't slow down in time to avoid hitting it. I'm terribly sorry, ma'am."

It seemed unreal, but I believed it. My life was over, my brand new life with my wonderful husband. I had lost my parents, and now my Jimmy.

I sank down on the sofa and looked around the living room. Jimmy and I had spent so many hours together in this room, working to meet deadlines, prioritizing our bills, watching old movies on T.V. Sometimes we had just goofed around, and we had made love. I could see Jimmy sitting on this sofa in his shorts and tee shirt with one arm around me and the other hand in a bowl of popcorn, watching a Wildcats game.

"Is there someone we can call for you, Mrs. Castlebrook?"

"No. Um, yes. You can call my husband's parents. They don't speak to me. Please make the call from here. I'd like to know if they care that their son is dead."

I went to the desk and took out our personal phone directory. One of the policemen dialed the number. I felt numb all over as I listened to him repeat to my husband's parents the same maddening message he had given me a few minutes earlier.

I couldn't fathom that my love had been snatched away from me so brutally. My entire world was gone. I hadn't gone out of my way to make friends since we moved to this lovely college town. Jimmy was all I needed. Of course, I had acquaintances: tenants in our building, other students from our classes, and teachers at the school where I taught, but no real friends.

The policemen drove me to the morgue. I was in shock, and the truth seemed surreal until the moment the sheet was pulled back, and I saw my darling lying there lifeless. Then stark reality hit me.

"Is this your husband, Mrs. Castlebrook?"

I tried to answer, but I couldn't speak. I nodded just before I fainted.

When I awoke, I was in a hospital room. The kindly face of a middle-aged doctor was looking down at me. I had no idea why I was there. The doctor told me that I had been brought to the hospital in a state of shock a month earlier. I needed Jimmy, but he wouldn't be coming to take me home. The doctor told me what had happened.

I was in therapy for days, and instead of getting better as time went by, I sank into a deep depression. I wouldn't eat, and the only way I could sleep was with the aid of heavy sedation. Nurses gave me lipstick, a mirror, combs and brushes, hoping that I would care how I looked and do something about it. But I didn't care. I was dead inside.

I don't know how long I stayed at the hospital in Lexington. There's still a gap in my memory, but that doesn't matter now. I vaguely recall my arrival at Still Waters, or maybe I think I remember because I've heard the story so many times. I don't know who is paying the tab. I suspect it's my in-laws, and they're doling out the exorbitant monthly payments to assuage their guilt.

I intend to write to them and advise them that they're off the hook now that I've regained my memory. As a matter of fact, I think I'll do that today. I'm also going to try to get in touch with Daniel's aunt to see if she can help me locate him.

"You've had an unusually traumatic life, young lady." Dr. Fitzpatrick took off his glasses and looked at me with the eyes of a friend. "You've come through the therapy like a real trooper."

"It was touch and go much of the time. I'm sorry I wasn't more cooperative."

He smiled. "I'm confident you'll pass the battery of exit tests with no problem. I know you're anxious to leave, but we won't be able to begin testing until next week. As soon as we have the results, you'll be ready to begin your new life. I'll schedule the tests to begin Monday morning at eight o'clock. How's that?"

"Great."

Chapter Thirty-seven

Dr. Fitzpatrick had been right about everything. The therapy he thought best had worked for me, and I had passed my exit exams with aplomb. The review board was nothing more than a formality.

I had written to Jimmy's parents, but hadn't received a reply, so I called information and learned that there were no Castlebrooks listed on Hilton Head Island. I didn't know anything else to do. If they had moved from the island recently, their mail would be forwarded. If not, at least I had tried.

I would be leaving Still Waters in two days, and I still didn't know my destination. Lexington was out of the question; it held too many memories. I couldn't be there without Jimmy.

I was sitting at my desk making lists of places I might consider when there was a knock on my door. I opened it, and two of my favorite people filled the doorway, smiling.

"Maddie, Doris, come in."

"I just want to wish you good luck, baggy britches," Maddie said.

"And I'm delivering mail. This just came to the business office." Doris handed me an envelope.

I ripped it open to find a cashier's check for fifty thousand dollars.

"Is anything the matter, Clemmie?" Doris asked. "You look pale."

I sat down on the edge of my bed at a loss for words and held up the check for their inspection.

"You lucky girl," Doris said. "You certainly won't have to hang around Louisville unless you want to. With this much money you can go wherever you like."

I knew the check must have been Jimmy's parents' reply to my letter. They were trying to salve their consciences. Very well. I'd take their money. I couldn't afford to be too proud, considering my circumstances.

Maddie turned me over to Doris so she could go back to work.

"The first thing I want to do is go on a real vacation," I said. "I've never done that."

We went to a travel agency and picked up a stack of brochures. Then Doris took me to get a new driver's license and to open a bank account. I would check into a hotel and take my time deciding where to begin my new life.

I had dinner with Maddie and Maria that evening. Maddie was helping Maria come down off her pills and open her heart to trust a friend. I could attest to the fact that Maddie was an expert at her work.

I stopped at Emma's table on my way out of the cafeteria to tell her goodbye.

"Good riddance to bad rubbish," she snarled. "You'll be back. You're just as crazy as the rest of us. You'll be back. Ack, boo, stupid, nut case, ack."

John was devouring his dinner in the usual manner. He didn't stop eating when I told him that I was leaving Still Waters. Ignoring his apathy, I bent down and hugged him.

"I love you, Clemmie," he said, and continued eating.

"I love you, too, John."

He looked down at his empty plate. "More! More chicken pot pie!"

Sitting at my desk, I began making a shopping list. Doris had promised to take me shopping for new clothes for my vacation. I hadn't decided where I wanted to go, but I wanted it to be someplace warm. I'd buy a few things suitable for cooler climates too since I hadn't made up my mind where to live.

It felt strange to sit at my desk and write something other than a journal entry. I missed it in an odd sort of way.

I was too excited to eat breakfast the next morning, so I ran to the cafeteria for a cup of coffee and went for a walk around the grounds. It was the end of August, and the sun didn't feel as hot as it had a few days ago.

"Good morning!" Doris hurried to meet me in the parking lot. She was all smiles.

She was something of a clothes horse and knew how to put together terrific-looking outfits. We had to go to a couple of specialty shops to find the warm weather clothes, and even then, the pickings were slim. I only needed a couple of outfits for the time being. I could shop as soon as I reached my destination.

We had lunch at a delightful tea room after finishing our shopping. Then Doris went to the center to conduct the afternoon activities.

I was admiring my new apparel when the floor attendant knocked on my door. She told me to come downstairs for a phone call. This was the first call I had received during my entire stay at Still Waters. I couldn't imagine who it could me.

"Hello."

"Clemmie?"

The voice was deeper than I remembered, but I knew its owner.

"Oh, Daniel." I felt tears of joy make their way down my cheeks. "When your aunt didn't answer my letter, I was afraid I'd never be able to find you."

"Tell me you're okay, Clemmie."

"I'm fabulous. I'm leaving Still Waters tomorrow."

"My aunt explained everything you wrote in the letter, so you don't have to rehash the whole thing."

"Daniel, how are you? Where are you?"

"I'm great. You won't believe what I'm about to tell you. I'm married and living in Savannah. My wife and I have a beautiful baby girl."

"That's wonderful. Tell me about them."

Daniel had survived a lot during his trek to manhood, and I was truly happy for him.

"My wife's name is Catherine. She's gorgeous, and she's the best mother in the world. Our six-month-old daughter is Suzanne, and she hung the moon."

"What line of work are you in?"

"I'm a construction worker for the time being. As soon as Suzanne's a little older, Catherine will return to work as a paralegal and I'll begin my college career. We'll be moving to Macon, because that's where I'll be attending school. I'm going to be a civil engineer, Clemmie. I want to build bridges."

"Oh, Daniel, I'm so proud of you."

"Where will you go when you leave Still Waters?"

"I haven't decided where I want to live, but I'm leaving on my vacation bright and early tomorrow morning."

"And where might that be?"

"I didn't know the answer to that question until just this minute. I've suddenly developed an insatiable craving for fresh shrimp. You don't happen to know of a place where I could buy a whole bucketful, do you?"

Daniel laughed. "You bet I do, and it's not far from where we live."

My best friend and I talked for a few more minutes, making plans for the next day. He and his wife and baby would meet me at the airport in Savannah. Then we would head for Hilton Head Island.

Catherine thought Daniel and I were joking when we told her that we intended to have dinner in the woods. She seemed a little nervous when her husband parked the car and started into the dense foliage with their baby daughter and a bucket of shrimp.

"Where's he taking us?" she asked me.

I grinned. "To meet the best cook and one of the best people in the world."

I took her hand, and led her into the forest. Daniel looked back over his shoulder at the two of us and smiled.

"Hey, Clemmie, got your flashlight?" he asked.

"Got it."

"Why do we need a flashlight?" Catherine asked.

"Because it'll be dark and spooky when we come back through these woods tonight," Daniel teased.

A few minutes later we reached the clearing. Daniel and I looked fondly at the familiar surroundings. Nothing seemed to have changed.

"Where are you two taking me?" Catherine sounded truly concerned. "This is the middle of a jungle."

A loud squawk rang out, and Catherine jumped back, causing me to lose my balance.

"Now, you've done it," Daniel said. "We're in deep trouble."

"Don't be scarin' my settin' hen." Mama Rae stood on her porch with hands on her hips.

She's not afraid of anything, I thought. I knew she didn't have a gun, or any sort of weapon. Then I remembered: she didn't need weapons; she had black magic.

She shielded her eyes from the sun's late afternoon glare and walked toward us. Was her stride slower, or less purposeful? I couldn't tell, but I didn't think so.

"Mama Rae," Daniel said.

She kept up her march toward us.

"It's us, Mama Rae," I said.

Our old friend wore a long skirt and her slouch hat, but her earlobes sparkled. She was wearing Mama's diamond studs. She opened her arms, and Daniel and I rushed into them.

"I knew you'd come back to the islan'," she said.

Acknowledgement

I wish to thank the late Dorothy Breen for generously sharing her knowledge of the early history of Hilton Head Island.

CPSIA information can be obtained at www.ICGtesting.com
Printed in the USA
BVOW022141090412

287278BV00002B/1/P